Praise for Michael Pye's *The Drowning Room*

"A wonderful novel . . . a Horatio Alger life story with plenty
of sex, unspeakable sadness, and a feminist twist. . . . If you
can write as well as Michael Pye . . . you should never want for
readers."
                                    —*The Boston Sunday Globe*

"Dark and exhilarating . . . an extraordinary life and book, full
of struggle, wonder, color and sorrow—all described with detail
so vivid every sensation leaps off the page."
                                    —*Detroit Free Press*

"Haunting. . . . Pye's portrait of early New York is a memorable
one of easy death and hard life. . . . His character, Gretje
Reyniers, emerges as a rogue New Yorker for all generations."
                                    —*Time Out New York*

"Imaginatively conceived . . . Pye has constructed a complex
and sympathetic portrait of a woman driven . . . by the harsh re-
alities of seventeenth-century survival . . . Pye takes scrupulous
pleasure in re-creating the scenes and textures and aromas of those
times."   —*The Philadelphia Inquirer*

"A tour de force. . . . Gretje's story is one of survival by an
outcast, one whose independent life and none-too-careful loves
are seen by others as only scandalous behavior."
                                    —*The Dallas Morning News*

"Throughout, the prose is seamlessly marvelous—rich and Ra-
belaisian in its capturing of the sights and ever-present smells of
the seventeenth century."   —*The Hartford Courant*

"Terrific . . . ostensibly a seventeenth-century picaresque, the
novel also cartwheels acrobatically into darker, more profound
visions . . . the story rises and falls without the least creak of
strain, poetic yet brisk."   —*Portland Oregonian*

PENGUIN BOOKS

THE DROWNING ROOM

Michael Pye, journalist, novelist, broadcaster, and historian, is the author of eight books, including *Maximum City: The Biography of New York*. He divides his time between New York and Portugal.

MICHAEL PYE

THE DROWNING ROOM

PENGUIN BOOKS

PENGUIN BOOKS

Published by the Penguin Group

Penguin Books USA Inc., 375 Hudson Street,
New York, New York 10014, U.S.A.
Penguin Books Ltd, 27 Wrights Lane, London W8 5TZ, England
Penguin Books Australia Ltd, Ringwood, Victoria, Australia
Penguin Books Canada Ltd, 10 Alcorn Avenue,
Toronto, Ontario, Canada M4V 3B2
Penguin Books (N.Z.) Ltd, 182–190 Wairau Road, Auckland 10, New Zealand

Penguin Books Ltd, Registered Offices: Harmondsworth, Middlesex, England

First published in Great Britain by Granta Books
in association with Penguin Books Ltd 1995
First published in the United States of America by Granta Books in association
with Viking Penguin, a division of Penguin Books USA Inc. 1996
Published in Penguin Books (U.S.A.) 1997

1 3 5 7 9 10 8 6 4 2

THE LIBRARY OF CONGRESS HAS CATALOGUED THE AMERICAN
HARDCOVER EDITION AS FOLLOWS:
Pye, Michael, 1946–
The drowning room/Michael Pye.
p.   cm.
ISBN 0-670-86598-2 (hc.)
ISBN 0 14 01.4149 9 (pbk.)
1. Reyniers, Gretje—Fiction.   2. Dutch Americans—New York (N.Y.)—
History—17th century—Fiction.   3. Women—New York (N.Y.)—History—
17th century—Fiction.   [1. New York (N.Y.)—History—Colonial period,
ca. 1600–1775—Fiction.]   I. Title.
PR6066.Y4D76   1996
823'.914—dc20   95–45263

Printed in the United States of America
Set in Adobe Garamond

For John,
who also lived with Gretje

ONE

'RIGHT!' SHE THINKS.

Her legs go like scissors, the bed curtains fly open and Gretje Reyniers examines the day. Too cold, too quiet, she thinks, too much light off the snow, too many people waiting. And there's someone lying dead in the yard. 'Someone' doesn't quite cover it. She can feel a whole night's cold along her side, where Anthony almost always used to be.

The white cockatoo, brought up on the last boat from Curaçao, hangs by the stove in the corner of the room, forever turning on its perch to keep in the warm draught. Its feathers look smudged. The bird begins to scream.

Gretje shouts for milk and bread.

She sees the shock of red on the bird's head, which makes her think about wounds. 'Nonsense,' she says out loud. But Anthony's lying out back in a box, stashed like a bit of cargo. He has to wait there until the ground breaks enough to bury him.

Tomas trots in with food. He's a sallow boy, clinging to the world through chores, mute and with an empty face. She thanks him, but under her breath; he doesn't always

7

hear what is said to him, because his memories are at least as real to him as the food or the cold. She sits up on the edge of the bed, breaks the bread into the warm milk and drinks breakfast from the bowl. The warm milk soaks down through the vaults of her belly. She puts the bowl on a stool, and the bird clatters down to eat.

This morning she's got to walk out there in the town and show herself: Gretje Reyniers, the new widow. It's one thing to be in the safe empire of her house, quite another to be out where people's eyes are bright enough to draw blood. They'll be hoping for a performance, of course. Since the harbour froze, they've been starved of performances.

She wakes herself up with cold water and washes carefully under her arms and her breasts. Still alive, she thinks, still solid. She pulls on a plain coat and takes a deep breath before opening the door.

The sky's black, the light brilliant. The cold settles on her skin like an oil. She's waiting, just waiting, for the first bark of an accusation, though she knows exactly what makes people forget about a sensational past: the thought of what she owns today. She pulls all her property around her like a cloak, every stuiver of her capital, all the houses and even, in these bitter, hungry days, every turnip and onion in her store. All that credit lets her strut along. She dares them even to think about her.

The clerk at the fort says: 'Good morning.' Then he adds: 'Good morning, Mevrouw. Madam.'

She smiles weakly, which she thinks is proper. The clerk can't quite bring himself to sympathize or commiserate, because after all, the man Anthony has gone to God, which is a blessing, and what's left is the town whore.

She scratches her name on the paper: Gretje Reyniers, Mevrouw Janssen. Widow.

There are papers on the clerk's table, and stuffed into books bound up in leather; nobody earns, nobody dies without papers. Gretje knows she's there, accused and recorded: how shockingly she landed in New Amsterdam, when she slandered, when she sued and when she was sued and slandered back, debts welshed on and debts demanded, some minor assaults, nights with a bottle too much inside her. Now she's there as the Widow. She has two lives: her own, and the one that cannot die as long as there are clerks to keep the papers.

The clerk helps her to a chair. He's a bit premature, but she can sense what he's trying to tell her. Everyone wants a widow, especially one with property and money to lend, who's young enough for children and doesn't want them. He's saying, by his attentions, that he doesn't want to be overlooked.

SHE BUSTLES INTO the square of the fort. No soldiers moving; they're not paid enough to brave the cold. The high sod walls, rotten as they are, look almost solid with the frost; the snow gives them a neat white line. Beyond the walls, the town seems clean and brilliant and unnatural. The air hurts Gretje's teeth.

Three sailors slink past like foxes. A big woman wallows in the snow. A couple of Scots traders fuss with weights. They all have the shifty, sideways look of people who are hungry and peevish, who've been trapped too long by the ice in a town that's no more than a trading post. She can feel hunger and envy marching down the street as bold as she is.

The town is hungry, but Gretje is hollow, too. Only it's sorrow that knots up her bowels, a feeling so strong it's like something living and kicking inside her. If ever she gave it birth, it would make the whole town cry.

She doesn't understand. She was never bundled up with her husband. She's still Gretje Reyniers, entire in her skin. But this morning, she's perfectly lonely.

She gulps at the air, and it stops her breath. She makes herself see things, all things, even familiar things—sees them with eyes so wide it looks as if she's used belladonna. Here's a black, tidal ditch, the stench frozen into it; a sad copy of an Amsterdam canal, so everyone calls it Herengracht. Here are a few stone gabled houses, thrown on the ground like dice. The ice has glassed the trees. She smells coffee on the air.

Here's the Minister's wife, a hard dumpling of a woman, trying, with a bit of God's grace, to cross the street without slipping. She's going to come up and pity Gretje in a minute. Gretje tolerates that less well than the usual smug abuse and stalks briskly on. The Minister's wife follows, a sermon frothing on her lips, a pair of dogs running mockingly behind her. Out of the corner of her eye, Gretje sees the Minister's wife blundering on to black ice, frowning. She thinks the frown makes her invisible. But she's skidding, teetering, then her arms flail backwards and she's down on the ground, holding the dogs off with her stare. She's quite forgotten her sermon for the day.

Gretje sails on through the snow. The houses throw shadows that protect her, but then the houses peter out. There are wide rivers on either side of the island of Manhattan, and woods and fields and hills. The whole great wild is much too close to her house.

She comes home shivering.

Tomas is at the door. He's agitated, but you can never tell why with Tomas: maybe he burnt a loaf, or remembered seeing his parents killed, or his heart just started racing. Past and present are equally real to him, all the time.

She storms through the room, bits of cold still hanging in her cloak. There's someone sitting at the table. She rushes on through the stables, all misted with the breath of the horse and the cows, to the land at the back of the house. The trees look neat, pruned and edged by winter. The coffin is set out in the snow.

Gretje sneezes. She knows she has to hold everything together by sheer will, that she can't let her attention falter even for a moment. But out here, with the cold and the coffin, her will fails.

She scrabbles at the coffin, trying to claw the frost and the snow out of the wood as though they were nails, and pulls up the lid, working carefully now. There he is: the dark, alarming face of Anthony Janssen, known as the Turk. She touches him, lightly. She wants to stop the cold from wiping away his face and freezing the blue eyes into white. She thinks she is looking down through the eyes into the hollows of his body.

He's here, each muscle of him, and yet she's still alone. She wants comfort. She goes sprawling into the coffin, covering him, as though she could warm him back to life. She wants him back to occupy this space inside her where now there is only a shrieking grief. The ice of his body seeps into her clothes.

THE NEXT MINUTE, when she comes round, is like the bright, achy moment after drinking. There is an angel at the door of the house. She thinks for a second it's the gin sending visions, but she hasn't been drinking, and the angel won't go away. It is white, vague, made of unused skin and muscles, haloed with blond hair and smiling.

'Get out,' Gretje says. The angel moves sharpish, like a nervous dog, but doesn't leave. 'Who are you?' Gretje says.

The angel waits a minute. 'Pieter,' it says.

Gretje pulls herself up on the cold coffin walls; she looks as if she's practising tricks. But she's thinking.

'Pieter' means she's talking to a boy, although between the big hands and the fat that shadows the hips, she cannot be quite sure. The eyes are like those of a painted child: huge and black. He's thin, mostly. He could be a tulip that's been forced and blanched in a cupboard.

More tart than angel, Gretje decides. She hauls herself out of the coffin and feels the full bite of the cold.

'What are you doing here?'

She knows he won't answer; that would be much too easy.

'You want food?'

He nods. He's of this world, at least.

'Go and ask Tomas.'

'He gave me something.'

Whoever he is, Anthony is none of his business. She picks up the coffin lid and slams it in place.

Anthony's dead, which makes her furious, most of all that she survived him. She doesn't want to have to deal with him. But maybe she'll make him jealous as she never could in life, flirt a little with this boy. She brushes off a dusting of frost, and a faint, wormy smell, from her skirt, and totes herself heavily back into the house.

Tomas makes the boy sit down and gives him beer.

'I'm glad to be here,' Pieter says. Molly, Gretje thinks. A sideshow in trousers.

She strips off her cold, wet clothes, checking each layer until she finds something dry; then she parcels herself up carefully again.

The cockatoo beats up from his perch and settles on Pieter's shoulder, nibbling at the child's ear. Tomas looks on lovingly. Gretje thinks the horn of the beak and the skin of the ear look alike: translucent, full of blood. Alive.

THERE'S A LIVING to consider.

This time, she's unceremonious. She goes out wrapped in felts and furs, tails and heads at her neck and her hips and her legs, all tussling and brawling like a litter of young. She's a stall on the move.

She walks to the second house on Bridge Street. The house is quiet, hoping she'll go on by, but she charges at the door, crashes up the stairs like a storm in motion and rousts out the Scottish traders from their gable rooms.

'You pay rent or you don't stay here,' she says.

One of the traders, his clothes hung on bones, tries courtliness. 'We were sorry to hear about the tragic—'

'Rent,' Gretje says.

A round man, the kind who feels every bit of his fat as a distant, unsafe frontier, says: 'But it's deathly cold.' Pause. 'We can't go anywhere. We have to wait until the thaw.' It isn't working; he pauses again. 'You know we can't bring in goods and we can't do business until then, and anyway nobody's got money to do business here.'

'Out,' Gretje says.

They line up, trying to look huge and indifferent all at once. Gretje picks up a chair.

'You don't get the benefit of what you haven't paid for,' she says. 'I'll take the chair before I'll let you use it.'

They shift uneasily.

'On your mercy, Ma'am. In the memory of your dear departed husband—'

She smashes the chair down on the floor, and it breaks into spears and splinters. She says: 'You get out in an hour, or I bring the sheriff.'

'You're a cold woman,' the thin man says.

The four men watch her like generals watch a fort, looking for weakness, but in their minds, they're already packing.

IN THE TAVERN later, people tap their noses, smile obliquely, shrug knowingly, until one of the Scotsmen punches a Dutchmen out of irritation and makes him say something.

'You know Gretje,' the Dutchman says.

He won't say more, and the Scotsman balls up his fist.

'Gretje Reyniers,' the Dutchman says. 'Her husband died.' He makes a small song of the word 'died'.

The Scotsman lets his fist land in the Dutchman's gut, almost tenderly. Beer flies.

'All right,' the Dutchman says, recovering himself and taking the Scotsman's drink with righteous propriety, 'She's a whore, and that man of hers died very suddenly.'

Shrugs, smiles, winks.

'You mean she killed him?' the Scotsman says, and the Dutchman looks shocked.

'She's from Amsterdam, originally,' he says.

SHE'S RED WITH action, but now she's stalled; so she takes down the bottle of rosa solis and settles by the stove.

Pieter is going to ask questions, for sure; that's what children do. She might even be tempted to give him answers, which is never safe. It would be good to have some distraction from her own thoughts which she keeps tasting, tonguing, like the pulp and blood when a tooth's been pulled.

On the wall is a painting. She knows Pieter is trying to decide what she sees in it, but he sees only a city square—the

Dam in Amsterdam in winter—and skies that are slate grey and busy with wind. The Dam is lit from all sides as though it were a stage, its arcades dark except for the faint bright sigh of a skirt. Across the way the gables of the houses rise like steps to Heaven, all brilliant with snow. And in front, despite the bleak cold and the low sun, business. A horse, head down, tugs at a sledge of bales. A dog stands guard over a man pushing a woman across the snow. Burghers assemble in twos and threes, and beside them are pedlars with trays of shiny, hanging things. There are men wrapped up in cloaks, and dogs shifting from paw to paw on the iced ground, and horses tethered by the store. A souvenir of Patria, out here in a forgotten colony.

She knows Pieter can't see into her memories, can't know what the picture means, or why she and Anthony brought it over when they first had money. She knows, but she still can't be entirely sure. For she lands at the Dam, and her mind goes walking far beyond the edges of the paint. Right and left, there's a canal tight with ice, and people playing; a baby in a bassinet being pushed by a matron in an apron; two fishermen trudging back from the day with nets at their shoulders and baskets in their hands, and the ghost of a white heron at their side; a man wrapped in a cloak with a chimney hat who is looking into the distance; children in brilliant red and blue carving up the new ice with their blades and forcing the day to stay open a little longer; and a dark figure with blue eyes gliding away on his quick blades, very sure and powerful.

Tomas stands in a corner of the room, rubbing his eyes with the backs of his hands, as though he is trying to wipe things out of sight.

'Tell me a story,' Pieter says.

Gretje takes some more rosa solis, hoping she'll sleep.

Pieter's sitting at the table, eyes bright with candle-light. She tries not to stare at him, but she's begun to work things out.

It's two weeks since the last ship tied up at the slips, and the harbour froze shut; since then, nothing's moved. Even the Indians don't go out stalking in this tricky, shifting snow; and nobody could have ridden into town. Unless he came off the ice in the sea, he can't be here.

If he is here, and she half-opens her eyes just in case he isn't any more, then he can't be in this house. It is two days since Anthony died, a day when everybody stays away— out of fear they might be reminded of a duty, out of embarrassment at her grief and the knowledge that good Christians don't miss the dead but cheer them on to Heaven, out of not yet knowing what the others will think about the wild woman Gretje on her own. He can't be in the house.

He says sweetly: 'Tell me your story.' She knows he's serious. He doesn't seem to realize he's impossible.

SHE HAS ONE of those orderly dreams, as though she were figuring how to explain herself before a magistrate: the name of the body is Anthony Janssen, this is how and where he died. But that's not what she's explaining in the dream. She's explaining herself.

She doesn't remember being born, but the dream has a space for the birth—to a soldier in one of Prince Maurice's regiments and a woman who's just her mother, nothing more. When she was a baby, the regiment was posted away, under orders to leave women and children behind. So she always thought she knew her father better than other children know theirs, because she could imagine him just as she wanted; there was nothing mundane to discover, that he farted or cut himself shaving or drank too much beer. Her mother, on the other hand, was always there. In the end, that is why Gretje killed her.

She wonders if her mother expected that.

Her memories of this mother were all wrapped up in the ordinary—sweeping the sand on the pavement, squatting on the wood commode, telling half-remembered stories of miracles in Amsterdam and Jesus in the manger. But Gretje counts up the wary looks, the times she was sent to be with someone else, a line of honorary aunts. She grew up white, fair, round, like a child is supposed to, but she knew her mother never trusted her.

In 1624, Gretje was twelve. She knows the year because it was a plague year, and the sickness set them on the move. You couldn't stay where people were bloated and dying; you got out as quickly as possible, in the hope that you were not ordained for death, before you had the signs that would make other villages turn you away. Besides, a village broken up by the plague couldn't prosper, or even feed itself. You were better off on the road. At least travellers could glean off the harvested fields, and ask for bread and help.

The plague settled in their village in the early spring. Gretje's mother went to ask for the shoes—the village had three pairs, for anyone who was walking away on business—and she set off as though she knew what she was doing. She tugged along Gretje, who wasn't fooled; she was dressed too neatly for the road. She carried a basket, and a couple of pamphlets about a famous rape and a famous murder that she'd bought at a fair; she read them in the middle of the day when she rested.

They went from village to village, trying to look like respectable people who had fallen on hard times, trying to be trusted even though they might be carrying God's judgemental plague along with them. The fourth day on the road, Gretje began to bleed for the first time, and her mother said it was just as well. Her mother never did explain things, and Gretje was left to spackle the world together with whatever facts or notions came to hand.

The eleventh day on the road, her mother tried to jump a passing cart, and the thick iron wheels ran, grandly and slowly, over her leg.

There was a surgeon in the village, and he tugged at the leg but he could do nothing with it. He shrugged and asked who was paying. Gretje's mother said the church would pay, and the surgeon asked which church precisely and how could he be sure? Gretje's mother said: 'The Lord will provide.' The surgeon said Gretje's mother might well be a Papist. Gretje's mother glared at him.

'You could give me a crutch,' she said.

'Don't have crutches. You need a carpenter.'

Gretje's mother looked at her leg, which stuck out at a wrong angle. 'I'd have been better off with a carpenter from the start,' she said.

On the twelfth day, her mother propped herself on a plank because she did not want to stop walking, but after a mile or so she gave up. She sent Gretje off to ask for food in the next village, but even after a full hour of walking, there was no next village. The whole country was supposed to be crammed tight with people, so Gretje thought, and here she was cruising the one void on the map.

She came back with young nettles and grass. Her mother sent her off again, and this time she came back with bread and a bit of hard cheese. Her mother looked at them fastidiously, made a show of asking no questions, and then lay down in a patch of wild garlic, surrounded by the green shine of leaves and the starry white flowers.

Night came, and Gretje lay rooting round the cupboards of her mind for bits of information. Oak for stitch,
she remembered, parsley for swelling. The ground was cold
and wet. On her mother's leg, bone had broken into
splinters that stuck through the skin, and a black scab had
settled around them. Gretje lay down by her mother's head
and kissed her mother's hair and smelt a comforting
kitchen history of soot. She looked up and tried to drown
her eyes in the white dawn. A beetle ran under her back.
The leg stank.

Oak for stitch; she could run for ever. Parsley for
swelling; she could make the leg good again. In the
meantime, she was hungry and she hunted in the basket
under her mother's head. Her mother looked towards her
but not at her, a blank and ruminative look. She tugged at
the basket. Her mother seemed to be trying out a word.
The basket moved, her mother's head fell forward and her
eyes closed again. There was a knife in the basket, blade
gone black where it ought to be brilliant, and a bit of old
bread. The knife would not cut the bread.

Gretje stood up, brushed the dry bits of grass from her
smock. Her mother's head was still resting forward, her leg
out like a yard-arm from her body, and she was snoring.
Maybe somebody would find her and help her. Maybe
somebody would find her and think she was a soldier's
woman, which she was, and take her away.

Gretje looked down at her mother, with a new, cold
lens. The woman no longer looked good. It wasn't just the
mud, her snores, the darkened fringe of skin around the
eyes; she wasn't like a mother should be, not reliable, not
necessarily right. She couldn't care for Gretje any more.

Oak for stitch; a little oak, chewed before running,

and a man may run as he chooses without his sides being clamped by wind. Parsley for swelling, for the mound of her mother's belly, for the rot round the broken bone, for the swell under her breasts as she breathed. If parsley stopped the swelling, then Gretje wouldn't have to worry about her mother any more.

She was afraid of that thought. She looked round, waiting to see the Devil somewhere close. He would know precisely what must now be done, and he would be sure about it, not like the vague lessons she had sometimes been taught; 'Honour thy father and thy mother,' she remembered, which was useless now. Father was glamorous in a parade, but somewhere else, and mother lay in the garlic like a pork roast.

The country spread out like a pancake, silvery where the water stood and green where there were fields. Gretje looked for omens. She could pick at a flower, count the petals. She could watch for magpies, whether they came one by one or together. There was always something in the clatter and movement of towns that told you what would happen next, even if it were only the sound of a cart before it turned the corner; out here she had to imagine the next thing.

The sun broke through a ring of black cloud, above her but a little to the right. She stared. The light broke into rays, like the Light from God in Heaven in some Bible print. Down below the light there must be the next thing to do, she knew it, but the light caught water. Now she knew which way to look, she looked harder. The water was framed by broad earth dykes, and people were walking along them, between the secular towers of windmills.

Her mother lay on her side now, not snoring, but with her breath coming patchy and harsh. Suppose she died, she must be buried and prayed over; there were rules for these things. Gretje could remember only one thing: seeing a cross of straw on someone's doorstep after a death. She looked across at where the sun had briefly shone down and saw the people standing now along the ridge of the dyke, watching the water. She kept looking, as though only her looking kept the people there. She picked up wires of brown grass and wound them together into a cross.

She put it on her mother's breast, still not looking. Her mother snorted awake and blinked. Gretje smiled awkwardly. Her mother tried to move her leg and her face crumpled with pain. She tried to lever herself up, but the cross seemed very heavy.

THE DRINK WEARS off abruptly, and Pieter's curd of a face hangs between the curtains.

'You fell asleep,' he says accusingly. 'We put you into bed.'

He won't leave her. He's looking into her bed, her eyes, her dreams; her memory, even. He can tell she's been remembering things she'd rather forget.

'I wanted you to tell me a story,' he says.

Gretje turns over heavily. Anything she says gives him the advantage. She can feel him watching. Even so she can't quite stop herself dreaming.

IN HER DREAM she's running down the slight, tussocky rise of the hill, looking for all those people on the dyke. She can't see the shafts of gold, Bible light any more, but she knows the direction.

Then she isn't dreaming. She's remembering.

She ran along a track with deep ruts and then on gravelled road, and when a hedge blocked the view across the remorseless flatland, she simply guessed her way. Only one

house was visible, and that was abandoned, yet she could
see people up ahead, a townful all storming down to the
water. They had baskets in their arms and dogs running
among them.

She scrambled up the dyke, expecting to see some
omen: a great beached fish, a cow that had given birth to
ten calves, the moon trapped in water—or a flood and a
rainbow, with sinners being picked out of the water by
good men in rowing-boats. But she stood in a crowd of
women looking down on water caught between dykes.

'You forgot your basket?' a girl said grandly.

'I don't need one.'

'You'll use your hands?' The girl took her hands and
spread them open. 'They're too small.'

'My hands—'

'You'll get it when you get home.'

'I'm not going home.' She shouldn't have said that,
shouldn't have drawn attention to herself. But the girl was
not interested in her except as something to patronize, like
a pet or a child.

'It won't be long,' one of the women said, in order to
keep the children quiet.

Gretje was used to water that ran where it was put,
steered into channels and canals that still flowed, but here
the water lay still and grim in a long, wide box. On the far
dyke stood wooden contraptions with gears and levers, and
chains of buckets; beside them, the men waiting wore
broken boots and rusted clothes, as though they'd been at
war. She'd seen water break dykes, and she'd heard stories of
its awful force, but here it looked broken.

Around Gretje, the women wore such neat white head-
bands that they could not be working, and some of the men
were in serious Sunday black. She told herself they'd come

to see the water punished, to see it schooled never to flood again. She stood ready to beat the water with her hands.

There was a shot on the far side, a puff of smoke. The crowd on the dyke went quiet. Across the water a flag came up on a thin pole. The stillness echoed. Some red-eyed ducks went screaming up. The men by the machines had taken hold of a great lever and were pulling it down to the ground, slowly, and then letting it rise of its own momentum; then pulling it down, faster, their muscles hard and straining like wood under weight, and letting it rise; then pulling again, and the lever seemed to move more easily. The levers rose and fell all around. The windmills began to turn.

There was a smell of beer behind Gretje that was barely laced up inside a man. He went giddily down the dyke as though his belly were pulling him, and threw himself flat on the water. He did not sink. Gretje stared at him. He lay there, quite still, face down, until someone went after him, turned him over and saved him from drowning. And now she could see that the water was only a few inches deep, and it was creeping back from the land, inch by slow inch. A black tangle of silt appeared under it.

A dominie said: 'God be praised.' He was pushed aside. From the ground, he said: 'For the feeding of the damned multitude.'

For the still, grim box between the dykes had broken into life. Fish seethed over and under each other, gasping for the chance to be safe as the water shrank. The women pulled off their shoes and tucked their skirts up, changing from matrons to fishwives in a minute, deep in the glittering mess of tails and fins. They carried big silver perch tenderly and clung on to the tails of dace with a washerwoman's grip. As the water shrank slowly inside its cage, the fish grew furious with panic, beating against the women's bare legs and bruising them. They piled together, or they tried out the air. Gretje put her hand into the mouth of a long, shining fish and felt silk and bone, but she lost her grip; then she clung on to a fat perch and went running to the dry land with it.

Below her, the new black earth was like metal being worked, the light catching it and shaping it minute to minute, the dull silver of the fish like money hiding in the mud. She found a stone and smashed the head of her perch, leaving one big, red eye intact. She watched the matrons tripping and sliding on their gross harvest. The water had almost gone from the edges of the cage, and the fish were hopeless, flopping instead of seething, falling back after each great gasp of breath, and in among them the women, too, were tired and sordid. Their trophies jerked in the baskets.

The dominie towered above Gretje, or so it seemed, because he had the advantage of the slope. 'That's a fine fish,' he said.

'It's my fish.'

The dominie said: 'Plenty more in the water.'

Gretje aimed her knee at the baggy folds between his legs and went scrambling past him. The dominie was startled still for a moment, but then he lost his footing and came down in a slow roll, looking prissily dismayed as he reached the mud.

There was still a sheen of water on the polder, and the air was full of the smell of damp and rot. Gretje began to run: oak in her pocket against the stitch, the fish cradled in her arms so she could never make good speed. She expected angry people after her, but all she could hear—or imagine, anyway—was the sound of the fish turning up the mud to find air, of the matrons smiling to themselves as they took up the fish, of the machines groaning and tugging, and the dominie putting away the things of the earth. In a mile or so, she could look back and see only silver and black in the polder.

The fish was for her mother. Of course.

Gretje went back the way she had come, and found a tree for shelter. She tried to break the bones of the fish and take off its head. The skin wouldn't come away from the flesh, which clung to the bones, and when she bit the fish, she tasted something bitter and viscous and mulberry-coloured.

Her mother had the knife.

She started to run again.

SHE SNUFFS OUT the candle very carefully, catching a little of the hot wax on her fingers and sniffing it. She makes an inventory of all the smells on her body.

She barks through the curtains, even though there might be nobody there. 'You can go back where you came from, wherever that is. Just go back.'

She hears Pieter speaking softly. He might just be saying: 'I love you.'

GRETJE DREAMS OF Pieter's eyes, dark as wells, but then she sees the eyes belong to her. She's staring out from the back of a cart, trying to see where she is.

As she remembers it, she didn't choose to leave her mother; she just did. She couldn't live on the fish. She couldn't do anything to help. She needed to be somewhere more secure, and that meant a place with houses to shelter her and somewhere to hide. She didn't want her mother to catch her, either, because she wasn't sure it was right to run. So she found a carter coming back from the dyke and she asked if she could ride to town with him.

He told her the names of places, as if that explained everything. He talked about making arrangements to meet someone where one street crosses another, but she was used to a single straight village street. She was alarmed by all these roads that cut each other up confusingly.

She thinks she could tell Pieter this, offer it up to keep him quiet. She could tell him exactly what she saw: barges, cows, a woman sculling a boat full of barrels while a man sucked on his pipe; a wrought-iron gate, a high lamp, a wall with pillars and coats of arms; the line of a canal, a broad wall and the shadow of a windmill. All this, the carter said, as the cart rocked on, was 'Amsterdam'. And this 'Amsterdam' had streets, houses, stalls, carts, dogs and the smell of bread so that if she could only look hard enough, think hard enough, she could put together these bits and pieces and the city would seem as usual as home.

The cart rattled to a stop.

'Out,' the driver said. 'You know where you're going?'

'Yes,' Gretje said.

'A girl shouldn't lose her mother,' he said.

The carter's thought was automatic, barely thought at all, but it scared Gretje into a run. In the din of the street she made out a shout that seemed to aim for her, as though girls didn't run here, and caution told her to slow down. She was alert as a scared deer, and that made her feel the wet and cold and hunger all the more; she wore each sensation. She was absorbed in the tallness of the houses, the shuddering of the cartwheels, the bullying press of people, the signs that hung outside the shops with a black man's face, a unicorn, golden sheep and hands clasped to show trustworthiness. She was blinded with signs. She heard the notes of bells break against each other in the air.

There was nowhere to stop walking. She knew she had

no money, which meant she could not stop and buy food or anything to drink. The shops were edgy at the sight of a dirty child who did not know what she was doing. Once she turned a corner, and a boy was playing with a hoop. She watched for a moment. He turned to her and beat the hoop until it spun. She stood quite still. He picked up the hoop and ran.

The bells stopped making music and began to toll. She was among the boats now, their masts racked up against the sky like beanpoles ready for the spring; most of the time she could tell only what things were like, not what they were. The masts were sometimes hung with slack grey cloth, and sometimes they were topped with flags. There was the dark, pervasive smell of stale water. The view and the smells would not change for the next half-mile, and she could let herself feel tired. She half-expected the men working the decks would notice her and tell her to get on her way but they did not even look in her direction.

She thought in the careful, all-consuming way of children who lay out a universe in their minds to make sure they have a place in it. She tried to imagine the plan of the city, but it kept slipping away; all the stolid stone and wood in the streets seemed to have discovered a wonderful power to have uncertain shape. The gulls wheeled and screamed around her, and she wondered if here in the city they could be omens, like magpies in the fields.

She smelt leather, chickens, fish, bread, shit, heat, some sweet oil and powder, old cabbage, sour and stagnant water, the airless smell of tarpaulins. There were all too many clues.

There was a church bulking up above the houses, crowned with metal thorns for spires. She walked the length of the ships, their decks and sails crammed tight like a street, and crossed into a wide square. She was back among crowds, criss-crossing and selling: cheese on a sledge, tickets for a madhouse, genever from cups on a tray, a man carrying fat, blind rats on a stick. Men in puffed black and wide beaver hats strutted past; they must be important. There were women in cloaks that caught the light. A boy went bustling over the square on some serious errand, a pail in his hand. She could see who sold, who bought, who could demand, who could only offer, but knowing this didn't change things. It only reminded her that, until she had somewhere to sleep, she was the beggar in the foreground.

The church blocked the street out of the square: a high intimidation made out of straight stone. It made her look up so far and so sharply she thought her neck would snap. So, since she could not look up, she looked humble. The stones on the floor were cut with words. The air was cool and still and went up to plain vaults. There seemed to be many rooms but without walls, extending like the plan of something grander. Light that was ordinary in the streets came through the high, clear windows like a blessing.

She had to be noticed.

There were seven people sitting on pews by the pulpit. Nobody looked like a minister or so much unlike one that she could afford to ignore them. Since she was a beggar and in need of kindness, she did not straighten her hair or lick-wash her face, although for a moment she wanted to; she simply stood by the end of the pews, far enough away to seem like a sign or a memory and not like a brat. She could smell meat on one woman's clothes, and her eyes conveniently began to water.

Out of the sky-high walls of the church there came a sudden roar, huge and calamitous. Gretje knew she ought to fall to her knees, but she didn't. One of the people in the pews stood up and stalked to the door as though the noise had offended him. The sound came again. She knew it was only music and not the voice of God but she was taking no risks. She ran to the door as though the notes were sweeping her out of the church and she caught at the sleeve of the man who was leaving.

'Please,' she said.

He looked through her.

'I've lost my mother,' she said.

He dug into his pockets for a small coin and went off across the square like a man on stilts, not bending even at the knee.

She held on to the coin.

Then she felt the air change. She was used to the way the wind softens just before a storm and then begins to beat in at windows, but it was not that kind of change. For a start, it wasn't familiar, so it couldn't be natural. The change hung all around her, even when she walked into the square, or back along the street of ships where she had smelt old salt rope and wood. She was hungry and cold, and the whole town taunted her with the smell of buns and stew.

She cut down an alley to a small canal. The water laced through the town and sat there. A shallow lighter came by, tugged by a horse, and the mud at the canal bottom began to stir and whirl under the green water, and there was the stench of dumped shit, but it was sweetened with Christmas smells. There were no bakeries she could see, and the warehouse fronts were shuttered up, but still the town was privileged with warm spice. She began to be afraid, as if the scent were a ghost. She smelt her hands, and the wild garlic was blotted out by a wind full of spice and soot. The scent was excusing her, invading her, promising all kinds of things and she was sure for a moment of the Devil's closeness. She smelt mace, nutmeg, cinnamon and fire.

She hugged the sides of the street, where the gables arched over the pavement with great hooks. A little rain put patches on the cobbles. Everything in general seemed urgent, her walk, her breathing, keeping out of the rain and the spicy wind, but still she knew nothing in particular; so she was urgently walking nowhere. The nowhere she wanted would be cleaned of these brilliant spices, would be a nowhere for a child with nothing and a body that was close to exhaustion. She could lie down and sleep at last.

The bells rang out. In the village they meant funerals. She had a notion that people died in the city every half-hour, and the real business of the place was mourning. She crossed a long bridge and came into a lane of water that went off at right angles.

A row of black brick warehouses stood along the canal. Nobody was about on the streets any more, and the line of the canal was straight; she felt that she could know where she was. She had grown used to the smell, which was ominous on the wind but faintly sweet in her mouth. The doors down to the basement were open at one of the warehouses, and she looked in.

Down steps, she saw great brick tanks full of still liquid. Where light fell, there were dead rainbows cramped on the surface. Oil, she said out loud; she'd seen oil. She walked down into the basement. The tanks seemed to stretch away like fields, rich and stinking. There was nobody around, and it was dry here. The smell, she began to think, was what she deserved, and besides, it kept away the town and all the judgemental men and women and the question of where to go next. In the corner of the basement, there was a ladder. She climbed it carefully.

The floor above was wood that had been washed and salted; it was brittle. She looked at it carefully in order to see nothing else. She saw the nails with particular attention: straight iron claws, driven down with great force. Someone had carved a picture into the wood, but it was so rough that she could not make out what it was meant to be. The floor was flaking where the ladder cut up through the wood.

She glanced up. She was among bones: vaults, arches, shelters, naves, tombs and windows of bones, cluttered in heaps and standing high enough to seem like the stone church she had just left. She touched some that were solid as rock and some that caught like whips. Beyond the bones she could hear men moving around; she pulled her hand back. She sat down in the curve of a great rib. She had wanted omens and here she sat among the bones of ominous creatures, so huge she could not begin to imagine their living state. Their meaning went vaulting up above her until it was so huge and shapeless that it was like no meaning at all. It was even comforting. Other people would be disgusted, even afraid, and they would stay away.

PIETER BRINGS HER morning milk the next day.

'That's Tomas's job,' she says.

Pieter says: 'I got up first.'

Gretje asks: 'Where did you sleep?'

'On the chair.'

'You're too tall to sleep on the chair.'

'I managed.'

Gretje is drinking her milk more delicately. She sits up like a city lady.

'How did you get here, anyway?'

'I'm from Amsterdam. I came on the boat.'

'There's been no boat for weeks.'

'I was trying to find you.'

'It's not a big town.'

'I stayed on the boat. I had a friend.'

'You'd have frozen on the boat,' she said. 'You'd be dead.'

'We had a fire.'

Pieter takes up the bowl. Gretje says: 'Give some to the bird.' Feathers clatter and the bird comes down to Pieter's shoulder and kisses his ear.

Gretje shouts: 'Who are you?'

Pieter starts. 'I'm Pieter,' he says. 'I've always been Pieter.'

'And why did you want to find me?'

Pieter says nothing.

'Did you want to find me in particular?'

Pieter nods.

'I don't have a duty to you, you know. I can put you out any time. Send you down to the fort and see if you like living with the soldiers.' She looks at him, and wonders: whether the breasts will turn to muscle or milk, how the long blond legs are going to be strong. She notices the large hands.

She thinks he should be terrified. He has been in this icy America for weeks, he says, no way to get out or get back, and his warmth and life depend on her. And all her feelings are untidy, like linens when the cat's been in the cupboard, just sobs and peace and screams and desolation, certainly anger, maybe love.

'Get out,' she says to Pieter. He's not surprised when she does something surprising. He goes to the street door at once.

She stands by the stove, warming her hands. Tears come up out of her gut and she feels her whole face twist and tear with them. She gulps for air and pushes her hands down to the hot stove to feel a pain besides this sense of being hollowed out.

Tomas shouts at her.

USUALLY, SHE MAKES order out of her life with work, with acts that follow so closely on each other that there is no break. But now Anthony's gone, there's a whole book of silences between each minute, and she drags in the past to fill it. She's grateful for the comfort of things that are done with.

That morning in Amsterdam, her first morning, she woke up in the whale store, and the smell startled her: the stench of dead flesh rendered into oil. But she'll never have to do that again. She saw the shadow of the bones in the bright light from the windows, but now that's just a picture in her head. She remembers the faint sounds of men moving about the tanks of black oil.

Someone climbed the ladder, someone found her.

It happened to be someone kind, so she's happy to remember him. She forgets how she crept under a cave of bones when she first heard him coming, trying to be so still she'd be invisible; or how he stopped on the ladder for a moment, shouted something about starting the fires; and how she hated him for making her wait to see him. She should have run before anyone came, gone back to the streets where she was safe.

The man saw her at once; anything living was conspicuous in the bone store. He called to her as if she were a pet. She came out of her cave reluctantly, ready to duck away if there was trouble. He said: 'You can't sleep here.'

But he did have a wife who worked the fish market, so Gretje got work. She stood back while the wife threw a knife around a cod and tore out the oily vitals and sliced the flesh and bone. The heads went in a bucket, with their needle teeth snatching the air. Gretje carried off baskets of flesh and offal, in a parade of children who smelt of oil and cooked salt. She took a barrow of guts to the street of ships, and let it sluice down the walls to the water: her mark on the city.

She was bone tired by the evening. The man and his wife weren't offering a bed; they seemed to think it was easy for a child to find somewhere to sleep. So she crossed the docks to Warmoesstraat, and its fat, sure houses made of stone. She looked in through windows: a room with metal cups for sale, one with bales stacked high like hay for the winter, another with people writing in a row. She was too tired to want to understand.

But between the houses ran lanes with gates on to ramshackle yards and left-over buildings of wood. It was like finding a barnyard in the city. Anyone could run into the barns a dozen ways, through the wet basements, the hoists and high windows, the doors left a bit ajar; and there was always an escape.

Gretje walked in. There were two girls, Lysbeth and Marieke, who said there was room for her. Nobody asked questions, nobody seemed too anxious about money. She ate some turnips and bread and sat in torchlight by the door with the two girls. They played marbles, careful with the stones because they were scarce in the sand under Amsterdam.

When it was time to go to sleep, she had a bag of straw on a dry, wooden floor. She heard the boards creaking and breathing around her, someone crammed on to each ledge and into each corner, the beds butting up against each other. She felt safe in a great storehouse of children.

The next morning, someone she didn't know asked for money, and she paid from her earnings at the fish stall. A few people asked her who she was—not where she came from, what she was doing, how old she was or which church she belonged to, only who she was. She went out hungry to work.

By the time she came back, that simple question—who are you?—was buried in her mind and itching like a chigger. She had once been a child, but now she lived by herself. Nobody cosseted her like a child. She had once been a daughter, but her father had shipped out, and her mother was mislaid, so there was no percentage in that. She bled, so she was a woman, so Lysbeth said; but she had no idea what to do about it except to clean up the blood and make sure it did not show. She had a sense that it might be better, for the moment, to be a child in this dormitory. Being a woman could mean trouble.

Otherwise, her name was Gretje, and her job was carrying fish. Fishwives seemed to be set aside, loved mostly by the men who brought home the smell of dead whales, or fishermen, or the fish merchants: who didn't notice the smell of fish oil. Just working the fish markets put her in a class and category and made the answer obvious when people asked who she was. But perhaps she could be with other people and be someone else and—

The three girls told piecemeal stories. Beggars spoke French, Lysbeth said. They spoke French and came from Paris and knew everything. 'To work is to pray,' said Marieke, who'd learned she could get beer and sometimes small coins by letting men touch her and touching them back. Gretje said she'd seen the woman upstairs, the big, white billow of a woman who did laundry, lying down on her bed with the notary from the end of Warmoesstraat. Marieke, knowing, said she knew about that; they'd be married if the notary was not such a snob. She also knew the woman was going to have a child. And Lysbeth, unworldly and dark and kind, said: 'She isn't. The doctor came and he cut her foot and bled the mother vein. So she won't have the baby.' And so they spun a tapestry of a world

35

out of the bits they collected, a great picture of events.

'I'm not going to carry fish,' Gretje said.

Lysbeth thought for a moment. 'You'll go to the Spinhuis. They'll lock you up and make you spin, and your fingers will get cut until you have no more fingers, and the men will all come to stare at you. You'd learn to read, though.'

'My mother used to read,' Gretje said. 'She had stories about a murder and a rape in Delft. She taught me to read.'

Gretje paused: 'I could beg like the French,' she said.

'And then?'

'I'd have money every day. Solid money.'

'For solid money,' Marieke said, 'people expect something in return.'

'I could give them anything,' Gretje said. 'I could be anyone they wanted.'

The girls looked at her as though she was stupid. 'You're Gretje,' they said.

'YOU'LL HAVE TO be useful,' Gretje says.

Pieter sits in a roundel of yellow light, Gretje in the dark. His hands seem huge in their own shadows.

'You'll have to work.'

'I can work.'

Gretje knows she is about to make a mistake.

'I can do things,' Pieter says. 'You can teach me.'

She savours the moment, the smell of burnt air around the stove and the comfortable, stifling feel of the room. But she can sense the trap that's waiting: someone to care for.

'My daughter Maria is in Amsterdam,' she says. 'She goes to school.'

She could tell Pieter everything.

'Yes,' Pieter says.

She pulls back. If there's one thing she knows, it's a bargain: she wants to know what he'll give if she gives up her story.

'You could tell me,' Pieter says.

She laces her hands. She's out of the habit of trusting.

'Come on,' Pieter says, all brisk and sensible.

GRETJE LEFT THE fish market and took to the streets for a month or two. She was new enough to turn up at corners as the almost respectable child, the lost one, who was distinctly Dutch and understood the annoyance with all the French beggars, the one who was clean because she had only just lost her mother. So kind people gave her money and didn't ask for anything because they thought she might still be saved.

She went out on the spit of land that closed off the harbour, where a coppice of gibbets stood. She stood among the bodies and stared at the slack tongues, popped eyes. Sometimes a breathless gentleman would give her a coin.

She stood by the arcades of the Town Hall, on the square by the weighhouse and the New Church. She made herself look lost. She said she could not find her mother, which was true, and she walked demurely. She spent some money on starch so she would look like the other proper children. There was no gold, but she made a living.

She went to pray in the New Church, where she had once been lost, and stood at the inside of the door, out of the wind, and cried. The gentry could either drop coins in a silent, official box, or else get thanks from a poor, lost child who looked like their daughter. Some of them chose the girl.

The trouble with all this propriety was the women. Other girls worked the men, and men were at least vulnerable when they were needy. But a certain kind of matron thought Gretje would make the perfect servant: quiet, decorous, industrious. Each time she went out to work her particular beat, she ran the risk of being taken at face value and taken home to sweep.

On a cold afternoon, she went home with Mevrouw Van Wely, a puppet of a woman with a steel rod bent inside her, compliant and defiant all at once, who confused other people almost as much as she herself was confused. Mijnheer Van Wely dealt in pewter, or rather he sat in a workshop and smelted, formed, polished and soldered it. Upstairs, Mevrouw Van Wely simpered at the customers to remind them of their moral duty to buy something. Gretje earned her keep by not laughing.

It wasn't the Van Welys she served, though, as much as their house—a tyrant machine, always in need of sanding, dusting, sweeping, polishing, washing, airing and warming; the parlour hardly ever entered but laid out like a show with special things; the kitchen neatly maintained as though meat and blood and leaves and earth never strayed there; the stone pavement outside neatly sanded each time it rained. The linen chest was ordered like a library. The cellar was scrubbed out on Fridays, the smell of used mud briefly hidden by lye and soap. Since Gretje had the best eyes, she was set to crawl across each floor, looking for insect eggs, inch by inch.

It was easy to get used to the house, because it was all-absorbing; she started to think of Mevrouw Van Wely as its servant, as caught as Gretje in the routine. Every action was rewarded, in a way; she was always warm, because she dragged the peat down to the fires from the attic, and cleaned away the soot and ashes; she was fed because she cut potatoes; safe because she locked the windows at night;

she expected salvation because there was no time for sin.
She was even peaceful. In her mother's kitchen, there was
always her mother's need—for a child's hugs and kisses, for
being remembered, for being touched—that hung around
like an old, scabby dog. She liked its absence.

Still, the rules made Gretje nervous. She walked about
defiantly, expecting someone to disapprove. She was
wrapped up in grey and sent out on errands and she
brought back the cold of the air all around her and worried
someone would notice. She found a kitten, a tiger that
jumped and crept under her skirt and fought her hand and
lay on her like a nursing baby; she giggled at it, lost herself
in its sweet, dependent ways, and put it back on the street.
It cried, an unbearable high cry full of terror. She brushed
the hairs carefully off her grey skirt.

THE HOUSE WAS not perfect, of course. The workshop
brought antimony and lead into it and stone sinks full of
molten metal. The air, sweetened and cleaned in most
other rooms, stank of heat. Van Wely sweated over his
leather apron. He worked with a second man and a boy.
When they were upstairs, their bodies were so polite they
might as well have been drawings on paper; in the
workshop, they had form and force.

Sometimes when Gretje finished what she had been
told to do and found herself in a room where there was
nobody to tell her what to do next, she went down to the
workshop, always quickly as though she had been sent
there. She stood in the shadows at the back. Between her
and the forge hung pots, moulds, chisels tied by their
handles that stabbed at the air in the draught from the
street. She smelt mud, and the basement smell, the men,
heat and the separate smell of hot metal.

There was sometimes light from the metal. She had seen gold shine like that in the backs of churches, and on one rich woman's neck. She climbed on the shelves of brown and grey-green moulds, each numbered and marked, and she looked down. Van Wely took a plank on a stick and drew it across the sink of metal. He seemed to pull the gold away and leave behind a boiling mirror. She wanted to see herself but she was afraid of the heat. The men took up the mirror in ladles and poured it into some kind of crock. She wanted to know where the gold had gone from the skim of the pewter and where her face would go if she had looked into the mirror. She would be trapped between the thin skins of the crock for ever: wide-eyed, accused by the heat. The men set the crock aside.

Van Wely saw her.

'I wanted to see,' she said.

He took another form and flooded it with the metal until the mirror had gone. She let herself down from the shelves.

The boy, Hendrick, who was tapping at moulds on a table, said: 'Hey!' She was standing over the hot bench. 'You'll burn.' She could feel her face as red as shame. 'What do you want?' he asked.

She knew enough not to say that she wanted to see where the mirror had gone, and whether her face was caught there. She was terribly afraid to leave such a clear memorial. Anyone who could read her face for long enough would see her mother under the weight of that brown grass cross.

'I'll show you something,' Hendrick said, and Van Wely stared out of the door.

Hendrick tapped and pried at a mould, lifted it carefully apart and out came a dull arc of metal, as lifeless as a plastered wall but smoother. 'You take this,' he said, talking more loudly now because Van Wely did not seem disposed to interfere for the moment, 'and you solder it together and then you polish it.' He bustled around Van Wely, which was risky manners, and picked up a form that had already been put together. He put it on to the lathe. 'You can work the lathe,' he said, because usually that was the job he had to do.

Gretje worked the treadle. The dead metal turned. Hendrick took up a fine chisel and held it against the metal. There was a faint shower of metal on to the bench. The metal turned, and the chisel lay against it. Where the chisel had been, a sheen began to spread down the shape of the vase, a fine mirrored sheen that caught distinctly the shape of the light through the door. Gretje stared. The mirror would carry everything about her; it might even show where her mother lay. She would not, under any circumstances, show that she was alarmed.

The boy told her to speed up the treadle; she wasn't sure if he told her in words or by his gestures. His eyes were clamped to the metal on the lathe. She could feel the disarray in her neat, grey clothes, the salve of sweat on her body; she was aware of her flesh against the raw linen.

'There,' Hendrick said.

'Gretje!'

Mevrouw Van Wely stood at the workshop door, humming psalms.

'I'm coming, Ma'am,' Gretje said. She followed the woman's broad back at just enough distance to look back and smile. But Van Wely was up now and checking the moulds, and Hendrick was shadowing him at his side, ready to be Van Wely if he ever could.

She skinned parsnips, she ran errands and, in the late afternoon, she cut off from bringing back coffee from

Warmoesstraat and went to the barn where she had slept when she first came to Amsterdam. The house leaned at wider and wider angles from its stone neighbours, the kind of place that landlords would not suffer much longer, and then everyone would have to find a house like the Van Welys' to serve.

She gave the barn meaning, just as she was slowly beginning to give meaning to other quarters. Give her time and she could appropriate the whole city, just by living.

Lysbeth, the dark girl, sat at the doorway, picking through Marieke's hair for nits, as though she were weaving cleanness between the strands.

Gretje said: 'It's a fine day.'

'They let you out?'

'I come and go as I—'

Marieke looked at her shrewdly, and Lysbeth worked on.

'How are things?'

Marieke said: 'Good, good.'

Lysbeth looked up from her work. Gretje saw her familiar face, but she saw it whitened—with powder, or sickness, she could not tell. The paleness made Lysbeth's deep, kind eyes seem bruised. The change startled Gretje. She walked away, not a friend, but a proper gentlewoman's servant out on an errand.

'Things are good,' Lysbeth was shouting after her. 'Things really are good.'

MEVROUW VAN WELY loved to teach. She taught by example, by the din of repeated orders, by proverbs, homilies, legends and sometimes a Bible story; she taught the sanctity of all indoors. She started sentences with 'When you marry,' because she felt responsible for Gretje.

There was a small case of books, and sometimes, when Mevrouw Van Wely was busy in the shop, Gretje took one down to read. Her mother's stories had been easier than this Bible, this book of saints; she had known the words almost off by heart so that she hardly had to sound them at all. But she persevered. She read about the revolution of the meek, the dragon at the end of the world, the murder of Abel. In the book of saints and legends, she read about the Amsterdam miracle, but she was not entirely sure how Jesus could be coughed into a fire.

Mevrouw Van Wely said: 'Don't play with the books.'

'I was reading,' Gretje said. For once, she looked properly at Mevrouw Van Wely.

Mevrouw was pretty, small and swaddled up in domestic grey and white; there was life in her eyes but she seemed to apologize for it, like a large, uncertain girl.

'The books aren't for you,' she said.

'My mother taught me to read.'

The two stood unnaturally still.

'That's good,' Mevrouw Van Wely said, the kindness painted on her voice. 'It's good to read.'

But pliant, quiet Gretje had acquired this shadowy mother, and dragged her into the room: a woman never before considered. She had a skill that was not appropriate and access to what should be locked away behind bars of print. Gretje knew she had done something unforgivable, while doing something quite ordinary, which meant she had not grasped the rules of the house after all.

'Which book were you reading?' Mevrouw went to the case as if she were going to check that the book was not damaged or missing.

'The book of legends,' Gretje said.

The shop bell sounded, and Mevrouw went away. The

transaction was unusually brusque. When Mevrouw came back, Gretje was careful to have the broom in her hand.

'You should have asked,' Mevrouw said. Then, with an effort, she added: 'You should read the Bible. I could find passages for you.'

They sat pressed side by side, warm and assured, in a world of thunder and ruin, with cities fallen, sons slaughtered, women turned to salt, suffering humanity cased up in the belly of huge fish and a diet of plagues. They proceeded to the love of God, and the sacrifice of women. Mevrouw put her arm around Gretje's waist. 'I'm going to have a baby,' she said. Then she pulled her arm back as though she was afraid she had made some mistake.

Gretje kissed her, which did not happen again.

THE SPICES WERE taken out of the kitchen, and the old cheese, at the orders of Mijnheer Van Wely. He worried that spice would startle his wife's body and hurt the child. Where once the house itself had been the tyrant, now the baby seemed to rule the household and change all its ways, including those of its passive, clever mother. The cook made stewed rhubarb and stewed apple and stewed prunes in the interests of the wife's bowels. Since Mevrouw was not young any more, there was the possibility that her womb had dried up, so she took fat fish, goose fat, capons in their warm yellow casing of fat and quantities of butter. Her body, once kept private under layers of linen, was now a public matter, debated and treated with each dish that came out of the kitchen. She once said she wanted to dance, just dance alone, and Mijnheer came stomping up from the workshop to lecture her on the terrible consequences of women's sin of dancing. The baby would surely die. 'You might as well go riding,' he said.

She went to hug him, and he said: 'There are a lot of things we have to do without.' She sat down abruptly, as though she had been pushed.

Mijnheer went back to the workshop, his shoulders four-square rigid with duty, and shouted at the man and the boy about the dirt on the moulds and the failure to bring up antimony to set in the pewter and the fact that the door was open to the street, although Gretje knew he would have bawled them out for nothing. He shouldn't be in the house at all; in the house he added up only to the scuffing on floors, the dirtying of dishes, a heavy duty of laundry.

Gretje slipped past them, stood in corners and on landings, trying to be invisible; she wanted, in the way of a frightened child, to have the grown-ups act with such decorum that she did not need to know anything about them beyond their orders. She could feel desires and anger like honoured strangers in the house. She was faintly jealous.

And as Mevrouw grew larger, belly pushing up huge under her breasts, the mechanics of the house fell more and more dependent on Gretje—not just her muscles, but also her decisions. She worked particularly on the room where the birthing chair stood, the curtains pulled around it. She scrubbed the floor, and the wood of the chair where it was cut away for the midwife to work, plumped up the pillows and kept them in fresh linen every day, shook out the curtains and hung them from the window even though the days were cold. The tyrant house had to be maintained and somehow insulated, by sweeping, washing, picking, sanding, polishing, from all the drama and expectation that had been unleashed inside it.

Mevrouw still served in the shop and kept the books. When a customer came, she pushed herself up from her chair with a plump, domestic smile and knew what a huge advantage she carried in her belly when people smiled. They didn't like to quarrel down the price any more.

HER EYES FEEL swollen, her feet hurt, she can't think any more, she feels bruised through her head and body. Pieter is solicitous, but he's insistent.

She says: 'You don't want to know about the baby, do you?'

Pieter says: 'Yes.'

'It isn't a boy's story.'

'Tell me anyway.'

The stable cat settles in Pieter's lap to get the warmth from the candles.

MEVROUW TOLD GRETJE to go for a midwife. It was winter, but the leaves on the lindens along the canal had held and they chimed like icicles. The midwife bundled herself up with great deliberation and assembled bottles and tongs. When she had made quite clear that she did not simply jump when she was told, she came out to the street and began to canter almost faster than Gretje could manage, kicking up her heels under billowing black like a fast, fat horse. The wind scoured their faces.

The midwife left fur and wool like a trail in the hallway, outraging the house, and went to breathe her mare's breath in the face of Mevrouw.

Gretje stood on the margins. The contractions had started, Mevrouw said; she could feel them like a hand turning inside her. 'Good,' the midwife said. She prescribed purges to make the contractions come faster, and Gretje went for castor oil and senna; Mevrouw drank, went pale, winced at the next contraction and farted hugely. Gretje's instinct was to open the windows and air the house, but

the cold was too strong. Mevrouw sat agonizing on the
pillows, not yet in pain enough to forget her embarrassment at her loosening bowels. The midwife sent Gretje
to the kitchen again, this time to prepare waters from the
saffron and aniseed she had ordered. Gretje put the fine red
stamens into a glass that suited them and poured water
from the fire, but the glass cracked open. She tried again,
this time in a pewter cup.

'This'll make you quieter,' the midwife said. Mevrouw
took the saffron water and drank it. 'It's like spices,' she
said. 'That's because it is spices,' the midwife said. Mevrouw
said: 'They're coming more quickly now.' The midwife drew
the curtains round the chair. 'Can you read?' she asked
Gretje, and Gretje nodded. 'Then lay out tincture of myrrh
and aloe. There's a label on the bottle. Melt some butter.
Warm some wine.'

Gretje looked puzzled. 'Some warm wine in a bowl,' the
midwife said. 'Some warm wine in a glass for Mevrouw Van
Wely and some for me. It's her first, so it'll be a long day.'

The lamps were lit.

Van Wely paraded to some city event in black and a
ruff, because he would never miss such a thing, but he
came scampering back, alarmed and eager, laden with a ton
of his gentleman's manners but with his face bright as a
boy's. The midwife said it would be indecent for him to
move the curtains. He stood among the smells of the
room—violets, sweat, honey, aloes, saffron, aniseed, shit
and burning oil—and he spoke to his wife through the curtains, and she grunted and farted back.

There was a kingdom in the house now into which
nobody could pass, except for Mevrouw and the midwife,
and both were taking wine. When the midwife next came
through the curtains, she was smiling.

'The swaddling strips,' the midwife said. Gretje looked blank. 'The swaddling strips,' the midwife said again. In the service of the little, curtained kingdom, Gretje and Mijnheer Van Wely both cantered away on vital missions, embassies who brought back linen and silk and warmed wine. The kingdom was surrounded with a treasury of oils and butter. 'How is she?' Van Wely kept asking. 'How is the baby doing?' The lights danced in his eyes, and showed him nothing.

For fourteen hours, they walked back and forth through the room. Gretje brought broth, wine and bread. She thought of conjuring shows in which amazing things happen just out of sight, behind curtains that bump and billow. She thought of the pain she heard in Mevrouw's voice. She thought sentimentally of little babies, and smelt blood. She leaned for a moment on the wicker of the crib and the wall seemed to give, and she straightened herself up quickly; she checked that the linen was perfect. She did not want to be tired. From inside the curtains came sounds like a shipwreck and sounds like a cowhouse. It was vulgar, ecstatic, ordinary, miraculous and ridiculous, and not one of those qualities could for a moment be divorced from all the others. Gretje thought, with the big thinking of a fourteen-year-old, that this was the experience that everyone has, and therefore all experience must be like this.

'It's moving,' the midwife bellowed.

Van Wely said he'd go for a doctor because it was taking so long, and from inside the curtains went up a stream of spiced and winy invective; he had to trust the midwife, the midwife said, or else everything was lost and, besides, what did a man know? She wanted more broth, now, for the mother, whose strength was flagging. As Gretje left the room, she saw the proper Van Wely, in his ruff and black, standing by the curtains and not daring to part them. He had a transparent look, like a man with no energy to waste, who has willed all the strength and patience to his wife for as long as she needs it. He was even breathing with her, and the sound of her breath was enormous.

Now Gretje was the outsider, separate from events and separate from the house. She heard a scream, and the midwife said: 'It's turned. Push. Push.' She heard terrible breathing and a struggle, something being tugged and coaxed and tugged again: the baby, she thought. The women's voices had gone from a deep purr of encouragement to sounds of an inhuman pitch. Van Wely, at the curtains, was pale as water. 'Warm wine,' the midwife shouted, 'warm water. Warm butter.' Gretje dashed for everything, noticing where she spilled the liquids in her hurry. As she came back to the room, she heard a baby cry.

The curtains around the stool were thrown back, and the lamps had been brought together like a church picture. There was a child, washed in the warm water, smeared with oil, resting in swaddling-clothes for the sake of its limbs and now lying on the breasts of its exhausted mother. The faces were joyful and sure. Below was a rupture of blood and cloth, black and vivid, a mess of various cleaning oils and the butter that helped the child finally to slip out. The midwife had scrubbed her hands, but there was still a blackness under the nails. All this, Gretje saw quickly. Having seen it, she was quite unprepared for the way her heart seemed to force up under her ribs.

She brought more water. She brought wine for Mijnheer Van Wely. She helped Mevrouw on to a bed with clean white linen which was stained immediately. She opened the windows to air the house, and when she felt the

49

dawn cold, she snapped them closed because the immaculate house was going to have to accept these marks and smells. Below, the cold had seized the water on the narrow canal, and the heat from the window went out for a moment in the torchlight like a man's visible breath.

She wanted to hold the baby, but the midwife did not approve. She wanted to comfort all of them; she had never felt such kindness. She even connected, for a brief moment, this birth with her own birth, this pain with her mother's pain; but she set the connection aside, because she could not put joy back into her mother's life.

She caught the shape of her own face reflected in the pewter mug. Her look of guilt had been caught in the metal, put in the shop and sold away to a housewife for some dinner. It need never trouble her again.

She took up paper and lace to say that a boy had been born, and she nailed it to the outside of the door. She stood back. The door seemed to glint like glass. The air was scoured by the cold, but through it came the smell that once alarmed her in the city: spices and fire and soot.

She went up the ladders to her room where she meant to lie down but she could not rest. The house snored under her; its boards shifted like sleepers. Her window was closed tightly, and it let out only on to a landing with its own windows to the outside, but still the smell of spice stood in the room like a visitor.

She knew now that it came from the warehouses of the East India Company, where they burnt up the cinnamon and nutmeg and cloves to make sure the price never fell. It was the smell of plenty being spoilt. But to her, it was the smell of Christmas, livening the senses whether you wanted it or not. She wrapped herself in everything she had, crept down into the hallway and across the pavement, tied blades on her shoes and let herself gently down on to the ice, wondering if November cold was enough to set the water truly solid.

She could go anywhere this morning. The house was asleep, and the streets were almost empty, and she was warm with joy. The ice was new and therefore reliable, not cut up by rash boats and careless skaters. She trusted in speed. The white of the dawn turned to silver and then to red, and the red suffused the sky and began to die back, and above her was a clear blue. She sang under her breath. She had all the life in the world.

Ahead of her on the ice was one other skater. She saw the line of his body, and a dark, dark face. He smiled at her, as though they were conspirators. She slowed a little. His eyes were blue like paint. He turned around on his blades and went soaring away. She thought of Mevrouw in the chair, her mother in the garlic and then of the charcoal shadows on the skater's face. Just for the moment, a bit regretfully, she turned back.

GRETJE WAKES UP long before dawn. All she wants is to be with Anthony: dark Anthony, skating away. She pulls coats around her, almost forgets her shoes and goes out into the snow which throws back the very faint grey light in the sky.

Pieter sits on the coffin. He is whittling a stick. He looks placidly towards her and the knife cuts, cuts, cuts, cuts.

TWO

SHE BOWLS PIETER along like a hoop before a stick, and he's scared to hold back, scared to move on; he looks very young, all scared and petulant and soft. She shoves him into the fort, and into the room where the Colony Secretary sits at his desk by a slow fire.

'I want this boy off my hands,' Gretje says.

The Colony Secretary stretches.

'This boy is nothing to do with me. Nothing. He arrived on my doorstep, and in charity I looked after him, and he's been nothing, nothing but trouble.'

'He asked for you, Mevrouw. You took him in. No doubt you could pay his passage—'

'There are no ships moving, and you know it.'

'I know.'

'Then what are you going to do?'

The Secretary says: 'Nothing, Mevrouw. You can shelter the boy until the thaw. Then we'll see.'

'I refuse.'

'Mevrouw,' the Colony Secretary says, 'I didn't want to disturb you in your mourning. But since you're here—' He makes a play of shuffling the papers on his desk.

'I have to make an inquiry,' he says, 'into the death of Mijnheer Anthony Janssen, known as the Turk.'

'Yes,' Gretje says.

She's careful how she looks and speaks, more like a serving girl than the rich widow.

'The boy,' he says, 'can go.'

Pieter skids out.

'If it had been anyone else—' the Secretary says.

'Mijnheer,' she says, keeping her head down. She's used to the law as a public shouting-match, where you know what everyone wants; and she isn't sure about the Secretary.

'What was Janssen doing anyway?'

'He went out after deer. It's been a hard winter.'

'Took a gun?'

'Of course.'

'He went out in the snow, alone?'

Don't pause, she thinks. 'He was going round the farms on the Bowery. He thought there'd be deer come down for the grain.'

The Secretary prints a word on his paper.

'He was a strong man? Not an old man?'

She assumes the Secretary will see grief and shock in her face. But that's if he can bring himself to look at a whore's face. She wonders if she ought to try some other way. She thinks about settling in his lap and wriggling carefully, almost innocently for his pleasure, like a serving girl; he likes that. His stub of a cock will distract him, and then the wet in his lap will embarrass him, and that will be that.

'He was strong.' Gretje blanks her eyes, trying to keep his questions out of her head.

'He was healthy?'

She says nothing.

'And you found him dead.'

'Yes.'

'How did you come to find him?'

'He went out on a Thursday,' Gretje says. 'On the Friday he wasn't back.'

'You didn't give the alarm.'

Gretje shrugs.

'I suppose it came as no surprise,' the Secretary says, 'to you.'

Gretje says nothing.

'And the Friday morning, you started to worry?'

'He said he wasn't going far.'

'He hadn't gone far?'

'A mile, two miles. I don't know exactly. I followed the tracks. In this weather the tracks are good for weeks.'

'I didn't know you were a tracker.'

'I—' Gretje lets it pass.

'Where did you find the body?'

'The road was buried. I was past the barns, I know that. I was on a slope and I slid, and he was there. I slid down and came up against him, eye to eye.'

'The body,' the Secretary says. 'Were there wounds?'

She remembers the Turk's body alongside her own, not just by sight. She says: 'I couldn't see wounds.'

'Any other tracks?'

'I don't know.'

'How could you not know?'

'There were tracks, of course there were tracks. But I don't know who made them.'

'But you could track your husband?'

This is not going well, and Gretje knows it.

The Secretary writes: 'No wounds.'

'No sign of Indians, I suppose?'

'No.'

'But then you're friends with the Indians, aren't you?'

'No more than anyone else who does business.'

'Business,' the Secretary repeats and writes something down with great elaboration.

She can see he's afraid, but that is the nature of his job, afraid he'll miss something—smugglers, Indians, Englishmen making unauthorized voyages, trouble before it starts—and be blamed in Amsterdam later. Then he's afraid of Indians, challenges, soldiers, the sailors frozen in the town and the people who live here. He wants everything ordered on paper.

'I want that boy out of my house,' Gretje says.

'In this weather,' the Secretary says, 'that would be murder.'

The word hangs in the air for a while.

The Secretary says: 'I shall need to see your husband's body.'

'The boy is the Company's responsibility. You brought him here.'

The Secretary picks up a paper. 'There seems to be some question,' he says, chiselling each word as though for a monument, 'about the status of some property on Bridge Street.'

'In other words,' Gretje says, 'you want me to be quiet.'

The Secretary shrugs.

'I could have a soldier take you home,' he said. 'Or two, if you need the money.'

She's out in the street almost before she can breathe. But she doesn't brood on the Secretary's smugness. She's thinking of Pieter, who spends the night guarding the body

55

of a man he couldn't have known, who takes the task away from Gretje who paid for it with her grief.

The town and the ice both seem to stretch and creak, and there is a faint wind that chimes in the ice on the branches.

The smoke from the houses seems tentative.

She finds herself wretched in the skin of her coats. It isn't lice, for once. It is sorrow.

ONCE SHE'S HOME, she slops down the soup that Tomas has made and fidgets with the bread.

Pieter says: 'I didn't do anything wrong.'

This is her house. She doesn't have to explain.

'You don't want me here.'

Gretje says: 'You be careful. You leave here, and there's nowhere else except a cell in the fort.'

'I could do things—'

'So you said.'

'I'd help.'

'There's nothing to do until the ships start moving again,' Gretje says, and it's the simple truth. Life's frozen, like the harbour.

'Then talk to me,' Pieter says.

She doesn't care to give him anything that's personal and close to her heart. But she doesn't want to stay stuck in this moment, with Anthony out back in a box like a cargo you can't sell or ship.

So she summons up order, a New Year in Amsterdam in the Van Welys' house when she'd lived there long enough to take it for granted. She tells how she broke the seals on the parlour and aired it out, made the fires, polished the cups and vases, cleaned down the windows and lit the lamps in daytime so that the family was as brilliant as a picture.

Then she opened the door to the year.

Pieter likes order. She can tell.

Mijnheer Van Wely went out walking with the men, house to house, looking for friends, and Mevrouw stayed at home, guarded by a fat, soft, bawling baby with a single tooth. She ran to the baby's cries, lived by the quick stinking grind of his digestion. He had the fragile skin of an early apple, and she prayed over the faintest mark.

Three broad men trudged in. There was nobody to treat them politely, and Gretje was too young to flirt, so she poured spiced wine. The three men, notary, notary and apothecary, blustered about the good year coming, the shipping and the dividends.

Between their boots, so shocking it went unseen, a mouse scuttled over the perfect polish of the floor, tiny feet skeetering and scrabbling. Mevrouw stood up, apologized for her inattention, smiled much too bravely and heard the baby cry. Gretje went to take the baby, and Mevrouw snatched at him. The three men finished their wine. The house was still again, except for the sly eye of the baby.

Gretje stood by the shutters. There was a blanket of soft damp in the air, with no edge of frost. There would be no dark bodies rushing along the iced canals, nothing to remember. A horse and sled passed, wooden runners barking against the cobblestones, and when it had gone she realized the silence was not perfect. She could hear the walls. Inside the frame of the house things fell softly, tumbling and catching. She tried to hear where the sound began and ended, so that something could be done, but as she crossed and recrossed the parlour, she began to think the tiny sounds were woven round the whole room. Mevrouw Van Wely, meanwhile, lay with the baby. Gretje's attention flickered from wall to corner to wall. There was a scuttling overhead like angry feathers.

The bell sounded.

Inside the parlour, the mouse was frantic at the skirting-boards, trying to find a way back out of all the dangerous polish and into the soft brick ladder of the wall. Gretje flapped her skirts, herding it fiercely. It beat against the wall. She went for a broom, and smacked the floor and swept murderously.

The bell sounded again.

Gretje bounded into the hall, mouse flying before the broom, and flung open the door. She swept the mouse down the steps between two gentlemen in black and white who expected to be taken very seriously. She smacked the step with the broom. The gentlemen tried to smile through the drink they'd taken, but it was difficult. She said: 'This way.' They toiled up the steps and into the hallway, and Gretje tried to compose herself, taking their hats and cloaks and setting the broom by the wall. They stood expectantly.

The stairs at the end of the hall rose steeply like a ladder. There was a painting in the hallway of *The prosperity of the nation at sea, or general shipping*. The parlour door was shut. There was a sound at the top of the stairs, nothing in particular, that was muddled with echoes of itself until it was loud.

Gretje opened the parlour door. The gentlemen looked in on Mevrouw Van Wely and then back along the hall.

The polish and the sharp angles were all gone from the stairs. Instead, the mice came down like water in a torrent, a rush of bounding, scuffling, jumping things, a grey mass lit up with a galaxy of black eyes.

Mevrouw Van Wely had risen and put down the baby. 'Welcome!' she said.

The gentlemen were transfixed.

The torrent ran on past the parlour door, over the cloaks and down to the street. Gretje kicked after them.

'Happy New Year,' said the gentlemen faintly.

GRETJE EXPECTED TO be sent away after that, but, instead, Mevrouw was tired and ashamed, and Gretje cleaned, decided and bought for the house as though it were her own. When she came home by Warmoesstraat and looked into the shops piled with silks and corduroy and cottons, the shopkeepers courted her.

She walked down by the old wooden house in case Marieke and Lysbeth were there. Lysbeth, she was told, was pregnant and had gone up to some village near Groningen. Marieke had muddled herself up with girls from the orphanage and been sent to be a servant in the East Indies. Gretje shrugged. She came home full of nostalgia.

She was fretful at being the one who did what the house required, who felt responsible for the floors, the sausages, the gleam of the door and the linen for the crib. She could often hear the whisper in the walls, a faint catching and scrambling. On some days, she dawdled in the streets. If she just gave herself time, then something would happen: an omen, a great thunderstorm, a woman tossed by a bull and giving birth in the air, a terrible flood, a sea creature with words written on its flanks and a blade in its head, or a brawl between sailors and the big white women who kept them company.

On Fridays, she cleaned out the workroom with lye. She liked Fridays; there was nothing to stop her talking to Hendrick, the thin boy who worked there. She smiled at him, he smiled at her. He said his name was Hendrick, which she knew already, but he didn't have much to say. He kissed her. She wasn't stirred, except by curiosity to see where kisses led. She pretended to be busy.

Late one Friday, she met Hendrick in one of the cupboards and he undressed quickly. He was thin as quills, in his shanks and his cock, but she liked the fact of his body if not the body itself. He didn't fuss, which she liked. He just hammered into her like a nail, and her eyes were wide open. When he'd done, she mopped up the blood and lye on the floor and went away humming.

THAT NIGHT, SHE made the parlour immaculate again. She sat down for a moment in the finest chair, knowing she would clean it later. The room was as careful and proper as she remembered her own mother as being—she had meant to have proper memories of her, but other things broke in. She recalled a hot day in spring, her mother calling her in from the street and telling her to sit in the one fine chair where nobody had ever sat except her father. She smelt gin on her mother's breath.

Gretje sat anxiously in the chair, while her mother went scouring round the room for her father's clay pipe and scorched, pummelled pouch for tobacco. She handed Gretje the pipe, and she noticed the intricate square rose that was carved on its bowl and thought she could trim it into a whistle.

Her mother told Gretje to take out the old strands of tobacco in the pouch, which were brittle and raw, pack them into the pipe and light it. Gretje tried. She sucked on the stem of the pipe and the dottle and the bitter leaves and the smoke made her retch. Her mother glared. She made the tobacco glow in the bowl and felt she would suffocate.

Her mother turned away. She smelt the smoke and sobbed, and went down suddenly on the floor like a cover with nothing under it.

The memory of her mother's pain made Gretje shiver, and she pulled herself back to the comfort of the Van Welys' parlour. It was time to escape. She was tired of going out in the streets as a proper, respectful servant, and feeling all her blood and energy confined by starched skirts and a servant's manner. She wanted to skip and dance. Where once she'd been comforted by the certain things she did each day, she was coming to hate her deep involvement in all the needs and concerns of people for whom she did not particularly care. She dreamed of the house slipping down into the sand and the mud, falling past its own foundations, and down into a grave of struts and leathers. If the house ever fell, she'd be free.

She went out to buy fish and came back slowly. As she reached the corner before Van Wely's house, there was a smell of fire. Men were bailing water from the canal in leather buckets, making a chain, hand to hand, as though lives and afterlives depended on it.

The Van Welys' house was hidden in roils of black smoke and flickers of flame like lightning through thunderclouds. Water sluiced on to the timbers, in through the windows, on the stone walls. The smoke danced in the air and cleared briefly to show the paint that was flaring on the high gable, the polished door that was now charred like meat. In among the men who were bustling and shouting she could see Mevrouw Van Wely with the baby in her arms; but Mevrouw was staring up at the fire, and the baby was a terrible weight. Gretje went to her side, laid down the fish and said: 'Goodbye.'

Mevrouw was fascinated by all the imperfections creeping into her house, and by the fact that fire both made them and exposed them to an outdoor world. She said: 'It started in the workshop. Some linen caught fire. You left linen in the workshop, by the fires.'

Gretje thought for a moment.

'Did you?' Mevrouw said.

Gretje said nothing at all. She meant no particular harm but she watched the tongues and the tails of the fire as it ate the house and she knew they would want to have someone to blame—someone young, someone who was nobody, somebody who could be part of the household at one moment and thrown out to the Spinhuis the next.

'Did you?' Mevrouw said.

Gretje walked away.

It was wicked, she thought later, to leave Mevrouw Van Wely, always so perfectly absorbed and organized, with doubt in her mind. But she had to save herself. A ruined house would need retribution.

She stopped a minute at the corner, to look at the bustle and racket and the sweltering line of men toting buckets to the fire, and the way the flames came back up through the water as it hit the beams. She could see Gretje, douce and helpful, standing still by Mevrouw Van Wely and offering to take the baby from her arms.

So she abandoned that Gretje, like a snake puts off a skin. One minute she was inside the whole intricate domestic world, the baby, the shop, the pewter and shiny tiles and careful stoves, the orders and the regularity of a house that was also a life. Then the house was on fire, and she walked.

She stopped by the arcade at the Town Hall, smoke in her hair, and collected a few coins from the passers-by on the grounds of being exactly what she was: a girl with prospects who's just had bad luck. She calculated she had enough for a night. That gave her the right to walk without a purpose, like the luxurious women who passed in a cloud of violets and ambergris and powder; but she had a greater luxury than that. She wasn't expected, so she could walk anonymously anywhere. She walked down the street of ships, towards the great warehouses where the whalebones stood and the whale oil was kept in brick reservoirs, the places she had slept first in the city.

It didn't seem likely that she had left linen in the workroom, but she couldn't be sure. It was a long time since she had had to think about the mechanical routines of the house, or since there had been anything as remarkable as a birth or a death or a party to disturb those routines. Now she had left, she hardly remembered them at all.

Five ships down the line, she stopped. A man was standing at the prow of a boat, arms stretched out like Jesus. He had a dark face, the features like charcoal on a sallow white, and his eyes were perfectly blue. He was strong and balanced perfectly. He smiled at her; she smiled back. He jumped down from the bows and swung on to the street. She said: 'I saw you skating once.'

He said: 'I like skating.'

She said: 'What do you like doing in summer?'

He said: 'You want to go for a drink?'

She said: 'I don't know.'

He said: 'What else have you got to do?'

She said: 'I've got everything to do, but I'd like a drink.'

He said: 'You smell of smoke.'

'Gretje,' she said.

'Anthony,' he said. 'They call me "The Turk".'

They walked briskly out by the whalehouses to the taverns by the Haarlemmerpoort where she had first entered the city. They sat at a corner by the door, where the breeze came off the green water.

She said: 'The house where I work burnt down today.'

He asked for beer; they offered Lübeck, Groningen, Lon, Dort or Delft. She didn't know the names, so she nodded. She said: 'I'm not going back.'

She liked the way his eyes remade her. In her domestic grey, she had no breasts and no hips; she was a child. But in his eyes, she was a plump, white girl all smiling and round. She hardly had a face in the house, because she was always slightly looking down; but he said her face was pretty. She began to laugh and he hoped she was a little drunk.

'What's your boat called?'

'The *Soutberg*,' he said.

'It's a small boat.'

'Small boats go everywhere,' he said.

At the next table men were shaking dice and then peering into the cup to check their score.

'You're very dark. I mean, you have dark eyes.'

'My mother was from the Barbary Coast. A Barbary woman. My father was a pirate.'

'My father was a soldier. My mother wasn't anything.'

So each knew the other was alone.

She said: 'I never went to a tavern before.'

SHE IS VEXED. One minute she's sitting in the tavern, happily remembering, and the next she finds Pieter there. She can feel the pull of his mind on her memories.

'You don't want to hear all this,' she says.

'I do.'

She's said much too much. She's told him about Anthony the Turk, and now it's too late to wonder what she ought to leave out, what's so safe and distant it could have no more consequences and what might bring her down to the courtroom again. It is easy to tell a stranger everything, if the stranger goes away again, and stays away. But this is a hard winter when nobody can travel, in a small town where everybody knows everything. There are no strangers, not even Pieter.

'I could listen all day,' Pieter says.

He's warm, he's fed, he has nothing to do; why shouldn't he sit in the fug of the room and indulge her as she paints her past on the hours? But he's not indulging her. He wants something specific. He doesn't interrupt; perhaps he's getting what he wants. Or perhaps this is all a ploy to make sure he stays warm and fed.

She thinks: he'll give himself away soon, surely?

'WHERE ARE YOU going to sleep tonight?' Anthony asked.

'I used to stay in a house down by Warmoesstraat, close to the water. The back of the house hung over the water. When we wanted to piss—'

'I sleep on the boat,' he said.

The bells sang out the half-hour.

'I can go anywhere and do anything,' Gretje said.

Anthony looked puzzled.

'I'm sure of it,' she said. She was, too, with him.

'You could go to the East Indies, but you'd have to be a servant. You could work in a tavern, but you'd be better off in Amsterdam than anywhere else. You could go to Curaçao or to America.'

'Did you ever go to the East Indies?'

He asked for more beer. 'No,' he said. 'But I know about them. Sailors tell sailors everything.'

'I wish people would tell me things. I know about the house, that's all.'

'That's useful.'

She was leaning on him, her breath hot on his face, her smile insistent.

'What's the most terrible thing you know?' she asked.

He drank off his beer. 'Not having a drink,' he said.

'I don't mean that,' Gretje said. 'I mean something terrible.'

He paused: 'I don't know what you mean.' She looked at him contemptuously, as though that was an old trick.

He said: 'Drowning.'

She sat back, expectant.

'They throw a man off a ship to drown. I've seen it. In the middle of the ocean, and he hangs there in the water, just watching the boat move away.' Anthony drank.

'Go on.' She was beginning to see into the men's world.

'There's a room in the prison,' Anthony said. 'They take murderers there. It's down in the cellars, under the level of the water. They open a sluice, and the water comes in. They leave you there.' He looked solemn and afraid.

'Yes?'

'There's a pump, and either you work it or you drown. You stop, you drown. You get tired, your muscles won't work, and the water comes up over the pump, and you have to dive down to save your life and you drown pumping.'

Gretje was dizzy. She could taste his terror and in it she saw at last what kept the streets straight and the city ordered, what guaranteed civility among the ruffed and starched gentry. She always knew there must be some such secret thing.

She whispered: 'Were you ever there?'

'I was in a hurricane once.'

'I have to go,' she said.

'You don't have anywhere to go.'

She said: 'I still have to go.'

He walked with her to the street of ships. 'We don't sail for four days,' he said. She waved to him. He saluted.

The sun went down, and the buildings came to life in torchlight and lamplight, each doorway a flicker of shadows, each window a clear picture, the high gables lit like gross crowns. She never had nights in the city before this. She heard the bells and the talk. The front of a palace was a life story in the light. She was dazzled and fascinated. She remembered the Turk's startling eyes, and also his hands, even though she did not remember looking at them.

She looked down steps and saw people in yellow, waxy light all laughing and staring and shouting and drinking. Around their boots, and the feet of the tables and the chairs, lapped a faint grey water. The canals were rising with the tide, and the basement water with them. Two women shouted that they wanted to dance, and a Jew from Poland played a fiddle. A man at the doorway, with a ponderous accent, told Gretje that all Dutch women were mad for dancing, and looked her up and down.

She thought: he knows about the drowning room.

The women were up now, lumbering from side to side, faster and faster, their dance like some crushing machine, and their clogs broke the water and made it rush into their skirts and their stockings. The splashing caught the men at their tables, but the drink kept them quiet and warm. The women were spinning now, arms at each other's waists, shouting and laughing. The men watched. The women were furious, and they caught up the water and made it dance with them in the light from the oil-lamps and the candles; they were dancing in a fine cloud of light.

THAT NIGHT, THERE were slashes of lightning, a shooting star when the sky cleared, and thunder rumbling through the streets like a parade. Rain never came.

Gretje went back to the old wooden house off

Warmoesstraat. She wasn't used to sleeping on boards any more. She fancied nails were catching at her skirt, and the nails belonged to the hands of a great beast that was sailing a ship called the *Soutberg*. By the morning, she had dreamed about drowning and she woke up shivering in the heat.

She walked down Warmoesstraat to see if the shop-keepers knew she was no longer the proper servant girl, but a woman on her own with nobody to vouch for her; but she spoilt the test by looking too curious. She bought some cheese on Van Wely's credit, which solved the problem of food.

Out of habit, she walked to the house. It was done for, she could see that. It had burnt down to its plan in spars and platforms of charcoal. It smelt of the canal which had been emptied over it. She looked down into the basement and saw a glint of some shiny thing among the ash and rubble.

'You!'

Mijnheer Van Wely, dirty but starched, came lumbering out of the ruins, trying to pull what rank he had left.

'You! Gretje! Girl!'

Gretje turned around. For a moment, she thought she need not answer to that old name. But she was still tied to it by all the good Dorcas grey that Van Wely had bought her.

'Fire-raiser!' Van Wely said. 'Thief!'

Gretje said: 'I didn't take anything.'

Van Wely said: 'You took every fucking thing from us.'

'I didn't steal. I don't steal.'

'You came off the streets, you stayed in our house, and all the time—'

Gretje was close to the narrow water of the canal. 'I don't know you,' she said.

'Never trust a serving girl,' Van Wely shouted to the street. 'They're tarts. They're teases. They're thieves. You let them into the house, everything's gone.'

A few gentry waddled by, avoiding the scandal of shouts. A couple of streetgirls watched, in case an audience formed and they could work the crowd.

Van Wely crossed the pavement with huge deliberation, the good burger pregnant with law, and he went to strike Gretje. She dipped, like a curtsy. He held his balance for a moment on the edge of the canal but then he plumped forward and found himself floating on the thick green water.

Gretje ran. A few gentlemen made half-hearted attempts to pull Van Wely to the canal bank, but he wasn't in danger. He was ludicrous, like a dead cloth balloon, and gentlemen don't laugh at gentlemen.

In the muddy water, Van Wely was screaming at the air and the willows. 'Ran away,' he was howling. 'Proof. That's proof.'

But Gretje was three turnings, sixteen possibilities away, in a city that branched and twisted.

Van Wely pulled himself back on to land. 'She's a devil,' he said. 'You can see it in her eyes. You can tell by the way she walks—'

But Gretje was walking, eyes down, in the skin of a douce maid.

'You'll take her into your house and that's the end of everything,' he said, his voice down now to avoid more scandal. 'They're all the same.'

Van Wely, she thought, could heap all the blame on to Gretje, and wash his own sins away, but that Gretje burnt down with the house. Like a martyr, she thought, and giggled.

The trouble was that this whole big city was none too

big. She could half-remember half the faces on this street. She hadn't the time to find a roof and set up with work as a laundry girl or a seamstress, and she had no money, so Van Wely would know to look for her in the territory of beggars and streetgirls. And she didn't know anyone well enough now that Lysbeth and Marieke had gone. Maybe the street-girls would hide her, but maybe they'd sell her on.

Since she wanted to be with the Turk in any case, she went to find him.

He was sunning himself on the deck. She shouted to him, and he stretched. She shouted his name. He looked up casually. She shouted: 'I'm going away,' and he scrambled to his feet. He put such force into jumping to the shore that he landed too big and too close.

'You can't go away,' he said.

Gretje said: 'I've had enough of Amsterdam.'

'Then I'll come,' he said. 'I've got money.'

She wanted to walk by walls, to cross streets suddenly and stop in doorways out of the light, so Anthony did not need to ask if there was trouble. He liked trouble. He used his big shoulders to shield her from people passing by. She didn't press him on when he would go back to the ship, or if he would, and he didn't ask her anything at all. It seemed like perfect complicity.

They cut out of the shelter of the city, through the broad walls. The city was a ship moored in all the new land and trim water; they abandoned it in its dock of stone. They walked briskly on straight, flat roads.

'You're not going home,' Anthony said, 'are you?'

'WHAT DID HE look like?' Pieter asks.

Gretje can't answer. To her, he doesn't have a single face that she can catch in a few, strong words; he was in her sight and in her memory all those years, and what she studied was the brightness and rest, the joy, anger, smiles, scowls, exhaustion, hope that was in his face. She can't generalize all that life and hand it over.

'Did he look like he looks now?'

Perhaps he's just interested, that's all, in how men change.

'How do you know what he looks like?' Gretje asks, sharply. He can't have seen into the coffin, not unless he opened it for himself.

Pieter shrugs.

'I said: how do you know?'

'Tomas said—'

'Tomas can't speak.'

He shifts, wretched, on his chair as though he knows the slap is coming, and it comes. He's startled. He rubs the smudge of red on his cheek.

He thought he'd set such a trap: led her into weaving a comfortable version of her past, warm enough, engaging enough to keep her mind off what was missing. It was almost as though Anthony would be back when the sea thawed.

Then he shocked her with the fact of dead Anthony.

She saw through him. This past, this feeling, was precisely where she did not want him trespassing. She sees that Pieter is alarmingly still. He may be a child, but that just means he has more time left to lose than she does.

SHE MIGHT AS well be asleep. She's still, curled up in the down of her bed. Inside the stillness, the steady breath, there's just a splinter of consciousness. She could tell herself she is dreaming, but really she's thinking. She's not happy dreaming with Pieter in the house.

It helps to think about Anthony.

She strides out with him, out of Amsterdam the day after the fire, moving, always moving, heart and lungs like a machine, until the business of moving becomes the same thing as the purpose of moving.

She was surrounded by a low, flat horizon, whichever way she looked, and against it there were windmills slowly turning against a huge sky and, once, scaffolding in the middle of nothing with no workmen, as though somebody had thought about a house and then forgotten. This was the emptiness she remembered when her mother sent her away for cheese and water. To Anthony, she was occupied only with the moment, with the sun and the rising wind on her face and not wanting to stop, but she kept glimpsing a body under a hedge, abandoned in the shine of the wild garlic. The sight shocked her and stopped the whole exhilaration of moving, and she felt stranded in the open land.

She sits up in bed, listening hard.

Behind them a cart came rattling, its wheels disputing with the stone road. The Turk waved to the driver and then stood in his way to make sure he stopped, and asked for a ride because the girl was tired. 'Tired?' the driver said, full of meaning. 'She's been walking,' the Turk said. 'Walking?' the driver said and sighed. He was surrounded by silence and water, and the Turk was the bigger and younger man, so he let them up and settled back to the reins, hunched over them as though he did not want to be seen. The Turk sat brashly beside him. Gretje bounced among last year's turnips in the back, legs apart to keep her balance on the pile, and Amsterdam forever in her sight even as it grew smaller and smaller.

'Going far?' the driver managed. He didn't expect much of an answer.

'Haarlem.'

'Got work there? Family?'

'I'm a sailor.'

'Oh.'

The cart hit ruts and tossed Gretje briefly in the air among the hard, purple roots.

'Been a sailor six years.'

'Everybody has to make a living. Married, are you?'

The Turk thought again. The driver decided he was not as bright as he might like to be.

'No.'

'Nice girl.'

'Yes.'

'Young.'

'Yes.'

'Sailors,' the driver said. 'Me, I have a bit of land. Sailors, they can get up and go through the door and they come back when they mean to come back, and their wives get on with living. Me, I go out the door and I come back when I'm told.'

'Yes,'

'Me, I want a bit of beer, I make my time, I persuade the woman, I hear a sermon, then I go down the tavern, and the woman and the sermon come with me and they drink my beer. You think that's fair?'

'It's not fair.'

'Sailors. You never know where you are.'

The Turk kept quiet. All they wanted from this man was a ride to the next best place where Gretje would stop being distracted. He looked back and smiled at her, but she was wedged across the load of turnips and her look down the road was enough to skin rabbits.

The driver said: 'I thought about being a sailor once.'

Gretje felt suspended on a line being drawn by the cart, a straight line leading back always to the city. She razed the city in her mind, made it black and sparse like the Van Welys' house.

'I said I thought about being a sailor,' the driver said.

The Turk said: 'I've seen a lot of places.'

'Know things, do you?' the driver said.

'I know places.'

'That's nothing. Anyone can know places.'

The Turk wanted to boast, but he also wanted to ride.

'I know about life,' the driver said. 'I know from preachers.'

SHE'S HARD AWAKE. She's thinking the damned Minister wouldn't have a funeral for Anthony because he'd gone to God, and there was nothing to mourn, or else to Hell, in which case there was nothing to do. She's thinking about preachers.

The grievance gets muddled with the story, and she can't stop the story. Whatever she thinks or does, she can hear the driver's voice.

'I know that either a man is saved, or a man is damned, and there's nothing to be done about it,' he said. The cart rattled, the turnips shuddered under her. 'But you take a baby, hasn't had time to think a sinful thought. If it's not on the list of the saved, if it's not among the elect, the preachers say it goes straight to Hell. So,' he said, checking slyly to see that the Turk was listening, which was the price of the ride, 'you can be innocent and you can still be damned. It doesn't do any good to stay away from sin. You follow me? Contrarily, if you're justified before the Lord and going to Heaven anyway, why worry?' He pulled an apple out of his shirt and mangled it with his loose teeth. 'Fuck all the girls and drink all the drink and maybe you get in a fight and you kill a man and it none of it matters because you're on the list or you're not. You think about that.'

The Turk had nothing to say. He looked ahead down the straight road, and Gretje looked back to the city, and together they held the line of the road in place.

'So,' the driver said. 'They come and they preach and they say God is sending the hail or the flood or the mice or the cold or the thunder, and it's all because of what you and I do. Always you and me, you ever notice that? We look at the wrong woman. We drink too much. We have a wrongful thought. Well if we're all damned anyway, what's the point of trying to save our skins? I ain't going to save Holland.

'You really going to Haarlem?'

The Turk shrugged.

'Because,' the driver said, 'I turn off the Haarlem road here. Wife and I could find you somewhere to sleep, if you need it.'

The cart jogged to a stop. Gretje looked vengefully at the Turk, and the Turk looked blandly back, and she said: 'I'm hungry.'

'There's food,' the driver said.

THAT NIGHT GRETJE lay in a broad manger. The straw prickled against her back, and she stretched as though she expected to touch somebody, something else in the straw, but her arms bumped against raw wood.

She thought of a dog's tongue, warm and slathering, then prickling and teasing. The tongue had points and force. She was afraid to open her eyes in case the first thing that she saw could command her life; her mother told stories like that. She opened her eyes. She was shouting, and the Turk told her to be quiet and he grinned.

The Turk held her. The world became sharp again very slowly, the edges of things separating out from the mass of shadow, the faint window light now clearly brighter than the dark of the manger.

'You never did that before?'

He was over her asking for thanks; his face was huge as a moon. Her breath stopped in her throat, and she struggled to take back control.

'You all right?'

She heard someone pounding on a door. She imagined anger, retribution, judgement; she would be prosecuted for being possessed, for having a spirit live inside her body, for failing to maintain and defend the holy tabernacle of the body as her mother did, when her father was gone (or so her mother said.)

The Turk went to the door, and Gretje felt desolate with nothing to touch.

AS IT HAPPENED, they didn't leave the next morning. The driver needed help with some stacking and loading, and the Turk volunteered. Gretje worked in the kitchen, quiet as a maid; she knew that part. The driver's wife looked as though she had fallen down into being old and the fall had cost her the line of her teeth, bruised eyes, broken limbs. She looked as Gretje's mother should look: a little bit alive, despite everything.

'You don't have brothers or sisters, do you?' the wife said.

'How do you know?'

'You watch people too much.'

'My mother died.'

'Everyone's mother dies.'

It seemed terrible that time could defeat people, better

that Gretje's mother had—and then Gretje realized she could not finish the sentence. She assumed her mother was dead, but not properly dead, enough for grief and mourning. But perhaps her mother had hobbled out from under the hedge and was living on the move somewhere, or begging, which she could easily do with her smashed leg, or even working. Impossible, she thought. All the memories that added up to her mother had to do with a kitchen, not unlike this kitchen, and a village and being settled. Her real mother died the day she started walking.

Four nights later, the driver came for the Turk and asked him to help rig a cover for the haystacks they had spent the day consolidating. It was an odd time, but the Turk was a guest and he went. After a few minutes, the driver came down to the manger where Gretje was lying in the dark.

The driver said: 'Be quiet.'

'I don't have any money,' Gretje said.

'Take your smock off.'

'You can't see anything. It's too dark.'

'What makes you think I want to see?'

'I thought men had to see.' She sat all tensed on the manger's edge. 'I'm still bruised from the cart,' she said.

'You two going to get married?'

'No.'

The driver said carefully: 'If I fucked you, and you were married, that would be adultery. A terrible thing. All the plagues of Egypt would come down on Holland.' He was pinching her thigh. 'Locusts, tides and blood.' She could feel the bruise starting. 'But if I fuck you now, that's nothing. That's just saying thank you.'

'It'll cost you,' Gretje said.

'You've had board and lodging.'

'I do this for a living,' she said. She meant to put him off, to suggest he was after something ordinary.

'You charge him?'

'He's a sailor,' Gretje said. It was a strange kind of bluff, she thought, since she worried mostly that the driver might believe what she said.

'How much?' the driver asked.

Gretje said: 'Amsterdam rates.'

'I wouldn't know Amsterdam rates.'

And nor did she. She came up suddenly against the end of her bluff.

She thought she could hear the older woman scuffling along the straw and tiles, and she said very loudly, 'Where's Anthony?'

'He's working.'

'And your wife?'

The old woman stood at the door, torch in hand. Perhaps her eyes had died and she could not quite make out the circumstances. Perhaps. The driver threw himself on top of Gretje, clawing and grabbing, and pushed into her. It was very sudden and it was over just as suddenly.

The old woman held a torch over the manger, and Gretje could see nothing but her face in a halo of gold. Instead of the powdery skin and dusty eyes, she looked alive again, almost young in her fury.

Gretje lay in the manger, very still. Driver and wife were gone half an hour before the Turk came back, sweaty and dusty, from the haystacks.

'Your friend the driver,' she said. 'He fucked me.'

She had to see Anthony's face, but he held the oil-lamp so that he could see hers.

Her mother's books did not cover such things. She'd read the lives of the saints in the Van Welys' house, but there

were always seraphs around rape at the very least, and sometimes the Virgin Mary herself, followed by a terrible death,
and then trumpets, flowers and gold. But Gretje was here on
her own: no reason or revelation that could tell her why.

The Turk, too, was puzzled. 'I'll get him,' he said,
because Gretje was with him. Then he wondered if Gretje
were trying to rile him, if her story were true and, if it were,
if maybe she were making a little money on the side.
Perhaps he should ask how much the driver gave her, and
ask for his share. He half-wished he had collected a definite
wife, a definite tart, and not this curious sexual friend.

'You want me to go after him?' he asked.

She wasn't sure. She wanted to hold the Turk and she
wanted him to stay away. More than anything, she wanted
to see his face.

As though nothing had happened, the driver arrived at
the door and he said: 'You'll want to come to the church.'

Anthony said: 'What did you do?'

The driver said: 'Never mind that. You come down to
the meeting if you want.'

GRETJE SITS IN a room where the air has long since been
used up by the stove. The airlessness helps her doze for a
moment and then she feels stifled. She shocks herself
awake. She's afraid of dying. Anthony died without her.
She'd counted on company.

Revenge seems like a grand idea; just an idea, not prac-
ticable, but worth thinking about and dreaming about.
She's fed up with angels like Pieter, whose very existence is
ungodly and unsafe. And she's fed up with Pieter if he's a
boy. She wants order back in her life in place of grief. She
wants to push grief out of her belly like a child, into the
world, so it can go and do harm to others.

79

When she's sure of her anger, she goes out to the yard.

The snow is a stage, lit with the mineral fires of the moon. On the snow, Tomas and Pieter dance slowly, absorbed in their turns and holding each other at a courtly distance, stiff and exact like figures on a carousel.

WHEN THE MEETING was over, they walked back through the village: Gretje and Anthony, the driver and his wife, listening to the chorus of psalms that still seeped through the walls of the houses. Each song had been worn and simplified by time, carrying the same plangent words. The whole village was like an instrument that's still untuned, the songs clashing each against the other's key and tempo, but still with an insistent sameness. Gretje shivered and began to hum.

'I've seen things at sea that weren't human or animal,' the Turk said. 'I've heard hammering on coffins at night in a churchyard.'

'I see faces sometimes,' Gretje said. 'Faces in the water.'

'And the mate on the *Soutberg* has a wife who has the gift. Sometimes she won't tell him what will happen on a voyage, and he knows enough to stay home on dry land.'

Gretje had to ask: 'When do you sail?'

'Very soon,' Anthony said.

'You know where you're going?'

'They said America. I don't know. I'll be back.'

'You carry passengers?'

Anthony hugged her.

The driver was braying something sanctimonious to his wife. Anthony said: 'Sin finds out the sinner in the strangest ways.'

'I wouldn't know,' the driver said. 'I don't have anything on my conscience.'

Gretje felt the pressure of Anthony's hand and said: 'Sometimes angels come in the night, in dreams.'

After an hour or so, when the huge, heavy moon had shifted appreciably in the sky, Gretje and Anthony got up, tidied themselves and felt around the walls and floor for anything useful. In the bedroom, the driver was in half-sleep, and he imagined rats in straw, where they belonged. Gretje and Anthony found rope, some kind of powdered rubble for rendering the walls, paint, some wood and a wicker basket. The driver turned over and clapped his arm over his wife. She let out air from every part of her.

Gretje and Anthony closed the barn door carefully behind them and stood by the hitching post.

'Now,' Gretje said. Anthony picked up a bit of rusted metal, a broken horseshoe, and heaved it at a window. At the same time he shrieked and whistled. Gretje began to bang slowly on a barrel with a heavy wooden spoon.

In the bed, the driver's wife settled under her dreams. But the driver was awake. He heard spirits out walking, or else robbers, and he had to get up, either to disprove them or to chase them off. He thought about taking a lamp or a torch but that would only alert them. He went very quietly.

He stepped into the softness of the night and paused. The tapping had stopped. Perhaps he imagined the shrieking. Other people should surely have been wakened by the noise, but nobody was stirring; or perhaps they had been too much in the presence of spirits to trust themselves out of doors before dawn. No animal or bird moved. The quiet started to sound loud.

Suddenly his mouth filled with cloth, his hands went behind him and fixed there, and he felt rope burning against him. He lost his nightshirt before he knew it and felt the cold on his body but he was too alarmed to shiver.

Cold and wet hit him in the balls and stayed there, hardening quickly.

'In the name of the Father,' he said.

There was rope round his wrists and ankles, and he was tied to the hitching post. He looked and looked, but he could not make out the shape of the things and devils that were doing all this. He tasted something old and all too natural in his mouth. He retched, and a new rope went round his balls, and he felt something attached to his head. From the smell, it must be the goat's head he hung, just to be safe, inside the barn door where nobody except the Devil could see it.

He said, outraged: 'I'm a bloody graven image.'

The village was silent again. Out towards Haarlem, Gretje and Anthony settled down to sleep by the road. 'Best,' the Turk said, taking over, 'to wait until dawn.'

'There might be another cart,' Gretje said, falling asleep.

When she woke at dawn, she wanted to see how the Devil unveiled sin in the morning, their masterpiece, all horned, unmanned and bristling with cold and alarm.

She said to the Turk: 'Thank you.'

GRETJE HAD THOUGHT nothing would ever take her back to Amsterdam, but there she was, going back in the dawn. Anthony was sailing, and she'd be with him until then and, when he'd gone, she would start a new life of some kind. You could go anywhere from Amsterdam.

This time, Gretje rode with the driver who was proud of a daughter who'd married the master of the house and was setting up as a merchant for herself. They passed a straggle of men and women in rotting cloaks, pushing a cart with pots and a chair and a cat, who looked at them calculatingly. 'Germans,' the driver said. 'You forget there's war sometimes.'

'I feel safe here,' Gretje said.

'So does every bloody body else.'

The cart stopped abruptly. 'I can't go any further,' this second driver said. 'I've gone out of my way as it is.'

They stood down from the cart and watched him drive away.

By the road stood a tower of brick and stone that shrank to a spire at the top. Gretje didn't like to ask the Turk, and the Turk did not explain why this particular tower could be a boundary as sure as a sea or a cliff. She stared at it: shallow, thin brick, stacked like slate, that ended in a metal spike. It was too intricate for a roadside with no definite mark for miles.

The Turk strode off. When he had gone a few hundred yards, she found the nerve to shout: 'I don't understand.'

He came running back, smiling so tenderly and hopefully she almost burnt. 'It is,' he said, 'a banishment post. You get banished from the city, you can't come past here.'

'But anyone could come past here.'

'Not if they're banished.'

'There aren't any soldiers.'

'You can come into the city on some days—the Feast of the Holy Miracle.'

'You know about this?'

'I know about the law.' He put his arms round her, assuming all the authority of the lover and the law. So she hacked at his shins and she ran off down the road.

THE COLONY SECRETARY dares not catch her eye. He is edgy in her house, even flanked by the two soldiers—determined to be official where he's been lecherous before. He's wondering, Gretje senses, if the soldiers also know the house.

'I'm sorry,' the Secretary says.

Gretje leads them through the stable.

'The ground's too hard for burying,' she says, for the sake of something to say. 'As soon as there's a thaw—'

'It's just as well,' the Secretary says. He is wondering if he should acknowledge that she is a widow, a woman with some delicacy of feeling, and send her away. 'If we had a doctor—'

Gretje waits, in case he has a sentence to finish and finds that, like Gretje, he does not.

The soldiers lift off the lid of the coffin.

Anthony should be alone, Gretje thinks. If anyone is going to be with him, it's her. She wanted to be in bed with the body the first night they brought him home, but one of the men started gabbling about gangrene. She wanted to lie there next to him, in the usual, necessary way.

'No wounds, you say.'

Gretje says: 'I didn't see any.'

The soldiers are staring at her. She steps forward to the coffin on its little bier of snow.

'You didn't see any wounds,' the Secretary says.

Anthony's skin is sallow and bloodless still, but there is a black, pulpy mark in his forehead. One of his sharp, blue eyes is gone.

She knows a body bleeds in the presence of a murderer. He wouldn't tell lies with his blood, she thinks. She can't look, can't not look, can't look, to see if he is bleeding.

'Cover him,' the Secretary says, and even he, round and pompous and clerkly, is touched by the horror on Gretje's face.

SHE LOST ANTHONY the day he went back to the *Soutberg* and started knotting rope and folding sail. She didn't wait around. Since she was in Amsterdam, she organized a living there—served and cleaned in a tavern where they never quite asked her to sell herself, felt a bit superior to the girls who danced and sold drink and fucked in the big disorderly musicos.

Then she began to be sick in the morning, and she tucked herself away in a small room, lightless in the back of a warren of houses and backhouses, and set up as a seamstress. She cramped her fingers together and made exact stitches, a skill she did not much want to remember.

Gretje was afraid then. Anything else that happened to her body could easily be corrected, or ignored; she had fancied herself in some other place even when the driver was fucking her, and it was only the sight of his wife's awful face that had held her in the same room. But this could not be ignored. Her shape changed and advertised what was happening to her. Sooner or later she would have a child, without benefit of a church to support her or a man to blame, and there would be those months when she would not be able to work. And the only people she knew now were the ones who wanted her to work.

She stooped over the linens as she sewed, and her eyes tussled with the stitches, and she felt always crumpled, hot, disordered and offended by her body and the tiny room in which it was hidden away. She wanted to be out of this cubicle and into the city again, able to stretch and wander. She was terrified that she would be hostage to the child, as Mevrouw Van Wely had been, and then she thought she already was imprisoned by its weight. She stitched lines of blue on to white: flowers, angles, stars and figures. She held on to their exactness. It crossed her mind that every craft rested on fears like hers.

Michael Pye

THERE IS A hole in Anthony's face that was not there before. Gretje had been afraid that animals would drag him out and scrabble at him, but that can't have happened; the body is frozen. The frost was meant to keep him perfect until the ground could be opened, and he could be buried as she remembered him. And now someone takes a hammer and a stick and shatters half the brilliance in his face.

The Secretary asks why she thought that Anthony was not wounded.

'He wasn't,' she says. 'Not when I found him.'

She knows the Secretary has no warrant. He knows she can't escape. They're at stalemate over a missing eye.

GRETJE STANDS AT the table, cramming bread into her mouth.

She is glad now to remember the days when she was pregnant for the first time. She worked, ate, slept and feared, had a neat, domestic life; she was without the books or plays or street-talk that could have distracted her or changed the language of her dreams. She had only the stock of a fifteen-year-old's mind.

She waited, as her mother waited for her father, waited for someone to salvage her, sure that nobody would come, as nobody came for her mother. She kept no mirror because the mirror would have told her she was very young, the milky white of her skin showing only a little chalk from the lack of air; she was obstinately plump, obstinately handsome; and this was not at all how she saw herself. She crept out like a hunchback to take in work from the usual houses. She worried mostly about finding corners where she could piss away the great load that lay on her bladder.

She persisted, though. That time passed, just as this present time will pass.

But she knows they will blame her for Anthony's death, if they can. They're all friends and defenders of Anthony, all of a sudden. Already they think her various sins have spoilt their community of godly souls. Each little fuck puts them all at the risk of Hell. From that, it's a small step to accuse her of the wrong use of a knife, of butchering her lover, and from there, a warrant is no step at all.

She needs a refuge. She remembers the room she had when she was pregnant, underground in an Amsterdam house which had begun as a couple of rooms and a narrow front, and then juggled its way upwards, downwards, hanging out at the back and gabled in front, still on its narrow base. She remembers that the summer was long; in the country they complained of drought cracking the land which usually had to be defended against water with such care. But at the end of summer there was sudden, drenching rain, as though the sky had silted up and then broken like a dyke over the whole of Holland.

In her room, Gretje had the pleasure of not knowing which particular sin the preachers blamed for the flood. But in her room, the floor began to seep like a sponge and a new smell began to stain the linens. Hollows in the packed earth filled up unexpectedly, drained, and filled again. The once-solid floor was suspect in places, and came away on her bare feet: black, stinking stuff. She collected the last bundle of linens, sniffed them and tied the dampest in the middle, and went off to make deliveries.

Paid, she stood blinking in the sunshine, big and self-conscious. But everyone else was blinking after the rains, and damp and grubby with mud. Two huge women went by hand in hand. She had money in her pocket, like everyone else up here in the streets. She couldn't possibly go back to the flood in her room.

A tarpaulin was lifted off steps and threw water on the pavement, blackbirds splashed in puddles, the bells sounded their usual half-hourly hymns but now they sounded like celebration. There were drums in the distance.

She crossed the bridge with her head down modestly and then, as she cut through the first side-street, she saw how people noticed her belly and made room for her. She had respect.

The drums were answered by a brassy sound. She always escaped the Van Welys' house for the kermis, and this, of all the fairs in Amsterdam, was going to be the grandest, the one which shook off the famous rains and shone. The brass cut the chatter on the streets.

She was tugged along by the excitement of the others, by their sense of glory in a few days when work and God and the tyranny of clocks and houses were all set aside, and the city filled up with its neighbours and its neighbours' neighbours. She heard laughter in choruses and modes as she had once heard psalms. The drumming mocked the rains, and the brass mocked the lightning, and the standing water threw back the brilliance of the light until the streets were dazzling, and she was glad to save her eyes among the shaded alleys of the fair. The tents caught little winds and shivered with promises.

She could smell plenty on the air, wonderful after her cramped room. There were cheeses bound in red and yellow, sausage hanging by beef on the racks and sliced to go on strong bread, and the last of the new herring, filleted and raw, and beer in barrels that smelt of oak and hops and malt, salty smells that bothered the taste buds; and the cold breath off the ice below the Mosel wines; and the sweat and digestion of round, big-boned people happy on the drink, lively on the food, smashing the brandy glasses on the table for the celebration of it, raucous in their jokes and their shouts. The world was loud and bright and overwhelming. A woman with no teeth asked her if she'd had a good time getting her belly. A seller of remedies for constrictions and disquiets pulled her on to his box and told the crowd she was lovely and peaceful and like a Madonna, and the whole crowd laughed; but the joke was not on her. She waved to the crowd, stood down, and took a cup of beer from his assistant. 'You can find the same peace,' the quack was shouting, 'and if you don't want to find it the usual way— and it takes five minutes and nine months—'

She pushed down to a clearing where a rope was stretched between trees, and a thin man with huge feet and a pole was edging along the rope, dressed like a clown. She watched him hang in the air, his feet clenching rope, veins and muscles working along the length of his thin legs, and she watched the huge effort that went into his smile.

The drums rolled again.

Smokers with their slim pipes sat back, drunk on tobacco. Boys came rollicking through the rows of tents. A man with a tiny head went past, with baskets slung on a stump arm and a claw hand and the widest trousers she had ever seen. There were flags, apples, dogs passing quickly, women in starched caps and ruffs who laughed like sailors, and a man in wonderful white and black, a burgher whose decorum was spelt out plainly in velvet and satin and fur.

Under the tightrope, a circle of men had formed around a kind of fighting ground. She could make out two men circling there, a slow dance with knives, and she heard shouts for the Englishman, shouts for the Turk. She tried to push forward, but the men would not part.

Metal caught the sun and the standing water so it gleamed from a dozen directions, a storm of points and blades. The men were laughing, but the laughs were excited. 'Turk!' someone shouted. One of the blades went down in the air, up in the water, dazzled in the sun and when it came back its glint seemed to be broken; so she knew, even though she could not see, that someone had drawn blood, either the Englishman or the Turk.

She tried walking round the crowd. She could see between the onlookers a jump, a slice, a twist of the body, nothing enough to make sense. One of the men seemed to trip, then to catch himself before the ground. The other lunged. All this time, it never crossed her mind that there might be other Turks who came off ships with big, broad knives and got into fights at the fair.

She elbowed her way through some men who were more drunk than the others, and she made it to the front of the crowd. She saw two men, muddy and cut, dancing on the balls of their feet and grunting, slashing the air around each other's bodies. One good cut, and the fight would be over; too many witnesses for murder.

The taller man feinted when the Turk cut towards him. A line of blood showed on his arm. Then the Turk seemed to tire, and the taller man came back fighting, trapping the Turk between stabs. The Turk turned in a circle, arm up round his eyes. The taller man came in stabbing with the right, punching with his left, as though he didn't need to defend himself any more.

The Turk threw himself forward, knife up, and he skidded face down in the mud. The men cheered. The taller man backed off; he was laughing at his enemy who'd sprawled on the ground. The crowd loosened their circle, and went on their way as if nothing had happened except a man falling.

Gretje pulled the Turk's face from the mud, and he

swallowed desperately, coughing and then gulping for air. He looked as though he had been eating out of the earth.

'It's Gretje,' she said.

'Oh God!' he said. She pulled him up, but he seemed reluctant to move, like a sack filled with beer. 'I slipped,' he said. 'Where's the Englishman?'

'They've all gone.'

'Oh God!' he said. He sounded half-ashamed. He said to her, very firmly, his breath full of grass and drink: 'I'm used to fighting on decks.'

'Get up,' she said.

He opened his eyes properly, and he saw the size of her and fell back down.

She said: 'Now get up and we'll go and buy something to eat. I'm always hungry.'

'Oh God!' he said again. She made sure that one foot went before the other, that he moved at a speed where natural grace took over from the beer and allowed him to seem like a plausible man. She reckoned they must look like they'd had too good a time at the fair, what with her belly, his cuts and the way they held each other up.

In the tents there were stacks of pewter cups and carved chairs, fans, faience with putti, chests and baskets and smoothing irons, calico, copper and Icelandic stockings. The merchants watched them go by and hoped: 'Next time.'

She sat him down at the mouth of a gambling tent and went off to get beer. He immediately proposed marriage. She said: 'It doesn't count if you're drunk.' He said: 'If I'm drunk, why did you buy me this beer?' She said: 'One more beer won't make any difference. Did he cut you?'

'He couldn't get near me.'

'That's because you were flat on the ground,' she said.

'I want to marry you.'

'You won't remember in the morning. Besides,' she said, 'the baby might not be yours.'

'I want to be married,' he said. 'I'd like to come back to someone when I come back.'

'And it doesn't make much difference when you're away?'

'I want to be married,' he said, slapping his cup on his thigh and lapping what spilled on the table.

'Nobody has to marry me.'

'What are you going to do when the baby's come?'

'What plenty of women do. I'll work and I'll look after the baby. I do sewing now.' She brushed her skirts carefully.

'We got into Amsterdam two days ago. I tried to find you but I didn't know where to start,' he said. 'Nobody came looking for the *Soutberg*.' The blood on his lip was black, almost blue. 'It's tough to find a girl, I mean one particular girl, in the city,' he said. 'I didn't know what you were doing now—'

'So you went to a few taverns and a few whorehouses just in case I was there?'

'What else could I do?' He was so large and reasonable and stupid with beer.

'When do you sail again?'

'In three weeks. We're going to Curaçao and New Amsterdam.'

'You find me again,' Gretje said, 'when you're sober. It doesn't count if you ask me to marry you while you're drunk.'

'How come you know so much about the law now?'

'Maybe I want to marry someone who stays at home. Maybe I'm married already. It's easy for you to say things; maybe you're married, too.'

He looked up as bleak as a spaniel. 'Me?' he said.

She tugged him along like a loose, reluctant boy behind all her flagrant roundness. 'I want to hear a proper story,' she said, stopping at a tent with pamphlets. He said: 'I don't read.' She said: 'You know nothing.' She picked up a picture of broken men hanged on a frame over fire, with stolid burghers posturing around them and a farmer stoking the flames. 'Witches,' he said. 'Very good,' she said. 'How sixty-four witches killed a thousand people, old and young, and six thousand animals.' She pointed and said: 'Son murders father and mother!' 'Terrible,' he said. 'Innocent girl beheaded at Steenwijk,' she read, and then, 'Innocent girl beheaded at Vlissingen.'

'It's a good job you're not innocent,' he said, and she cuffed him.

The weight of the baby had grown in a minute; it was taking Gretje's blood, and she felt dizzy. She backed between the tents. Anthony blocked off the passing crowd as best he could, but he needed the tent rope as a guideline for standing.

She saw a puzzle picture of faces and bodies, milling along. She saw, in particular, a woman laughing with a man. The woman was as tall as her mother, as broad as her mother, the same colouring and the same eyes. Gretje wanted to pitch herself forward and shout, but all her life was concentrating on this needy belly, and the woman took the man by his arm and went browsing and cruising away.

Gretje fainted on to Anthony, and Anthony lost his footing, and they lay in a rag-doll pile. That, she liked to remember.

THREE

GRETJE'S FINDING IT hard to keep Pieter out of her dreams. It doesn't matter where her mind drifts, he's there: on a ship, in a church, at a fair. And when she wakes, he's always about the house like a mirror, those eyes reflecting and complicating everything, impersonal as glass and mercury and perhaps as poisonous.

So Gretje is not going to be a lonely widow; but she's not grateful. It's reasonable Pieter should be at the end of the table when there's food, or by the stove in the evening, but it's also alarming. And Tomas shadows him; they've made an alliance.

Gretje gets out the rent books, exactly noting who has paid, and when, and whose dereliction would need the sheriff if there was any money at all circulating in the frozen town. Calculation is her way out of being seen. Besides, the columns are a map of her certainties, although she suspects that when she stops adding she'll see nothing much more than bricks and trouble.

When she looks up, Pieter is waiting.

He's too young to know what to expect. He's like one

of those customers who gets to the room and the bed, and strips half-naked and then wants her to make the moves and play at wanting him—the truly annoying kind.

Then Gretje cries, which startles her. She blots herself and takes a glass of rosa solis for her chest.

The rent books are not as solid as the houses, she reminds herself. They're just pictures. They're like the story she's told Pieter, more out of nervousness and emptiness than anything, which never quite matches what she can catch in her eyes and her mind, let alone what happened. She's cloaked herself in words.

She sits at table, reckoning to keep Pieter's interest. She won't give him too much, just enough; which is the whore's economy. She's secure in her trade.

But Anthony's still with her, a warmth on her side. And yet when she tries to call back in words this loose, gallivanting alliance over so many years, and tries to hook it into this Gretje Reyniers, stranded with a chest cold and a candle on a dead, frozen island, then nothing at all connects. She's grown out of her own story. It's the same with the sums in her books; they seem so far from all those needy men and hot thoughts that helped pay for them.

Gretje can feel the rosa solis warming her stomach, and it brings on regret. She thinks she should have chased after that woman at the kermis, just to know if she really was her mother. She thinks she misses the baby she left in Amsterdam, her daughter Anneke. She even misses Maria, her second child, who's in Amsterdam so she can have a better life. Most of all, she misses the things that really happened. She wants to know: whether she deserted her mother or her mother left her, whether she burnt down Van Wely's house, whether her first child grew in Amsterdam or died. She strokes herself, sniffs her sweat, tries to be connected again.

At least in Amsterdam, she could rest on the sheer angular system of the city. But here, there are hardly laws to break. In Amsterdam, you could be anonymous. Here, every move is notorious because people have whole winters to watch each other.

She glares at Pieter. If she wanted to, she could tell him a story: how she came into labour and gave birth, how the midwife said something sharp and the baby was gone, while Gretje still lay exhausted. She thinks now that she never really saw her daughter.

The Turk had paid three hundred guilders to put the infant in the orphanage, decent provision for a child too young to have a proper face, and went away to sea to earn the money. Gretje knew she didn't have time for sentiment, but she couldn't always make herself move, couldn't stop her eyes throwing up tears. Colours were a bit shabbier for a while, lights less bright. She would wake suddenly in the night, thinking only of stopping the baby's cries that she barely had a chance to hear. She felt furious, then furious with herself, then furious that she couldn't sleep, and then the tears came and she was pulled about the bed by misery, and she curled up and knotted all the muscles of her body as she did when she was a child, and the pain sobered her up.

She didn't have the time to be mad. She knew she could no more go about as a maid, because Van Wely was looking to hang a maid. She didn't like the idea of going about as a laundrywoman or a seamstress; she wanted to get out of basement rooms, and see some lights. She wasn't going to work the streets, either; she wanted indoor work.

Gretje Reyniers went down to the harbour to see Mary the Starcher because she needed a profession: whoring.

'YOU GOOD AT this?' Mary asked. She was a big woman.

'I'm good,' Gretje said.

'You're young enough.'

Mary the Starcher wore a high hat of feathers, gaudy like her paint, and a great many animals; she had an old look. She appraised Gretje, as Gretje had seen dealers appraise stones. 'But you'll need to work,' she said. 'You can't stay here unless you earn your keep which means you sell the drink and you hand me back half what the men give you. You get a room, you get dresses and feathers, you get paint and you even get protection. What's your name?'

'Gretje,' Gretje said.

'Your real name?'

Gretje paused.

'Doesn't worry me. You can make yourself up as you go.' The woman made it sound like a spell.

'I could clean as well,' Gretje said. 'I'm good at that.'

So she was hired to work for Mary the Starcher, who'd stiffened shirts before she stiffened men, who had seven girls mostly from the North all working in a house she called the High Court of Holland. The girls pushed syrup drinks and watered beer and took the men away to fuck them in their city rooms. 'Nothing else on these premises,' Mary said. 'Just promises.'

Gretje, who'd never bothered with words for herself before, now had dozens, mostly mussel and cunt and kwedio and pussy. She sat on the knees of men with big hats who fumbled under her dress as though they needed directions, and she made tables of sailors laugh, and there were men who liked her to cut and deal the cards because she looked so honest. She was the young one, the one who never seemed needy. They liked to try to get her drunk, but she knew exactly how to tip her drink into the sawdust bins and make sure the punter had more than he needed until he was poor and snoring. She even made a joke of it with the other girls. 'He sells grain, you sell fucking,' she said. 'I sell them a chance to do nothing in a whorehouse. You can sell anything if you try.'

The house lived off the sailors who came in from the Baltic and the North Sea, steady work and uninspiring, a conspiracy of fish-eaters to find warmth; but it came alive when the East India fleet was home. The air smelt of money. There were forests of candles burning. There was some point in the grandest kind of display, breasts bare and cushioned in velvet, legs swung across a chair, some pearls, a perfect white cap and an open smile; every satin inch a woman's certificate that she'd been found desirable before. The men came off the ships, standing like congregations on the lighters, ready and willing to be picked over.

But the fleets went out again, never quite when the house expected it, and the business went with them. Naturally, Mary the Starcher looked around for other work for her girls.

GRETJE TRIES SOMETHING different: she's put Pieter by the stove, given him the beer that Anthony liked, made a little, privileged man out of him, warm on his skin and in his belly.

'He had both his eyes yesterday,' she says reasonably. 'You know that. You could say that if they ask.'

Pieter doesn't say anything. The beer is strong; it makes him lazy-eyed and boneless.

'You could tell them.'

He won't answer her. This is such a simple thing, and he won't answer.

He belches sleepily.

She thinks of him whittling his stick in the yard by the

coffin, she thinks of Anthony lying stiff in his blind sleep, she thinks of someone taking a stick to those blue-paint eyes.

But she's given Pieter privileges in this house, and it's too soon to take them back. Besides, she's beginning to like having someone to hear what she's got to say. It's just that her story keeps taking her to dangerous places, things she wants nobody to know, and she tries to skirt about them without Pieter knowing that she's keeping something back.

So she tells him how the house went dark when the East India men sailed—less gold and shine, fewer candles, and it seemed colder because the bodies were not packed hotly together round the tables. It didn't seem such a privilege to be in a house when the house was half-empty.

Mary the Starcher called her upstairs to the parlour and told her to dress properly.

'Like a maid?' Gretje asked.

'Just clean and decent, if you can manage it.'

'Where am I going?'

Mary the Starcher said: 'An old friend of mine.'

'What am I supposed to do?'

'Do what you're told, and watch everyone. You'll like it. There's a carriage waiting.'

'But what do I do?'

'You're going to the theatre,' Mary said, 'and it's outside Amsterdam. You like fresh air, don't you? And face paint?'

GRETJE SAT INSIDE the carriage, away from the driver. This was glory: being alone. But it was terrifying, too. The landscape gave up the lines and horizons of the polders, and there were wooded lanes. She could tell there were trees behind the trees, that not every living thing had been planted to hide something else. The view turned prettily, scarily wild.

She delighted in the air. Then she wondered, seriously, if she would come back alive. Gretje Reyniers had been sold to somebody, maybe as a sexual pudding, or a kitchen maid, or a sacrifice, and sold by a madame who needed the money. All this comfort was just careful delivery.

The carriage rolled up to a grand brick house set close to the river, with new chestnuts planted among the old trees and a lake where the grounds had proved too swampy to drain. Gretje stood on the gravel for a moment, taking in the big, open order of the place. She couldn't see alleys or escapes.

She ducked into the servants' entrance for safety, but the servants wouldn't have her. A pair of busy girls made her wait at the door while they found out what she was there for and when they came back, they shooed her to the gardens, to a pavilion among the trees. They wouldn't say why.

Inside the pavilion, there was a smell of paint and camphor. At one end, red curtains framed a stage. A man came bustling up to her and asked why she was late; he was neat and thin, like an etching of himself.

'Mary told me to do what I'm told,' she said.

'Amateurs,' the man said.

'Nobody ever called me an amateur,' Gretje said.

'That's why you get to do the difficult bits,' the man said.

He walked her down between the seats in the theatre. The stage was lit with oil-lamps that threw gold light on an artificial sea. Thunder rolled. Light shot about like lightning.

Gretje said: 'You can't scare me.'

'I don't know why I'm bothering to tell you this, but this is a play. A play. In this play, there's a miracle at sea. There's a fearsome storm, people pray for their lives, and the Madonna appears in a great golden sun. You're the Madonna.'

'Oh,' Gretje said.

'So you come down from the flies in a big gold box, which opens if we're good and lucky, and there you are. With a baby.'

'A baby?'

'This baby.' He pushed a cloth dummy into her arms. Its eyes were painted blue. She held it carefully and looked about her with suspicion.

'Where are the other actors?'

'In the house or coming later. The actors are the gentry.'

'But I'm acting in the box.'

'You're in the box,' the man said, 'because the gentry wouldn't dream of doing anything so risky. They just ponce about and recite poems in front of you.'

'Is it dangerous?'

'You're bought and paid for.'

She climbed on to the stage, stepping over the rollers that carried painted waves, trying to step decorously because she'd been told to dress decent.

'The ladder,' the man shouted.

She started up the ladder into the dark above the stage. She couldn't see how to take the baby with her, so she tucked it in the belt of her dress. Below, a man turned a kind of mangle with strips of cloth and made the noise of wind, and another tipped a pipe of stones to sound like rain. She saw mirrors glinting.

After a dozen steps, she was above the bright paint, and up in a net of cables and hanging ropes and iron, like a ship's rigging. Her foot slipped on a rung, and she fixed her hands on the ladder and she suddenly didn't trust the ladder to stand up for much longer. She climbed faster.

At the top, among the enormous shadows from the

stage lamps below, there was a platform. There was nowhere else to go, although she looked carefully for somewhere else. She eased herself off the ladder and pitched on to the dark, narrow platform.

A box hung in front of the platform, something like a tea chest, one side cut away so that she could step into it. There was a chair, facing the audience and what looked like a solid wall. But that wall was painted in front to look like the sun, a simple circle when it was high above the stage and closed, from which spread out fine, golden beams in the stage light as it opened. It was pretty, she thought.

She sat down, and she put the baby to her breast for comfort.

Chains stuttered. The box jerked. It was dark where Gretje sat, and she imagined the baby alive. The blue of its eyes helped.

The box descended slowly. As it did so, the wall in front of Gretje began to pull apart in the middle, to open so she could see the flats and the machines around her. When it opened fully, she was staring out into a blaze of light.

The box settled on the stage, and she climbed out at once.

'We haven't finished,' the man said.

She couldn't see into the theatre past the flares at the edge of the stage.

'Get back in the box. We'll see how it looks going up.'

The waves began to turn on their rollers, and the lights flickered on and off in a mirror to make a storm, and the waves turned the other way on the rollers; the mangle made wind, and the pipe made rain. Gretje picked up the stuffed cloth baby and held it lovingly. The box shifted uneasily on the ground, but she didn't fret; she had a part she could play. A mother who hadn't lost her baby after all.

The box cleared the ground. Metal sheets shivered for thunder. But all those effects were for the man who sat out in the theatre, and the gentry who would join him one day. The front wall of the box closed up again, and, from where Gretje sat, high in the dark where nobody was meant to be noticed, she could hear the chains catching at the quiet.

She sat in her golden box, hanging where the false lightning made messages out of the smoke and the dust in the air. Her mouth opened in a perfect, terrified 'O'.

'WHY ARE YOU telling me this?' Pieter asks.

She thinks: because I remember it, because it's what lives in my mind, because it isn't to do with Anthony, because it's picturesque enough to interest you, because it defends me against other stories.

She says: 'It's my story. I'll tell it as I want.'

WHEN SHE WAS not wanted in the theatre, she stood down by the river. She watched water seep in and out of a little pocket in the banks and a swan come to feed, and there were irises in the water and mallows on the bank. She didn't stay long away from the house.

She slept bundled up with a couple of other servant girls, one fat, one sallow with a spiteful body, who kept as much distance as the bed would allow.

'I used to be a servant,' she said grandly.

'Got into trouble, did you?' the fat girl said.

'No.'

'Then why'd you leave?'

The whole point of these girls was what they didn't do. They didn't leave, for a start. They didn't go into the theatre because that was the Devil's temple. They didn't steal, whore or drink like other servant girls. They were still working, so they had never done whatever it was that Gretje had done, which must be terrible.

'Where do you work?' the sallow girl asked.

'For Mary the Starcher. I'm her maid.'

The sallow girl snorted. 'Maid,' she said.

'And why,' asked the fat girl, 'did they bring you here anyway?'

'I sit in a box and I fly up and down,' Gretje said. 'I don't know why they wanted me.'

'If you ask me,' the fat one said, 'they wanted someone who doesn't mind indecencies.' She looked oddly hopeful at the end of the bed.

'You know whose house this is?' the sallow one asked.

'Mary never told me.'

'You know what the man does?'

'I don't know.'

'He makes a fortune out of selling what's not his,' the sallow girl said. She'd have pursed her lips if she could have borne to stop talking. 'He sells grain that hasn't been grown yet and that he doesn't even own, and people buy it.'

Gretje said: 'I don't know his name, even.'

The fat girl stood over her. 'You don't need to know these things. You just ride up and ride down in your box.'

But the sallow girl wouldn't leave Gretje alone. 'You know who *she* is, don't you. She. The Mistress.'

'Mary never said—'

'She isn't married to him. She wears these hats with tall feathers and paints her face and she used to be on the streets but now she's so grand, she gets grander every day.'

Gretje said: 'Maybe that's how she knows Mary the Starcher.'

'Stupid name,' the fat one said, 'for a woman who gave up honest work long ago.'

'And how do you know?' Gretje asked. 'If you're down here in the country and never go to town and never did a bad thing in your life—'

'We know,' they said.

Gretje had the odd sense that she had failed them both.

'You could help with the silver,' the fat one said. 'You're not paid to do nothing.'

The girls dealt hints like cards. When Gretje came back from the little theatre, they asked what she had seen, and she said thunder and lightning and dust and sea, and they said again that it was clearly the Devil's work. But the Devil fascinated them. They wanted all the details. They were like one woman, facing backwards and forwards, always alert and troublesome, living as servants but thinking like grandees walking through a zoo. Everything horrified them. Everything excited them.

'You're wicked,' the fat girl said. 'You are, aren't you?'

The theatre became a place of refuge for Gretje. In her box, she was shut off from the world by planks and gilt and lights; she could be seen, but not as herself. Through the shadows and the lamps she could barely make out faces; none stayed still enough long enough to disconcert her.

On the night of the show she was waiting, high above the stage. She heard music and musicians laughing, she saw men and women in rich dress and she smelt tobacco and meat in the house as though it were a tavern. She felt grand, because they waited to see her. But all she saw of the show was the need to brace herself when the box started moving.

At the end, she was left hanging there as the gentry bowed and curtsied into the applause and the curtains closed. The music stopped. She could hear the chatter as the theatre emptied. She waited a while and then shouted to be let out. After a few long minutes, the box came shuddering down to the ground.

She clambered off the stage and sat where the audience had sat, trying to imagine what they had seen on that stage and whether it made a better show—with its mirror lights and its sounding steel sheets and its fake rolling waves— than all these rich people dressed up for dinner. The audience was the only show she could get to see, and she ran outside to enjoy it, a cloak pulled over her costume.

In front of the great brick house stood carriages, a cluttered parade of wheels, reins, horse muscle, men idling out of sight and a little mist of tobacco smoke. She walked on the other side of the drive, watching. The men were fussing with brushes on horses that shone already. An older man was shovelling dung from the driveway, serious as a surgeon. There were braziers against the damp.

A young man sat on the steps by one of the coaches: a plain, black box pulled by two horses. He looked awkward in his livery and didn't seem to be part of the easy club of the coachmen.

'Hendrick?' Gretje said.

He looked up. The braziers lit the driveway a little, and there were occasional torches between trees, but it was impossible to read a face clearly; so Gretje didn't know if she should run to him, or away as fast as she could, or if he was simply puzzled.

'Gretje,' Hendrick said very flatly.

'You're a coachman now?'

'No,' Hendrick said. He stood up diffidently to face her. 'Van Wely fancied himself at a grand party. So he hires a coach to pretend it's his, and of course he has to have a footman. So I'm the footman, all dressed up. I don't fool anyone, and he doesn't fool anyone, but he's happy.'

'Did you see me?' Gretje said.

'I just saw you. What do you mean?'

'Did you see me in the theatre?'

Hendrick shrugged. Gretje came in between the coaches, where the other men couldn't see, but where the light of a torch caught the back steps of the coach like a stage. She was still painted so she'd look innocent from a distance, still dressed in white under her cloak. She dropped the cloak.

Hendrick gaped, which settled his future.

THE NEXT MORNING, the glory had all gone along with the sense of holiday, and Gretje was sent to scrub out the theatre and rake the sand by its door. She was glad enough to be occupied. It was alarming to think she'd sat so publicly and stared out into an audience where Van Wely sat, all powerful and connected and, most likely, still furious. Maybe Hendrick would tell him about Gretje, maybe not. They had to talk about something in the workshop.

The two servant girls ran out of the house and called her. The mistress, they said, wanted to see her. They could taste scandal.

Gretje dusted herself down. She wasn't quite sure whether to throw down her rake, which a good servant never would do, or whether to stash it carefully and keep the mistress waiting. But if this woman had the power to make even Van Wely spend real money on his social climbing, she'd better run.

Only she couldn't run, not in these rooms that opened one into another, with their marble floors, black and white and exact, where she felt obliged to wait at each huge door. She came at last to windows that were open on the river and a little terrace.

'You're Gretje,' the mistress said.

'Ma'am,' Gretje said and looked up for the first time.

The mistress was piled up like money in a huge chair. She smelt of flowers Gretje didn't know, and she was implacably white.

'How's Mary?' she asked. 'I asked Mary for someone who looks like me.'

Gretje was startled by the idea that this woman could ever have been ordinary.

'Do you even know my name?' the mistress asked.

'I—'

'*Je m'appelle* Artesia.'

Gretje said: 'That's French.'

'My old name was Agt. A bit more basic,' Artesia said. 'But you get the fancy money, you get the fancy name.'

'Everybody says you're beautiful.'

Artesia laughed. It began in the wrinkling of the forehead, the drawing of lines and shadows in the deep and placid flesh and unsettled the chins. Then her breasts rose as one great device. The laugh made her huge belly heave and her legs open helplessly. She seemed to flood out of the chair.

'I mean you are, of course,' Gretje said.

'Everyone who's rich is as beautiful as they say they are. I'm rich and I say I'm beautiful. I'm the courtesan, the old procuress, the wicked woman living with a speculator and his money; of course I must be beautiful.'

'But—'

Artesia stood, and the commotion subsided. 'I used to be like you,' she said. 'I suppose you turn tricks and sell drink. Had a baby yet? Had the pox?'

Gretje said: 'I play cards, too, and I clean.'

'All those talents,' Artesia said. 'You can act, too.'

'I never did before last night.'

'Balls,' Artesia said. 'I act when I go out there. People look at me and they see a duchess. Even the ones I sucked off twenty years ago see a duchess. They wouldn't dare see anything else. Why else would they be at my ball?' She fingered a cup made of green glass. 'Besides, I live with a man, and we're rich and we're blessed and maybe some of it will rub off on them. Or perhaps they just want money.

'That's why Mijnheer Van Wely was here last night,' she said. 'Little man.'

'Oh,' Gretje said.

'This morning I get a letter from Amsterdam asking if you're still here. He wants me to keep you here, or tell him where you're going next. This Van Wely, he's a follower?'

'No.'

'That's good. Followers just complicate your life. So he's trouble, then?'

'Thank you for telling me.'

'I won't be answering him. Of course.'

She stood, all broad and glorious against the windows, in triumphant command of each heavy pound of her being.

'I could stay,' Gretje said. 'I could work in the theatre. I mean, I could be like you. Like you were—'

Artesia said: 'You stupid child.'

NOW GRETJE HAS her own house, her own money, she can visit her memories of Artesia like a guest in a garden. She can see how the pictures hung in the corridor. But she remembers, too, how flustered she was in those days. She thought she was being invited over some boundary into a grander world; instead she was wondering if they'd even bother to ship her back to the city once they'd thrown her out.

The pictures were a nice distraction, at the time. There was Artesia in oils, younger, magnificent in some elegant

interior and with a plain, rich man; a curious picture of a
girl with oysters that made Gretje shiver; a godly interior,
two serious women at a linen chest and a serving girl
waiting for them, with a courtyard beyond that had been
swept and swept again; a household with a fire in the next
room, a dog at a platter, cards, hats and cheeses on the floor
while a woman with white breasts drank, a man smoked a
pipe, a fiddle played, and a monkey devil tinkered with the
clocks. Pictures, fixtures; things so certain they can be put
down and varnished over and hung up.

As she did then, she now dawdles in her mind before a
picture of some woman in a great room with gilt cups and
piles of polished fruit. She was fascinated by the notion
that anyone would paint, so elaborately, the purple of a
plum or the faint pink and white of an apple, when they
could have the real thing and its taste and smell from the
market. She looked at the woman's face. She could tell the
painted room was far away and maybe long ago, perhaps a
Bible truth she never knew, but whoever invented it must
have painted a real girl, an Amsterdam girl, someone she
might know. This girl had a name, a house, a time, maybe
children, opinions, an attitude to the artist, but she would
survive only in this thick field of paint. The painter had
stolen her.

Gretje came out of the house into a low, formal
garden, a few squares and triangles cut out of box.

She can still, as she sits by her own fireside, smell the
river running low.

NOBODY HELPS, SHE wants to tell Pieter. They show you
the world and take it away.

Nothing lasts, she wants to say. Nothing is sure. You
could find me out tomorrow and the me you found would

not really be me. Nothing lasts, except she lasted with Anthony; and what is she meant to make of that, now he's gone, now he's cold, now all the time that they once had together has turned against her.

Pieter wouldn't know. She hopes he doesn't know—all the reservations, complications, hallucinations and prevarications that go into loving one other. Gretje likes Love as a tart painted with wings, or Love as a commodity or Love as a great Christian notion that's simplified of smells or Love as a big fat word in a motto. Then, there's real Love. Selling it is one way out.

SHE WALKED BACK into the High Court of Holland, past the old street whores who hung about outside in case some punter was too drunk to find the proper door, or too poor to get past it.

'Things are picking up,' Mary the Starcher said. 'There's a new girl.'

Gretje said: 'It was a beautiful house, Artesia's.'

'This house is beautiful, too. Don't you forget it.'

'You want me to dress you?'

Gretje sorted out clothes and a wide hat with peacock feathers. She undid Mary's stays, and powdered her huge breasts carefully, and then packed the Starcher back into velvet and lace. Then she went down to the main room to see if anyone was in.

Marieke was waiting in a corner. She was dark, too dark to charge very much, and her hair was sunstruck; so she must be the new girl. The two of them embraced, carefully.

Marieke said she'd come back from the East Indies with the man she'd worked for, but she'd run away when they got to the docks in Amsterdam. She said she missed the old house on Warmoesstraat, her, Gretje and Lysbeth, who had gone up to Groningen to have her baby; but she couldn't go back to a place or a life like that.

'I want my freedom,' she said.

'It costs a lot, freedom,' Gretje said, already the cynic.

They sat down and remembered Lysbeth: dark, kind, slow Lysbeth who had always wanted to care for them. But then Marieke said East India was too hot, you couldn't walk for the insects in the grass and there were snakes and huge beasts, and it never grew cold enough to cover yourself and have that lovely sense of taking refuge under the bedclothes. Gretje said she'd had a baby, and that this sailor wanted to marry her, but she hadn't said yes or no, and then when the baby was born she'd sent it to the orphanage because there was nothing else she could do. She couldn't bring herself to call the baby 'she'.

They fought each other with stories. First, Marieke said she'd been pregnant in East India, but one of the local women knew the herbs that opened up the womb, and she'd pushed out this clot of a thing that might have grown.

Then Gretje: Amsterdam had been risky enough, even without insects, what with carriages and plague and knife fights.

Then Marieke, who insisted that Gretje couldn't imagine what East India was like, with no flatland and no winter and no canals and the whole world always relentlessly green.

Then Gretje: Marieke had been lucky to be looked after in a house. Gretje had to fend for herself.

Then each decided she needed an ally, after all.

The nightwork was steady, but together they had the notion they could buy their way to something better. They took everything the fishermen had, and the East India men were generous to the point of daftness; but when there was no more money in bed, they started to take in sewing and washing, until only Gretje had the muscle and time for it. Money would prove God's grace to her and let her out of the house. With money, she thought, she could afford to see her daughter, buy her out and take her off to some one-street village or some northern town; but the thought did not last long. First, she had to buy herself a life in which she was not buffeted about by every chance, nor ordered about, nor went about carefully now she was walking the city with linens in a basket and looking like a maid, in case the Van Welys recognized her.

The East India fleet cruised grandly out, and the house was left nervous. Girls fought over customers on a slack day. The price of the syrup they sold as drink came down to eleven stuivers for a while. Mary the Starcher said the city fathers caught morals like they caught the clap, and you just had to wait for the cure to get back to business. Some of the older women who needed the dark, who could never go back to working in a lit house, began to hang around the doors of the High Court of Holland as though they expected some calamity that would make them desirable again. Mary the Starcher hardened her features and bawled them out of the way, but the girls all sensed their presence. They seemed to be flocking.

Gretje, taking back washing, passed by the street of ships and looked around for the *Soutberg* as she often did. The Turk was off honouring his obligations, and she was honouring hers, and that was the natural order of things; she was busy as a tribute to him. But the *Soutberg* lay there: a slim, battered thing among the taller ships. She tried slipping past in the hope she would see he was there but not actually see him; she saw nobody. She went back to the house and put on her best whites and her crimson dress, the one she wore for the East India men, as though she didn't want him to recognize her if he came to the house. But then how could he afford to come to the High Court of Holland if he were still paying for the care of their daughter?

She thought of him coming to the house, and looking round the girls, one by one, and waiting to see if he would choose her.

She worked three hours in the house that night, waiting each minute for the Turk to arrive. When she could stand it no more, she slipped out into the street where she hoped, she said, not to run into him. She got Marieke to tell the Starcher that she was feeling sick, but the Starcher just said: 'She's too fertile. Doesn't matter what I do.' Marieke said: 'It's not that.' The Starcher said: 'She's been a good worker. Not too many tricks, but a lot of booze.' Marieke, a full year older, said: 'She's still young.'

Gretje ran into a scouring wind full of salt and rain. The streets were quiet, the doorways and the alley turns full of sheltering figures who were carefully not yet doing what they meant to do later.

She caught up with men walking, all in capes, with torches, all of them as decorous as an army in the rain. She covered her head and walked past them quickly, glancing back. It was the Watch, the city's conscience walking about to stop things; its members didn't need a band to keep them moving when they had such high moral purpose. Among them, she saw Mijnheer Van Wely, plumped up and furious, ready to take back the night from the moon if he had to.

She doubled back round the alleys and came in by the back way at the High Court of Holland, and went quickly down to the main room where Marieke was working. 'Get next door,' she said. 'The Watch are coming.'

'I'll tell the others,' Marieke said.

'You can't. Then they'll just look for all the girls some-where else.'

Marieke's punter was a farmer with a strong, huge belly, who liked to quiz the girls about what they could put inside them and keep a tally while he filled himself up with gin. 'Easy,' Marieke said. Then she whispered to him: 'Even you. I could.' He smirked and drank. She slipped her hand under the table, fondled his wallet with her fingers and rubbed his crotch with her forearm. The wallet was empty as the crotch. 'I'll get you a drink,' she said and went straight to where Mary the Starcher sat at the head of the room, always watching, face still as a painted picture behind which her eyes hid.

'No money at my table,' she said.

'He paid for the drinks?'

'Bottle by bottle.'

'I'll get the boys out.'

She raised a hand as though she were calling for drinks and two square-shaped men came forward, took up the farmer and left him outside. The rain scrabbled at the cobbles, and he started to snore in the gutter. Mary the Starcher's bouncers looked down the street and ducked inside.

For they had seen the Watch pounding down to the High Court of Holland, faces lit by torches and again from below by the shine of the street stones. The Watch blocked off the front door of the High Court, and someone with information went round to block off the rat-run that led out past the backhouse and into the alley. 'Like rats,' Van Wely was saying. 'They may run anywhere.' Then they waited for a moment, expecting that the warm room inside would somehow sense their presence.

But they didn't break into the High Court. They dodged to the right and spilled through the door of the next-door house, taking down the velvet curtain that served as windbreak with their boots, startled by the darkness and the smoke as the lights were all snuffed out at once.

Mary the Starcher asked where Marieke was. Nobody knew. Mary stood up and turned over a table and cleared out the men into the sharp rain. She took up some sewing which she had to hand.

'I had a live one, too,' one of the girls was saying. 'First real money in weeks.'

'At least you're free,' Mary said sententiously.

'I don't know why they went next door instead. We're a much better house.'

'I organize my luck,' Mary said.

Out in the rain, Gretje didn't like to turn back to the High Court of Holland. She was sure the Watch would be there. She had this story in her mind: that it was her fault. Hendrick told Van Wely, Van Wely made enquiries, and he'd come after her in particular, and not just general vice and sin. He would charge her with theft and arson and prostitution and lewdness; they'd put her in the Spinhuis or banish her from the city and either way, they'd make an example of her—brand her, flog her, show her off to the fair-time visitors as the best of all sideshows, the fallen women of the Spinhuis discovering God through labour, and making suggestions to the punters through the lattice in the door.

She went the back way, and the Watch were there, standing in the alley in the best shelter they could find. But they were not precisely behind the High Court of Holland; they were next door. They might just be trying to block any runs out of the High Court, but they seemed interested in the wrong door.

By telling Marieke to get next door to avoid the Watch, she'd sent her into the house that was being raided.

The next-door house was blank, dark instead of the usual welcoming lights, as good as silent in the rain when usually there was a fiddle and some shouting and the slap of dice and dominoes on the tables. Gretje stood with the cold rain invading her neck and she stared. The Watch had closed the next-door house with Marieke in it.

The older women, the ones nobody would take as whores any more, stood around the door like mourners. A light passed the one window in the gable of the house. The women stood in silence. Mary the Starcher came to the door of the High Court of Holland, saw them waiting, shivered and went back inside. The street was stretched so tight the rain seemed to bounce back to Heaven.

The next-door house opened up all at once, torches in every window. The Watch came out, surrounding a litter of girls, Marieke among them. She shrugged at Gretje and spat. Gretje thought she just meant to mean this was nothing, not Gretje's fault, but the old waiting whores saw the gesture and took it for an accusation.

The women of the house walked down the street with set faces, sometimes flirting out of habit. 'It's the game,' Marieke shouted. 'It's the luck of the fucking game.' Mary the Starcher stood at a window, saw the Watch retreating and the old, used whores, like crows in their capes, on the other side of the street. She closed the shutters and barred them.

The law marched into the dark, the houses blinded themselves for safety and Gretje stood in the persistent rain and she was alone. Across the street, the older women massed. Their only place was in this world of women and they stood ready to enforce the loyalty they could not escape. Gretje shivered for much longer than the cold could justify.

She tried to see their faces, but their whole trade was to hide their faces, obscure the state of their bodies, to be a hot hole in a back alley and nothing more; so even the shape of them was disguised and changing under their capes. She thought she saw a woman with nostrils set flat on her face and no nose at all. One of them said: 'Judas.'

Gretje said: 'I didn't do anything.'

The woman said: 'Didn't do anything to save them.'

Gretje said: 'You saw the Watch coming, too.'

Like crows on prey, the old whores closed their circle round Gretje.

The woman was tall, taller than most men, obliged to hide her great height with careful stooping. She seemed like one of those puppets that go about on stilts at fairgrounds. She hit out at Gretje, who moved back carefully. Another woman had a knife. The chorus of old women hung still for a moment.

Gretje said: 'I didn't talk to the Watch.'

The tall woman pulled Gretje to her, eyes huge, breath full of dead teeth and onions and the come of some desperate soldier. Gretje retched. 'Delicate, are we?' the woman said. The other women cackled. 'I'll show you,' she said. 'I'll show you.' She pushed Gretje down to her knees.

The woman's cape was enough to muddle her with the shadows, so that when it was gone, put aside into the arms of the waiting women, she was shockingly particular. She grabbed Gretje's head and pulled it to this side and to that side, making her eyes see everything. She stood there naked in the half-light, sheltered by anger from the cold rain. 'Read me,' she said, 'like a Bible.'

She had been branded, three times: dark burns and marks on both breasts, and on one arm. Her back was ridged and calloused from floggings. Her hair was gone, all

118

over her body, and her labia were swollen like another brand. Her angles and muscles were muddled with rolls of hard fat and she turned as Gretje had seen smart women turn in their finest dresses.

The rain suddenly stopped.

The old whores broke circle nervously, like women again instead of black birds. The soft, sieving sound of the rain was like camouflage. Without it, Gretje sensed, they had to look about, for police or for punters. They began to slip back into dark places, doorways or turnings, so a man couldn't shelter without brushing against them, so they were hidden when the Watch came.

Gretje stared at the tall woman avidly, and still she could not see the moment when the dress and the cloak put this particular body back into the muddle of the shadows.

The woman was gone. Gretje heard cackling.

She picked herself up. She was cold and wet, except for the hot damp around her eyes and between her legs. The cold stopped her breath. She was so used to being hidden by these streets and here she stood, alone in them, knowing that if she tried a door, the houses would throw her back. She went back, snuffling and doubtful, to the door of the High Court of Holland.

Mary said: 'Where did Marieke go?'

'She went next door.'

'Then I expect you want your money.'

Gretje nodded. She'd need money.

'You needn't think you can crawl back here.'

'I thought the Watch were coming here.'

'Then you should have warned me.'

'I warned Marieke. She's my friend.'

Mary the Starcher pushed some coins across the cloth

of the card-table and said: 'Fuck off.' She sat at her frame of embroidery, stabbing the needle in and out.

GRETJE COMES INTO the room suddenly. Pieter is head first, arse up, into a chest of linens and papers and treasures. The white cockatoo is shrieking, but only out of habit.

Pieter turns to her.

'You know me now, I suppose,' Gretje says.

He shrugs.

'Sit down,' she says. She surprises herself by her calm. 'There's nothing to find there.'

'I was looking for something.'

'I'm not hiding in the chest.'

He says: 'I have to help Tomas find the linen—'

'You're going to listen,' Gretje says.

'But I know—'

'I married in Amsterdam,' she says. 'I married Hendrick.'

She was glad to see Pieter look startled.

'You don't understand anything, do you? The Turk kept coming back, I expect. But how would I know? I didn't go down by the docks. I didn't go to the taverns and God knows I never wanted to remember where the High Court of Holland even stood.'

'I see,' Pieter says. She wonders what he could possibly see.

'You wanted a romance?'

'I have work to do.'

'It's a romance,' Gretje says. 'He saw me that one night and he saw anything but Gretje Reyniers. All in white I was and painted to look innocent; that's who he married. It's amazing what they manage in the theatre.' She wants something to smoke and calls Tomas. 'I ran into him again, of course, I had to. We talked, he seemed grateful. I don't know what kind of story he thought I had, but it didn't seem to matter. He said he wanted to leave Van Wely, because he wasn't getting anywhere, and in time he wanted his own business. He said he'd marry me.'

She took the pipe from Tomas and filled it slowly and lit it from the stove. 'He'd gone off to work for another pewterer because he knew I couldn't go back to the Van Welys. So there we were,' she says, 'packed up in the back-house, over the kitchen and the dining-room. He was good at his job so they put up with me, and I did some sewing and some laundry. There wasn't any money except what I kept from the house.'

Pieter says: 'Why?'

She knows what he's asking, and she answers before asking if she needs to answer. 'I was very tired. I was very young and I was terrified of each new day and that wouldn't do. It was easy to marry.'

'He looked after you?'

'Oh, yes.' She knows the story now. She organizes herself in her chair. 'He talked about opening his own shop. I'd do the books because he couldn't figure very well.'

The tobacco is charming her; her features grow lazy.

SHE REMEMBERS, TOO, the day all that caring and looking after and calculating came to an end. She was dressed up neat and modest, the starch speaking for her virtue. Her husband, Hendrick, wrapped his stick of a body in colours for once, red and yellow, and Gretje thought he looked more than ever like some temporary insect on a summer river: gawky, gaudy, articulated at the joints where other men had muscles. But she had grown attached to a warm bed and a familiar lover and a settled day.

Hendrick called her 'My love'; she called him 'You'. She

121

was afraid he would turn into another Van Wely, hugely ambitious but also careful, and always hanging between the two characters. But then she looked at the fool's colours he'd chosen for the day, and she smiled. He picked up the smile and made a song and a promise out of it. She sensed his happiness at her happiness, and she built on that. And so their marriage had gone on, like stairs, for five years.

She said: 'I'm always meeting people I know.'

'Old lovers, I suppose.' He was very sure of things.

'Sometimes,' she said slyly.

He looked at her face very closely, scrutinizing as he would examine metal for flaws. She said: 'Only sometimes,' because she felt sorry for him, but it didn't help.

That day, she wanted the confusion of the city. She wanted storytellers and beer and dancing. But she knew that would be the second thing they did. Hendrick had a moral centre as bony as his spine; he loved lessons. On certain days the Spinhuis was open to the public and the women prisoners were presented to the world. Hendrick wanted to go. She watched him sideways, wondering how he was excited by the fallen women, trying to be excited herself by the notion of Hendrick having a vice. But when she first saw him at the prison grilles, gawping into the courtyard like a fish, her guts came up against her heart like carts colliding.

She concentrated on the queue. Of course, there were men on their own, a handful of dominies and clerics who were perfect respectability, but mostly just men on their own. There were other people's mothers who looked almost lovingly at the prisoners, then remembered where they were and spat. Two boys stood at the grille and then ran out in panic when some ancient doxy undulated up, forgetting that her smile needed paint.

Some of the men slipped the warders some change and stayed longer.

The queue was easier to bear than the women. They were nameless, of course, their history reduced to the presumption of crime. Some sat making thread out of clumped wool, working the treadle, timing the wheel and deaf with concentration. The very young did this. They seemed respectable enough to join the queue and stare at themselves. Some of the older women sat about, glaring at the frieze of faces behind the grille, committing them to vengeful memories and half-hoping to catcall some past customer. They relied on the fact that the faces would pass in time. And some of the women were working, Gretje could see. They came up to the grille and they said, straight out, the things the men wanted to hear and never expected. The men stopped, smiled. They grew bigger, eyes and trousers.

She tugged at Hendrick's sleeve, but he was staring into the cage. He seemed alarmed and delighted by the women, by the beauty that temptation ought to carry and by the blankness in the eyes, the lightlessness of wickedness and sins. They were alive, but safe, like examples from a book of morals. They could not tug his sleeve, trip him, take his wallet or give him drugged drink or trick him into exhausting himself and spending himself in blood; he could never be tempted by them even though they were perfect examples of temptation. He was fascinated by the hope and glory that they managed to scratch together in the cells: a little colour, smuggled in, and cold water to bring pretty blood to the face. They managed to armour themselves in their trade. More than ever, he felt protected by the round plainness he adored in Gretje.

Gretje said: 'It isn't nice to stare.'

'It's a reminder,' Hendrick said.

Easy for him to say, with no vices in his past. 'I don't want to be reminded,' she said.

He put an arm around her shoulder. The line of moralists behind shoved forward and those ahead stood their ground. The prisoners caught the little battle of pushing and standing, and let on they were somehow flattered. One looked up from her wheel now the faces were more than glimpses, and she went red.

'Marieke,' Gretje said.

'Gretje Reyniers,' Marieke said in a loud, low voice that took the name and turned it into a growl.

She stood and came to the grille. Gretje, who thought of walking on, moved too late.

'Second time,' Marieke said. 'If they hadn't picked me up the first time, I wouldn't be here now.'

The ladies of the queue pushed forward, sensing a drama. This respectable matron might be a fake, tied to the mirror city locked beyond the grille. Or, even more stirring, there might be an innocent trapped in a dark jail. It was the stuff of woodcuts and pamphlets: Marieke should be pointing an accusing finger, Gretje should cower just a bit.

'I shouldn't have been caught the first time,' Marieke said.

'Is there anything you need?' Gretje asked.

'Yes. To be out of here.'

Gretje acted. She heaved a little, caught spit in her throat and made herself start to cry. The line of visitors changed sympathies: all at once there was one of them, polite and quiet, being bullied to tears by some harridan. The back of the queue began to ask loudly why there was a hold-up, they hadn't got all day.

Hendrick put his arm around her and helped her out

of the Spinhuis. At the canalside she stood looking on to the shine that overlay the water.

She said: 'I didn't like seeing her.' Hendrick just held her, and she liked the warmth.

But it wouldn't do any more. She had seen something terrible about the prison, how it held Marieke as she had been—the dark girl playing the men at the High Court of Holland. A little bad luck and Gretje, too, would be stuck with her record and nothing else.

Along the canal passed women and men in bright fair-time colours, and the lindens shivered in a soft breeze, and she knew she had felt safe because people were properly dressed, because they acted, loved, drank and ate and danced in character and class; their record was written on their clothes. But she was also confined by this order, reduced to a backhouse dweller, attendant to other people's linen, and none of them cared or even knew that she had also once been like Marieke.

She heard the drums and the half-hour bells.

Since she was more than she appeared, then so could other people be, and there was nothing to bind the world together. Even Hendrick could be almost anybody. The day was bright, the shade was kind, the city full of gentle order and she finally saw through the whole parade to the uncertainties beyond.

'We'll have a beer,' Hendrick said.

She walked on with him. But doors like the doors she'd polished now looked like black mirrors in a row, and the stones around brick around stones looked painted like a stage scene, and the leaves rustling made the sound of something hidden. Streets alive with people became alive in themselves. She sensed houses that moved to block the way and opened up alleys just to startle her.

Hendrick said: 'You're very quiet.'

'I was enjoying the sun,' she said.

He knew she was lying.

He tried to cheer her up, made to run off, long bones clicking like a puppet, but he saw how she was staring and he came back to hug her.

She couldn't stand all the comforting any more.

PIETER'S OUT OF the house, and she's glad. She doesn't need to puzzle over what she can tell him. If she wants to, she can do some forgetting.

But he trots in, cheeks grazed with the cold, a bit of paper in his hands. He doesn't give it to her, but he lets her know—the care with which he puts it on the table, the solemnity in his voice—that this piece of paper matters.

Gretje and Pieter jostle to be the second one to speak. Pieter is full of excitement at the paper he's brought. Gretje is faintly alarmed by papers. You can't ignore papers like talk.

Pieter smooths out the paper on the table. He puts one of the thick-stemmed glasses on it and walks out of the room ostentatiously.

She thinks: 'It's a trick.'

She's slicing an onion for the pot. She cuts the slices into fine, translucent dice. She goes on chopping until she has a wet dust on the board.

Then she picks up the paper, as she knew she would.

It is headed: 'Gretje Reyniers. Anthony Janssen.'

She stands up to read, thinking she can always slip the glass back on to the paper and pretend she was working at the table.

The paper is a list of all the times she or Anthony went to court, or were taken there, the evidence read against them and on their behalf—a copy from the Colonial Secretary's registers. There's the time the Minister's wife refused to enter a house because Gretje was there; the time Anthony's dog did violence to a pig, but it was a sorry old pig. Then there was the incident on the dockside when Gretje took a broom handle to measure the private parts of three sailors; if she'd been serious, she thinks, she would have done much more. And the time she stormed into the fort, shouting that she'd be the people's whore and she'd been the whore of the nobility long enough. Gretje sued for debts and was sued, slandered and was slandered.

Even her arrival in New Amsterdam is recorded: when she landed off the *Soutberg,* and the crew lined up on the side shouting that she'd do it for a tub of butter. She'd picked up her skirts and told them to kiss her arse—but what else was she supposed to do? They were just hoping.

This is as much of her life as officialdom knows: a mean thing, made up of spite and debt and scandal. There are dates by each entry. The writing looks like a clerk's writing; that costs money. Pieter couldn't ask for such a paper, couldn't pay for such a paper, and she wonders how he could come to be carrying it. She wants to ask, but that would mean admitting he knew how to snatch her attention. She feels uneasy.

He's checking her story. He knows there's nothing to be found out about Amsterdam and so he's ready to listen to her version; but now he knows what everyone knows about Gretje Reyniers in America. Anything she says, he can test.

Tomas lugs buckets into the room, ice that has thawed in the stables. Gretje tells him to fetch Pieter.

'Where were you?' she asks.

'I was down in the fort—'

'What were you doing there?'

'Playing,' Pieter says. They both know he's lying.

'Playing what?'

'On the ice.'

'Playing colf? Playing sledges?'

'I was playing.' He pulls back into himself.

'Who gave you this?' she says, pointing to the paper with her knife.

'Nobody. I found it.'

'You don't find pieces of paper,' Gretje says reasonably. 'There aren't so many pieces of paper in New Amsterdam.'

'I found it in the fort.'

'Who were you talking to?'

'I don't know.'

'Who wrote this out?'

'I don't know.' He is red with embarrassment now.

'You can't write like this.'

'I can write.'

She says: 'Leave the paper.'

He scuttles out of the room, and she can hear him calling for Tomas, Tomas, Tomas. She stands disconcerted. She has been noted down and recorded—everything everyone knows about Gretje Reyniers.

They are making the case against her.

SHE COULD DO that for herself, only it would be a very different story. For she knows exactly what all the proper people would consider shameful, and it's nothing on that official list. Instead, it's that day in Amsterdam when the city's fixed plan seemed to dissolve, and anybody could be anybody, and there was no point in accepting Hendrick and the backhouse any more. Five years she'd held Hendrick together with the force of her will, made him real instead of a boy apprentice, and now she wasn't at all sure that that was any achievement. So, abruptly, she stopped.

She had a cup of beer, and Hendrick had the same and he was grinning. They stood in a great square in Amsterdam that was all gabled and belled and busy, and she knew she had to run.

When she imagines it now, there's Hendrick. There is a bear, stepping from foot to foot like a dancing drunk, and a tightrope-walker, still struggling pointlessly from pole to pole. A man, standing under pictures of the mad, some of them more or less dressed, was selling lottery tickets. Hendrick pushed Gretje past. But she was sure she would have won.

Artesia is there in her imaginings, ample and indifferent like blancmange, propelled on a sled. Beside her trots Mijnheer Van Wely, knotted with compliments, trying breathily to keep up with Artesia's quick, strong attendants. Behind, there's Mevrouw Van Wely, in company with a red, bawling child, all wilful and loud; they stop at a stall selling toys.

That much is true, she knows. The child wanted drums, hobby-horses painted up to do battle, skittles and horns.

A stall sold books and pamphlets, nothing new, only old atrocities: women flayed by Spaniards, their skins used for drums; murders, rape and witchcraft done in villages. Whoredom destroys the city, said a guide to the whores of Amsterdam, listing every last bearer of destruction.

Hendrick said: 'Get me a good story.'

Gretje said: 'I'll give you a story.'

Van Wely's child was perched on a stoop, all excited now he had new toys and blowing bubbles from a pipe. The child put down the pipe and forgot about shiny bubbles. He took up his new bugle and blew. The sound surprised him. He blew again.

Big, placid horses started to shift about in their reins, to paw the cobbles. The bugle started a dray-horse forward when it shouldn't be moving, and a loose load of barrels went crashing and splintering on to the cobbles. There was beer flooding everywhere.

There's going to be trouble, Gretje thought.

She dodged a bit, lost Hendrick in the crowd, and she made sure of losing him properly by sidestepping down a tight alley-way. She pressed herself against the wall, half-expecting the wall would fall backwards and turn out as fragile as the city, the streets, the order that had once been such a friend.

At the end of the alley she could see people cantering about, Van Wely's boy being dragged off by the ear with his bugle in his mother's hand, a dray backing up. The great bear, chained at the neck, went ambling by without a keeper.

She heard Hendrick shouting: 'Gretje!'

God, he was loud enough when he wanted to be, definite enough. She wasn't going to lose him so easily.

Others took up the shout, beerily but seriously, as though they were shouting after a thief. She started moving, moving fast. She found she had company at speed in the scrimmage of walkers, company she'd never had to notice before when she walked at a decorous pace. There were children on errands, darting and weaving, adults who would not be stopped because they would have too much to explain, a stallholder out for vengeance with a great tin kettle that he brandished like a club. Her world was just these quick people, their panics and their crimes.

She thought of stopping, sashaying, pretending she'd just meant a joke when she lost Hendrick. But she liked running.

There were a dozen people shouting 'Gretje!' now, a

little army besieging the drinkers, playing continuo to the storytellers, worrying the tightrope-walker in his slow, grim progress across a rope that seemed to be sagging. The bear, gobbling grapes from a barrel, ignored them all. The dozen caught up a few more, all keen to see the city as a kind of puzzle, with someone to hunt called Gretje.

She was sighted flirting with a soldier, buying a lottery ticket, singing on a stage but not singing well; Hendrick grovelled for ruining the song. Someone saw her on the horse-drawn carousel, turning in a little carved boat, and Hendrick jumped the last wooden boat to ride off and save her. She was supposed to be down where the wrestlers were cracking bones, but the crowd was too busy with its bets to join the chase. Proper young wives were bothered because they might have been Gretje, and the only women who went unbothered were the working girls who needed to be bothered to make a living.

Gretje marched into the Old Church and sat down. She could do that quite devoutly and she wondered what else a truly devout person would do to fill the time until dark. It crossed her mind that the whole world was just as she had imagined it as a child. She held it all together. She was responsible for everything.

She was leaving; she knew that. The question was where, what destination she knew that wasn't either Amsterdam or the village where she was born.

In a while, they'd get tired of the game of hunting for Gretje. Someone would think Hendrick was just a drunk.

She'd test things one last time. She'd go home for money. If Hendrick found her, if he were there, she might think about staying. If there were nobody waiting, she'd take just enough for—and she stopped. Enough to travel on the *Soutberg*, she thought, to any place that wasn't

Amsterdam and any life that didn't involve Hendrick, or living in a backhouse, or doing the books, or seeing yourself reflected endlessly in the dim, imperfect shine of a metal as dull as pewter.

There was nobody at home when she got there.

She didn't know how much to take for passage on the *Soutberg*. She didn't know if the *Soutberg* was in harbour, or where it might go next, or if Anthony the Turk still sometimes worked on the boat. But she'd decided that everything would turn on the chance of whether Hendrick could beat her home, and he was not there. So everything was decided.

She took some clothes, the money she'd saved, leaving a bit for Hendrick because he needed the comfort of balanced books and cash in hand, and she didn't want to harm him. She threw on a heavy cloak, even on this brilliant day, because she might need it wherever she was going.

The gulls were mewing and diving all around the ships on the Rokin, and she had to bawl her business through their cries. The *Soutberg* wasn't there, a man said. Another said he knew Anthony the Turk, that he was in America, or maybe Goa. Another said the *Soutberg* was sailing, was standing just off the spit of land where the gibbets stood at the mouth of the harbour. There was a clerk who could help, in the office of the West India Company.

She never remembered West India men coming into the High Court of Holland; maybe they didn't feel as rich as the sailors who went East, or maybe there weren't as many of them. So she didn't have contacts in the great West India Company. But as it happened, she didn't need them; she needed only the small price of passage. The clerk said the Company needed settlers and he even seemed grateful. He wrote out a paper for her, did not ask her to sign anything and sent her down to the water again.

There was a lighter, a board of a boat, lying under the dock wall, and a pair of sailors helped her down to it. She sat there, red-faced and royal, staring out towards the open water as though she were chasing a vision and wanting to throw up. Amsterdam drifted back behind her, and she was on her own; the water was not enough to link her to the city. Besides, as the men rowed the lighter carefully between the bigger ships, she felt grandly conspicuous where she'd skulked so often. It seemed all wrong, being seen when you have nothing to sell.

But Hendrick saw the lighter from the shore. He had been home, he had seen the clothes and money gone and was terrified his wife had gone for ever; or else why should she go at all? Because he'd exhausted all his reason, he knew at once that this tiny, wrapped figure out in the harbour must be Gretje. He shouted: 'You go, you're dead!' He meant: 'You go, I'm dead!' The gulls shredded his cries long before they could reach the lighter, which was out of the shadows of hulls and into the almost open water.

The way she heard the story later, from some sailor who was staying the night, Hendrick pushed his way to the end of the dock wall. He'd be a hero. He threw off his shirt and he stood on the wall, posed to dive a heroic dive, board the lighter, bring her back.

Behind him, there was mild commotion: the bear getting in among the fish, his keeper chasing after him, the bear looking sly, the keeper not quite sure how to get a purchase on so much fur and muscle but wondering if a pail of beer would slow the animal down. All Hendrick could see was Gretje going slowly away, a blur of dark colour in the middle of a lighter with barrels of fish and biscuit on either side.

The bear cruised up by Hendrick, standing on its hind legs, perfectly willing to go into its dance.

The story was embellished, a famous staple of below-decks wit, but Gretje recognized Hendrick.

The bear cuffed him gently, but Hendrick was past noticing gentleness. He smelt its breath, saw its wild eyes and its huge paws flailing about like a drunk farmer, noticed the sharp claws at the end of its every friendly gesture. The bear was a monster to him, a story-book horror, not a fairground stunt. His eyes popped, his anger and fear sent him scarlet and dizzy, his legs abandoned him and he fell, but backwards and on to the land, no longer a hero swimming out to sea after his woman, but a drunk who'd cracked his head on the rusty blades of an anchor.

The bear ambled off, smelling beer.

Hendrick never moved again.

Gretje sailed on.

GRETJE WAKES UP in her dark house. The white cockatoo works shrieks out of its thin body. Gretje tells herself everything is fine and her whole life is legitimized by the papers, the houses, the rent books, the family, the rank of a widow whose credit and standing are good. Her life will be ordered again when she can just throw off this cold, this grief, this fist clenched hard inside her chest, this cough in the chest, this pain. She even sounds out the words: 'All right.'

She puts out a hand and finds cold wax, no tinder-box. The candle's gone, the shutters are closed against the cold, and there is no light in the room. Even the stove is dead, and she is sure she told Tomas to keep it burning. The room is dead. For a moment, she's horrified; she wants company in this stillness. She fancies she can hear the ice working against itself in the rivers, but even that sound has to be imagined hard. She wants breathing, bodies turning in sheets, the coughing, farting, roaring snores of some other human being.

She gets up from her chair, carefully. The stove may still be hot, so she skirts it. Her feet are numb on the tiles. Pieter and Tomas must have left her asleep, not covered her or woken her to take her to bed. She feels neglected, something she never had to feel when she didn't depend so much on kindness.

Her hip scrapes on wood, and she pulls away and feels along the edge of a table. She hopes to find a candle, the tinder-box, and then she can step to her bed and pull the curtains and defy the cold and damp and stillness to stop her sleeping.

Something moves. She doesn't stop because of course things move in a house—a dog, a cat, a child, a servant; the endless settling and bowing of a wooden frame and sometimes the scuttle of a rat looking for warmth; even the earth underneath the floor, cracking with frost. And there will be the echo of her own careful movements.

Her hand on the table catches in cold cloth. This time, she stops. The cloth is crisp with ice, but beginning to grow damp in places.

When Anthony died, she wanted to put him in their bed. His face had gone blank; she knew he had gone away. But she was not interested in what she could see. She wanted to be back where she belonged, lying by him. Tomas pulled her away.

This cold cloth is Anthony's shroud. This mound and length of flesh beyond the cloth is Anthony. He is laid out on the table as though he had crashed home drunk and fallen asleep, as though he were laid out to be visited by the town, cold like his own monument. Her fingers move circumspectly. She catches at a blanket, but nobody bothers to keep a corpse warm; and there is warmth.

She backs away and kicks against a bucket which

clatters and roars. She collides with the stove, and a bruise starts. She feels around her for light, any kind of light, finds the shutters and throws them open. The cold floods the room.

Pieter is curled on the table, a blanket over him, sleeping with the tall, broad body in the shroud. He looks up at Gretje as though he belongs there.

'There are dogs,' he says sleepily. 'Tomas saw their prints.'

She can't imagine what he means.

'Wolves,' he says. 'I know they have wolves here. They come into the town because they're hungry.'

'You were trying to save him from the dogs?'

She squats down, making sure she can see Pieter's face. This is the first time someone else has wanted to care for Anthony. A rival.

'The body has to go back,' she says.

Pieter seems to stretch out until he's guarding every inch of Anthony.

'He'll rot,' Gretje says. 'He'll spoil. You keep him out of the ice, and he'll fall apart until the bones come out of his skin.'

He glares at her, and she thinks she knows what he's thinking: that she wants Anthony gone, that only Pieter loves him.

'We'll see about it when it's light,' Gretje says, very tired suddenly. She means she'll see about Pieter, if she can.

FOUR

GRETJE JARRED AWAKE the second night out of Amsterdam, the world settled at a queer angle, wood tearing down its seams. Shouts. She could hear footsteps on deck and the sound of heavy ropes striking out across the deck.

A sailor came to the door of the stall.

'Gone aground,' he shouted into her face. 'Get on deck.' She must have looked puzzled, because he added: 'Sand bar. Of course.'

She wrapped herself in her cloak and went outside. They'd been going edgily through shallows for two long days, struggling out from the harbour to the deep, open water. They weren't even loaded yet; the cargo came on board when they got out of the Amsterdam lake to the sea at Texel. But already this nutshell of a ship, carrying people and biscuit, was stopped. Gretje thought: there's a warrant of sand out for me. She'd paid to ship out on the *Soutberg* because that was Anthony's home; there was no Anthony. Now she couldn't even ship out. She could just see herself trudging back, defeated, into the city.

Her whole future lay with a bunch of men who were

fussing at the foot of masts, finding intricate things to do with rigging, anything rather than take their orders and climb down to the cold, black water. Some were keeping very close to the small boats.

The captain bellowed: he'd told the pilots to throw the lead more often—what were they paid for?—ships got through with a fathom more draught. He had a good mind to pitch them off bodily and see if they could find their way home. Even out here in the wind his voice was huge and full; it was authority.

She watched the men as the voice forced them down the sides, big men going almost delicately, trying to stay shy of the sea like cats. Their job was to get a foothold on the sand bar where it wallowed to the surface like a great whale, and then put their muscle up against the *Soutberg* and push it bodily back to deep water.

They didn't like the idea at all. It was cold and dangerous. You never knew where sand might slip away and take you down, and sand will drown you far faster than water. Besides, shoving and manhandling big machines was the kind of work they got in the polders when there was no hope of a berth at sea. And once the *Soutberg* shifted, they were afraid it would somehow slip away, leaving them on sand that could vanish at any moment.

The captain stood on a raised deck, under a kind of sounding-board that made his ordinary voice sound thunderous. He was a troll, short and bow-legged under the weight of his rank and pride. Gretje sniffed. But the captain's will worked; the men went to walk on the water, grumbled but went, and all because of this tiny man, who walked like a goat, great belly slung on his joints. She couldn't look at him. He was like a toy, and she knew very well that between the sand, the currents, the men now flailing in the surf and the captain's orders, they could all still die.

The idea of death was a new one. Gretje counted her virtues.

First, she had been a good wife to Hendrick, as good as he expected, for longer than she liked to think.

She was surprised at how much light was left in the night. She could make out the surf tied around the hull and men trying to keep a footing on the sand and pressing their backs into the flat, scaly stern of the *Soutberg*, and a small boat sculling around with torches sparking and flaring. The last of the crew went down the ropes to the water.

Second, Gretje hadn't run away from Hendrick until she had to, and, besides, he was nothing when she left.

A boy shared her cabin, along with his mother and a minister's wife. He came up on deck and pressed alongside her. 'The tide'll take us up,' she told him.

'They've all left us,' the boy said.

'We'll be moving soon.'

She imagined the *Soutberg*, empty except for the women and the boy, drifting for ever on a sea without waves. Then she found she'd run out of virtues to list, and the ship was still fast on the back of this great whale of sand.

The boy was mouthing a prayer.

The ship, subtly but definitely, moved. But it shifted to the right side, not forwards, as though it were being pulled down to the water very slowly by its masts. In prints of shipwrecks, Gretje remembered, the ships always list this way.

Shouts. A man slipped off the edge of the sand, one minute standing, the next minute drowning with a caricature of a startled face. Men fell forward in the water as they tried to push, and the ship heaved back, and they lost

139

their footing in the soft sand. The ship shifted again, and Gretje braced herself hard against the deck and the rail. The sand was taking the ship down.

The boy was praying out loud.

The men below were tired and drenched, muscles seizing in the cold. The captain shouted, but he wasn't any longer what they most had to fear. They made a pack up against the stern of the *Soutberg*, the front line leaning on the next line, the next line getting a purchase on the men behind them, and they made the ship shake a little. And as it shook, it moved gently forward.

'Again!' the captain shouted.

Nobody in the water was sure what he could do. But they massed together again and shoved, and the ship began to slide as slowly and carefully as the day it was launched.

There was a scrambling rush below, knocking the bright torches off the small boat into the sea and coming close to turning it over, leaving some of the crew to wait on black sand while the *Soutberg* set sail for the sea at last.

GRETJE LIES IN her bed, curtains open, wrapped up in these adventures. When Pieter arrives at dawn, she's so calm she could shatter.

'You had no right,' she says.

He says nothing.

'You have to understand,' she says fiercely, 'you have to understand about Anthony and about me.'

He says: 'I want to understand.'

She wants to shake him again, ask why? why? why? But instead she tells him what happened. After all, this is the story that's sticking to her, that gives her relief from the sense of loss and occupies her mind, obsessively, always. It's something to share.

EACH DAY OF that voyage, Gretje walked to all the boundaries of the *Soutberg* and stared out. Her world became shapes sliding, an ice atlas in constant motion, slopes and crags that were close enough to touch at one moment and had disappeared in mist the next. On days when there was sun, the sea went from whitened green to the strong grey of storm clouds to something like unpolished jade, or pea soup from home. Then the water came down like hail on the bows. She tried to calculate what each colour meant before the great swell pitched the ship and the sky fell in on her.

'Not a lot of women in New Amsterdam,' the captain said. 'If you're any good at trading—'

'How long before we get there?'

'Six weeks, sometimes eight. We have biscuit for six, so you'd better hope the weather is good.'

Since money was low, she tried to make herself useful. She offered to play cards, but the men wouldn't gamble before they'd been paid. She couldn't understand the ones who spoke a polished kind of Dutch, with the spittle taken out, nor the ones the crew said spoke English. She walked among them hoping to be a temptation, but their minds were fixed on the balance of the tiny ship in a huge, bucking ocean, the ropes and tarpaulin; or so she thought. She went below once, and there were two sailors together, stripped to the waist, wet with work, in the light of a single candle. She lifted her skirts and said: 'You haven't smelt mussels for a bit, boys.'

The men were flexed to arm-wrestle. 'We're at sea,' one man said. 'What else is there to do?'

Gretje slipped a finger into her mouth.

'Maybe,' said one of the sailors, surrendering abruptly and letting his arm be forced down to the table, 'we like not having anything else to do.'

So the notion of landing with some extra money had to be set aside. She looked again at the tiny captain on his broad, bowed legs and the cabin-boy, about the same height, who kept to the cabin and made tea. Matched, she thought, for the duration.

'Why are you going to America?' one of the sailors asked her, accusingly.

'I had to think of somewhere.'

She took comfort at first in the company of other ships when they slipped past on silent business, but the crew explained why ships are silent at sea: how some were out hunting for prizes, how they would go indifferently past wrecks. She slept in a wooden stall with two other women and a boy, who never spoke to her once they had seen her trying to stir up the men. And the men were preoccupied with the grim business of keeping the salt and cold out of them. They swilled down beer and killed the crawling things in the bread and biscuit and quarrelled over how much salt bacon they could have, and whether it would last, and why the West India Company hired such mean masters. To Gretje, they all seemed too young, only painted over with their roughness.

The shapelessness of the sea was alarming in itself after the order of the polders, the familiar roads that went off so surely to the horizon. She missed horizons, and floors that do not buck and settle and rise again. She missed, most of all, the possibility of being anywhere else, especially when the sea came in like stones on the deck and everyone took to the cramped shelters. She was going a distance she could not imagine, but caught in a small, blind room.

Skins rubbed thin with fear and confinement and boredom and beer. Sometimes the sea was so loud, and the wind so insistent in the rigging that the life of the ship became a silent show. She saw two men on the wet deck, necks all inflamed and mouths wide open. She saw them slip around each other, watchful and flexed. One of them had a knife. The cabin door slammed shut and the fight was suspended.

The boy had to go out to be sick, and the door opened very briefly on a sailor lying on the deck, one leg buckled back under him. The boy came in again, terrified, and cried by his mother. It must, Gretje thought, be the first time he'd seen the consequences of a fight. They breathed each other's breath all night in the closed cabin.

Around dawn, she pushed the door open. One of the two fighting men was standing by the mast, eyes crushed shut, face warped with the sheer work of pain. One arm went up to the mast, and she could make out through the spray that the hand was pinned to the mast with a broad knife. She understood this much: he could almost bear being here on a bleak deck and held in place; he had lived a whole night of that. But he could not bear to repeat the pain of the metal passing through flesh. Since she could not take that pain away and she could not break the rules of discipline, she moved on. She thought the man's worst indignity was to look only half-crucified.

The women insisted on slamming the door shut. It was best to be confined in this box of familiar wood and nails, better than walking on deck where all the boundaries were water, ice and wind grown incomprehensibly huge. The morning passed. She could be sure it was morning because it came after the dawn, just as she was sure it had been evening after night had fallen; instead of bells that sang at the half-hour, she had only these two certainties. The rest of the day was fog and wet. Around what she thought was the middle of the day, she went out to get water and food.

The men had all assembled on the deck, the tiny captain between them. One fighter still hung from the mast; the other was laid out on the deck. The captain knelt, took a mirror and held it to the mouth of the still body. He stood on his toes to show the mirror to the man at the mast, who seemed to shout. The captain shouted. There was no distinct sound through the wind. Men tugged the body upright and brought coils of oiled rope. The man at the mast seemed to shrink back into himself, his hand fastened on the knife and his eyes now fixed open. The captain took great shrugging breaths, as he did when giving orders. The man at the mast tugged away from the wood, and the knife hung in his hand for a moment before clattering to the deck. The captain looked up to where corpse and fighter stood, eye to blind eye.

Once she had gone drinking with Anthony the Turk in a tavern by the Haarlem gate, and she had wanted to know, really know, what held the world of men together, and all he had told her was about the drowning room. It seemed extraordinary how she had felt then: excited, justified.

The captain gestured. The fighter was pushed face to face with the corpse, his breath in the dead mouth, his eyes caught on the other man's stare, and each came to support the other. The men married them with ropes. This new, single body stumbled to the side of the ship, pushed by the crew. The captain's voice came clear during a lull in the weather: 'Let justice be done!' The fighter was pleading through the dead man's beard, as though the victim was speaking for his killer.

The men looked as if they wanted to vomit their anger, to be anywhere but where they were and doing anything but what they were doing. It was shameful to tie a man to a corpse, and more shameful to be compelled to do so by some toy captain. And yet they did it, Gretje saw. She saw blood coming from the fighter's eyes. The new body pitched for a moment on the ship's wall and then fell. Only Gretje ran to the side to see it floating, bloating and turning in the stew of the waters, bounding against the ship's side as if in play and then lagging and disappearing in the seas astern. She imagined the fighter still howling down there. She thought how terrible it would be if he did break free of his friend and had to drown alone.

'I SUPPOSE,' GRETJE says, 'the Secretary gave you that paper.'

Pieter is soft, implacable; he can nag with his silence. She thinks of imps and demons that come into the house to trouble the order of the rooms, a monkey making trouble in a painting, a devil like a spider's skeleton hanging in a corner. She tries to put him in the place of the boy on the *Soutberg*, and somehow it doesn't work.

She thinks that it is terrible to accuse him of attacking Anthony's dead body. But then, it will be much more terrible if he has.

'They asked about you,' Pieter says.

'What business do you have with me?'

She is afraid of a simple answer, glad when he says only: 'They wanted to know. I told them I wanted to know, too.'

He's a spy.

'What is wrong with you?' she says. And then the real question comes back to her, even though she has been tamping it down like fire under damp wood. 'Who are you?' she says.

Pieter's quiet. Tomas moves in the room as a dog does, tactfully.

'Who are you?'

They are watching her. If the boy attacked Anthony, he

will attack her. But she can't throw him out into the snow, and he can always find her.

'What do you want?' she's screaming. 'Who are you?'

THE SEA WAS bright with light. The *Soutberg* skimmed along a coast of scrub and sand and low, blown trees, with the men and the passengers hanging at the side for the sake of a green smell.

The boy in her stall said: 'It won't be long now, will it?'

'I don't think so.'

They were pinched and dirty, clothes stiff with salt, faces broken out in boils and curious spacklings of red, like buried animals come back up to the spring sun. They stared at the land, trying to make out the city of New Amsterdam and draw themselves closer to it by sheer will.

'We'll know it when we see it, won't we?' the boy asked.

The men smiled at Gretje, teased her, used their imaginations to make her back into a clear, white girl again, the round, desirable kind. The captain was even solicitous. His boy was out on the deck with a mop, smiling offensively.

'Do you know where you'll live?'

'I never thought.'

'You can get a bed. You could talk to the Governor.'

'I don't know Governors.'

'You will,' the captain said, 'woman like you. The man's called Van Twiller. Wouter Van Twiller. Won't last long. He used to be a clerk with the West India Company, and they made him into a Governor. He drinks.'

'I won't know him.' She asked herself how much drink a man had to take before a sailor would comment on the fact.

'You're not going to a city,' the captain said. 'You know that, don't you?'

'It's called Amsterdam.'

'That's just a name,' the captain said.

THEY CAME THROUGH narrows to a bay. Eight men stood on a sandbank, struggling to land a flat, thrashing animal from the sea. They were brown, and almost naked. The animal had great, wide wings like a sea angel.

She saw the windmill first of all, a tiny sketch of a machine sitting on the line of the horizon. The crossed sails helped her see it when her eyes could barely make it out. She imagined an army of windmills on all the shores, rising up in magnificent ranks and orders. But after the windmill, there was almost nothing: no towers, no smoke, no barrier lined with merchantmen, no smell of burnt spice or whale-oil.

She washed her face carefully, grateful there was no mirror. She straightened her dress. She was afraid of going into a strange place while she was between exhaustion and exhilaration at being free at last of her stall. She saw at once what she would do if she were a settler—take advantage of newcomers, mark them out by their dirt and roughness, smell the panic on their breath.

Smoke rose between what seemed to be two channels of water. She made out a green mass that rose above the ground and was squared off; it was something built, with green walls that folded in and out sharply. In the absence of churches and palaces she was hungry for anything deliberate. She thought she could see a second windmill just beyond the green. But she knew already the ground was not steady like home; it seemed to hump and tumble and fall away. So the views and horizons were unreliable, shading mile by mile into different countries.

In the stall, the two wives were pulling decorous white out of their travelling chests, chattering about possibilities.

'Summers,' said one of them, 'so warm and so fresh.' 'The crabs on the shore,' the other said, 'they have claws that are blue and white, like the flag.' They colonized the bare shore with their stories, made it seem full of women exactly like them. Gretje shuddered. The women, smartly, asked who was meeting her.

Some of the men clustered round her on deck, joshing and even pinching; this late in the voyage, nothing had consequences any more. They said they'd like to see her on shore. She said there'd be a price; might as well get organized, she thought. They said she'd been trying to give it away for weeks, so why should they pay for it now? She asked if they knew where she could find Anthony the Turk, as if she'd not asked each man that question before. They said she wouldn't need Anthony, not after them. She said she hadn't needed them, anyway.

The green, angular mass was a fort; she could see that now. It even flew a flag. It stood on a point, or perhaps an island, between two distinct channels of water. To the right, she could see tentative cabins, made of wood. A rough wooden wharf defined itself with pulleys and ropes.

Gretje strode off the *Soutberg* with the men hanging over the side and shouting. 'You,' one of them said. 'You'd do it for a tub of butter.'

'I expect so,' she said, 'knowing what butter costs here.'

'Butter,' the men started shouting.

'You're the ones who need it. For fucking each other,' Gretje shouted back.

'Butter!'

The men were laughing, and she was hot with their attention. She lifted her skirts and flaunted the fine dimpled mass of her arse.

'Kiss my arse!'

A man on the dockside, decorous but frayed, made a note: the first time Gretje Reyniers was picked out to go in the records for something besides being born and getting married.

She walked along the green bulk of the fort—part sod, part stone, its sharp angles compromised with gaps where the walls had fallen, or been drenched, or simply collapsed under the strain of being anything as definite as a fort. She followed a voluble goat in and out of the bastion. There were stout houses inside, men she took for soldiers lounging around, a long stone storehouse, a guardhouse with lattice in its windows. The goat marched as easily as an officer through the men.

'Hey,' one of the soldiers shouted. He had nothing else to say.

She was looking for a shape in the city. She found staggered rows of wooden houses, but some of them held only horses. She found pits that smoked and held talk; she slept her first months in New Amsterdam in such a pit, its walls lined with bark. The man who owned it had built himself a house after two long winters underground.

Gretje found a wide, empty ditch that stank like a sewer. She found a line of ramshackle timbers stuck in mud, tied with rope and fixed with pegs. She found something like a street, and a drunk woman told her it was Broad Street. She thanked her. 'And that,' said the woman, pointing to the ditch, 'is going to be Herengracht, until it gets to Broad Street. Then, it's going to be Prinsengracht.' Gretje thought the woman must be stupid with drink if she could see mansions reflected in a ditch. Then she wondered if drink would help.

She asked about the town wall, and the woman showed her the line of timbers in the mud. There were tracks on the other side of the pilings. She asked about churches, out of curiosity. 'There's a church,' the woman said. She stood listening to the absence of bells.

The Watch was a single man who passed on the hour during the night, crying that all was well. Gretje lay awake, wondering what, out here, he could possibly mean.

THESE DAYS SHE dreams of getting clear of New Amsterdam. She walks to the river each day in the hope that the ice will have fractured. Today, she's not alone. The Minister pokes hopefully at the river with a stick, and Gretje watches him. He might not want to be interrupted. Then he's angry, flailing the stick against the ice. Then he throws the stick so that it skitters out across the ridges of ice.

'Minister Bogardus,' Gretje says, keeping her distance.

He turns on her.

'I want to talk about the boy Pieter,' Gretje says.

He begins to walk at a furious speed, kicking up the snow like lime dust. He stops, turns and walks back, furiously.

'I need to talk about the boy.'

'Mistress Reyniers,' the Minister Bogardus says, 'I have nothing to say to you.'

'The boy's been with me ten days. I don't know who he is, and he doesn't leave.'

'Nowhere to go. We all know that feeling.'

'He moved Anthony's body. The body has a new wound. He brought the body into the house.'

The Minister's eyes are uneasy.

'I want the boy out of my house.'

'Nowhere else for him. Tavern's full. My house is full. The whole town's full, until there's a thaw and the ships can get away. Up to now, you haven't had your share.'

'My husband died. I need my quiet.'

'What do you know about quiet?'

She stares at him. He's supposed to know her with the help of God, but he can't even tell that time has moved on since the Turk died, and she is not the same woman.

'I am a widow—'

'Everyone knows you, Gretje.' He judges her with a careful, parochial smile.

IT WAS WEEKS, she remembers, before she really arrived in New Amsterdam for the first time and agreed to share all its illusions. Then, she walked grandly by the canal as though it were clean water between lindens and palaces. She felt secure behind the line of the town wall; it became the limit of her world. She wanted to be reminded of the order and gold that lay across the ocean, and she wasn't the only one. Her landlord left a single picture on the wall of her pit, on a peg driven into the mud: a rough portrait of an Amsterdam house, all broad black lines, not detailed enough to be rich, but a reminder.

When the nights came, she wanted to be anywhere that wasn't buried in the earth. She walked down by the wharf and talked to sailors off the *Southerg*; they made suggestions about goods they could carry over, goods they could carry back, and how she could sell them without troubling the Excise. She made herself walk as if there were straight roads between the houses, even though the limits and angles of the city were all invisible at night. Straight roads, lamps and torches claimed the world as safe and human. But in this dark place, even faint light from stars could make the space between the houses seem wild.

But the night was also comfortable. The houses that sold beer filled up with kind, slack people, their eyes all blunt with drink, who were together too long for the obvious one-night tricks of the Amsterdam taverns, who laughed at nothing in particular, and danced without music. The soldiers came in from the fort and tried to drink away their boredom.

'I tell you,' one of them said, an older man who must have had a life before New Amsterdam. 'I'll tell you about this place.'

She listened, out of politeness.

'What's your name?' he asked, eventually.

'Gretje.'

'Simon.'

Gretje surprised herself by saying: 'You didn't ever know a man called Reyniers?'

Sometimes the party was cramped inside the small wooden houses and had to burst outdoors for the sake of sanity, where people could leap and fight and fall without the constraints they remembered too well from the ships. Sometimes, when the night was cold, people rasped against each other and you could watch the consequences growing in people's minds. A tall, thin woman, whom Gretje knew as the wife of someone called Thomas Beeche, filled up with drink and annoyance and started to say that a bed was a trap with the wrong husband. The woman glared at her husband, who lay, eyes open and mind shut, in a corner of the room. 'A trap,' she said. 'And someone, someone, someone has the fucking keys.' Thomas Beeche's face was the red of a fresh burn. She reached out and fumbled at his trousers, looking for the keys, she said, to get herself out of her bed.

Thomas Beeche woke and snorted. He saw his wife snatching at other men, not cleverly, like a whore, but angrily, and he stood up. From feet to head he seemed to stiffen with a husband's dignity.

'We'd best be going home,' he said.

'I'm looking for the keys.'

Thomas Beeche went to grab his wife and, slipping, hit her instead. She slid to one side. Beeche's fist travelled on, on a flight all its own, and ran up against the top of a sea captain's head.

The older soldier pulled Gretje out of the house and said: 'You don't want to be here when the guard comes.'

Gretje said: 'My father's name was Reyniers. He was a soldier.'

'Where'd he serve?'

'I don't know. I only knew him when he was at home.'

'Went off, did he?' The soldier grinned complacently. 'Us soldiers.'

GRETJE LET THE soldier guide her, let him show her things: the square of the fort, lit and broad, a closed field, and in the middle of it, the Governor himself: Wouter Van Twiller, who sagged from his huge shoulders. There were men circling him and the bottle that he held.

'Claret,' Van Twiller said. 'The finest claret from Bordeaux. You've none of you ever drank anything like this.' He knifed the wax and tugged at the cork. He said: 'A competition. Drink till you drop, and the last one standing wins.' He sat himself on the cannon at the centre of the compound and gulped wine.

'It's better when he's drunk,' the soldier said. 'Then we can't understand the orders.'

'I never saw governor-generals in Amsterdam,' Gretje said. 'I saw processions, though. Men in black and white. I never got very close to them.'

'Better that way,' said the soldier.

A cask of brandy was rolled into the compound, and

the three men with Van Twiller inhaled the rough spirit as much as they drank it. Van Twiller, bottle finished, came over to join them. They scrapped like hogs at a trough, tricky and greedy and utterly absorbed. One came up swaying and fell awkwardly against his companion, who shifted under the legs of his neighbour, who brushed against Van Twiller.

'Off,' Van Twiller bellowed.

The soldier said to Gretje: 'I don't get to talk much, except to the other soldiers. Sometimes the slaves. They give us the same houses as the slaves.'

'Where do you come from?'

'Delft.'

'I never went to Delft.'

'You're from Amsterdam, aren't you? All the pretty girls go to Amsterdam.'

'That's where I lived for a while.'

'You in trouble?'

'I'm looking for someone.'

The soldier laughed. 'You'll find him fast enough if he's here. He's got a thousand miles to hide that way,' he said, arms stretched out, 'and a thousand that way and a thousand the other way, and this is the only place to hide. You think anyone lives outside New Amsterdam?'

'Some people must.'

'Some people do, on the South River. Not many. You can soon tell if he's in among them.' The soldier slipped his arm round her. 'I had a daughter like you,' he said.

Van Twiller was stretched on his dignity like a canvas on a frame. He shouted: 'The Governor-General requires—'

'Brandy,' said one of the men. He had a hog-like look.

The Governor-General thought for a moment, nodded and said: 'Yes,' as though it were a Company proclamation.

'We all belong to the Company,' the soldier said. 'The cows belong, the soldiers belong, the slaves belong. The beavers in the water belong. The salt and the beer belongs. The Company owns us all. And that's the Company.' He shrugged towards Van Twiller, who was dancing in the space of his own shadow.

'I never knew much about the Company,' Gretje said. She had to remind herself, lolling here comfortably, that this man was not her father.

'You don't want to know,' the soldier said.

She supposed she'd accommodate him. His hand was on her breast.

'Sometimes I don't know why we're here,' he said. 'We're supposed to save America from Popery by stealing Spanish ships, but we don't do that. Then we're supposed to plant farms, but we don't do that, either. We stay because there's nowhere else to go, for the moment.'

Van Twiller's men were like hogs, bristled flesh all slick and flushed. Van Twiller, in the middle of them, was like red wax. One hog stood perfectly upright, glared at another, and threw a punch. All of them were suddenly down on the ground, twisting and howling. Forearms blocked windpipes, fists landed randomly, one reared up off the ground in another's arms and fell down in the mud. Soldiers ran forward to pull them apart and were dragged down into the punching and gouging. The barrel sat at the centre of the brawl, leaking on the ground.

Van Twiller bumbled to the cannon.

'He's stupid enough,' the soldier said. 'Let's move.'

But Gretje was fascinated. She was watching authority, the big man himself, who'd just fallen on a cannon, was trying to make a tinder-box function, was leaning back with an expression of panic, was putting fire to the gun.

Something like a cluster of bats went up in the air, and sparks flew. The men were very quiet. The sparks came down prettily around the square, on grass, on roofs of thatch. Van Twiller sat and watched. The men sat and watched. Thatch began to crackle like starch and then to smoke. Flames came up through the smoke and skipped across the roofs like a mayfly over water. The Governor-General and the men sat, watching still. They seemed neither fascinated nor shocked; they were stunned with brandy.

The light of the fire swept round the solid walls of the fort and brought them to a kind of shadowy life. Men came out of corners and houses, shouting and bringing buckets to form a line going hand to hand. And still the Governor-General sat, the fire flickering in his eyes.

The next morning, her landlord said to Gretje: 'The fort almost burnt down last night.'

'Wild,' Gretje said. For the first time in her life, she could add with conviction: 'It was nothing to do with me.'

GRETJE GOES OUT for stockfish from the Company store, Pieter alongside her; she will not leave him alone, and he clings to her. Between the houses people move stickily, cautiously, as though they were threatened by the brilliance and the blue shadows. People are stuck in full view of each other, unable to snub or cut or duck. Instead, they shout their gossip.

' . . . gambled it away. All of it. My husband's money, all gone, all his fault. He took it, he lost it. I hope he rots in Hell . . . '

'Cuckoo, cuckoo, cuckoo!'

'Your daughter—'

'You wouldn't believe it, but he lost every stuiver. Every last stuiver. And us all ready to sell up and get back to

Amsterdam and maybe ship out to the East Indies next time, out of this cold. Now we'll never be able to go. We'll be here for ever.'

'Cuckoo, cuckoo . . . '

A little woman, wired and twisted by anger, yells at a man about money. The frayed and respectable fiscal, always honoured for his power to ask for taxes, walks along in a chorus of 'Cuckoo, cuckoo.' A suggestion that might have passed as a whisper in dry streets, something about a daughter and her ways, clings to the right father. This morning you can more easily map these little wars than the streets under their white flood.

Gretje picks up her ration of the board-like stockfish and pushes Pieter ahead of her. She says, as a joke, he's to test the depth of the snow. Once he goes down in a drift to his waist, and she sees him as though he were drowning.

But he flounders out of the deep snow, and she smiles. The smile surprises her.

'Race you,' Pieter shouts.

'I've got the fish.'

'I'll carry it.'

They come back to the house all red and laughing. She jolts herself sensible when they get inside.

Tomas stands there, wistful.

She wonders how she could ever have thought them impish or devilish. She sees boys.

'Take the sledge,' Gretje says.

The sledge is for dragging butter and flour from the store, and in a hungry winter it lies unused in a corner of the stable. To get to it, Tomas shifts a barrel of old turnips.

The boys go out into the white day, and Gretje starts to wonder if it's wise to have so much time to think.

IT TOOK A few months for her to settle in America, to be almost comfortable with a bed and a purse. But it was a patchwork living: trading salt, slipping pelts to the sailors to take back on their own account, fucking the men who came through the port for a few days or weeks, including the English who stopped on their way up and down what they reckoned was their own, English coast. She held on to her money so that in the awkward weeks between ships she had money to lend.

The one thing that alarmed her was the prospect of order landing with all its wilful rules; which it did, on a cold autumn day when the light was gold and low. The Company pulled Van Twiller back to Amsterdam on the grounds that he was too drunk to govern and too negligent to care, and sent out a new Governor: Wilhelm Kieft. Talk came ahead of him: that he had been a merchant in La Rochelle, that he had gone bust. 'A good Protestant,' the Minister Bogardus said. 'Another deadbeat,' Gretje's landlord said.

Kieft looked about at the gaps in the fort, at the rot in the ships and the boathouse and the town wall, and he announced very loudly that he would organize the island. The rules he made, Gretje thought with some bitterness, could have been written with her own ruin in mind.

Sailors could not leave their ships after sunset unless their leave was approved by the new Governor. No employee of the Company could engage in the fur trade and, since all of them did, there were new penalties if they were caught: their wages, their personal goods, their trade goods would all be confiscated. And there were laws now against mutiny, theft, false testimony, slanderous language and adulterous intercourse, whether with heathens, blacks or other persons.

'Nothing left except to plant potatoes,' Gretje said.

Her landlord said: 'You'll find something.'

'I wanted to find something before winter.'

She had never bothered with authority before; it meant only trouble. But here there were no alley-ways and busy houses to hide her. She might as well meet the man, she thought. She picked up her grievances and went down to the fort, hopeful rather than indignant, and determined to play politics. Kieft could banish her; she could only bother him; so it was an uneven meeting unless, of course, he was at all susceptible. She dressed like a good girl, but friendly.

Kieft was furious. Before him were a scatter of papers, roughly written, and a ruddy-faced man who kept scratching his head.

'I bought the cattle,' the man was saying. 'I bought them from the free colonists and I'm taking them up river.'

'To some grandee's estate.'

'To Mr Van Rensellaer's land, granted him by the States General.'

'And you're taking them away from Manhattan?'

'Of course.'

'Where the servants of the Company and the people who answer to the States General are going hungry because there are no live cattle and no ground under cultivation and it's damn nearly winter.'

'Officially, there is no winter here. You just read what the Company put out.'

Kieft signed a paper to confiscate the cattle, and the man walked out, puzzled by his defeat.

Kieft said: 'It gets cold here at night,' and Gretje thought that was that; but it was not so simple.

Kieft was confined by his ideas; he creaked and showed the strain of his confinement, but he did not relax it. He believed in order. He believed in the Company for as long as they paid him. He seemed a melancholy man, pinched and careful, but he paid Gretje to be with him for an hour at a time.

She wanted to tell him stories of life in Amsterdam, but he wanted only lists and quantities: buildings, bells, monuments and obelisks, defences and canals and squares. She described the weighhouse as best she could, and its golden weather-vane, and the street of ships that led out to the Ij, and the lighters working along the canals between the merchant palaces, and the shops on Warmoesstraat. She wondered whether to tell him about the smell of burning spice and that other smell of dead whales; in the end, she ran out of things that were gilded and proud, and she talked about the warehouses full of the bones of great creatures, and the vats full of oil. But he did not expect her to conjure the city alive; he wanted an inventory. Suddenly his face was vermilion, his breath huffed through the tight 'O' of his mouth, and he jerked in the chair.

Then he said calmly: 'The next thing is the Indians. We build this fort, we pay for the sailors and the soldiers, we defend the damn Indians against their enemies, and what do they give us in return? Nothing. They should pay us for protection.'

All that order had made him a little mad.

When she left him, there was the start of winter in the wind. She went walking while she could, beyond the town's wooden fence to the farms. In some of them, the corn stalks still stood waiting to be dried for the cattle or for kindling, or the ground was bare and managed, or roots lay in clamps against the frost; but most of the fields she saw were empty, and their outlines had grown blurred with weeds. The hedges and fences were broken down by wind and sheer neglect. She looked for cattle but saw only a pair of heifers in the lee of a hut.

She stood very still. The sky grew darker. Deer passed gracefully before a thicket, stepping with care. The darkness was not because of clouds, she realized. It was an assembly of pigeons, as thick together as grass in a field, turning the sky to their own purplish sheen. They were plenty, but plenty going south to save their lives.

GRETJE CAN TASTE the emptiness of the house. It is a most peculiar sensation, a bit like the time after a tooth is pulled, a bit like sickness on a sea crossing; it is as though the criss-crossing of bodies on their daily business was what held up the walls and roof.

She pours some brandy into a mug and sets it on the stove.

She relished silence once, and being entire in her own skin, in her own bed, on her own, not being fucked or bothered; it was the sensation she carried out on the streets with her as a weapon. But now she's pacing the room, and thinking that she always lives around people and survives that way, and that she cannot bring herself to be grateful for the peace and space that Tomas and Pieter have left behind them. She's not good, for the moment, at being undistracted.

She sits in the rocking-chair and makes it jerk back and forwards. She can feel her skull like a cup of fragile bone. Her fingers are cold. The brandy is warming, and she can smell the sugary fumes. A little wind moves in the corner, and she shivers. She can see that the clouds are like flooded black ink.

She puts her cold hands under her skirt and her petticoat and excites herself brusquely, uncomfortably, for the sake of having some distinct sensation, but her mind won't follow her fingers.

Then memory takes over. She's in a beer shop in New

Amsterdam, with a life all organized for herself, a room in a new wooden house instead of the pit. Suddenly, there's Anthony the Turk. He comes up behind her, slaps her, says she could find him a bottle of wine if anyone could, and sits down waiting.

'BY THE WAY,' he said, 'you're a widow.'

She thought he was talking nonsense. 'I thought you were sailing on the *Soutberg*?'

He said: 'I am. We landed yesterday.' He had a dog sitting on his feet, a black mood with teeth and a tail.

She said: 'You want wine or brandy?'

He said: 'I'm just in time for winter.'

She said: 'We'll see.'

'I came to get warm.'

'I've heard that line before.'

'Then do what you did before.'

He said he was planning to settle for a while. He was tired of never being on land, or in a warm bed. He didn't want the cost and trouble of Amsterdam, and they said there was work here, and he was willing to work.

'Not much work in winter,' Gretje said.

'They have to move the pelts and count them,' Anthony said. 'And trim the lumber.'

'What do you mean I'm a widow?' Gretje said, hoping to ambush him.

'Your man Hendrick is dead.'

'You know how?'

'There's a story, but it sounds crazy to me. About him being drowned by a bear in Amsterdam harbour.'

'You know it was my Hendrick? How did you know about Hendrick?'

Anthony wouldn't say.

For the next hour they drank and talked like trading partners at a regular meeting. Then Gretje shouted at him for not telling her how her baby was doing in the orphanage. He said: 'She's fine. You never asked before.'

'I care about her.'

'I only said you hadn't asked before, so I didn't tell you.'

'Is she growing?'

'She's growing,' Anthony said. 'She's almost five.'

'She has fair hair?'

Anthony shrugged.

Gretje strode out of the house. The wind slashed at her face, and the ground was iced, and her stride uncertain. She was too full of feeling to calculate her balance and she went streaking down a rivulet of glassy ice, graceful, then flailing, then riding on her arse, then stopped at an awkward angle to the hard earth. She howled as loudly as she could at the moon, waited for a moment and began to shiver in case she had woken the dogs and wolves. She picked herself up. She could see the house door from where she stood and was sure Anthony had been watching.

She was almost asleep by the time he found her, locked by a pile of furs into her bed. He said: 'I came to get warm.'

'It'll cost you.'

It was too cold to fool with flesh exposed to air. They fumbled with fur and nightshirts, shirt and covers, bits of sheet and pillows until they had made of the bed a house within the house.

'It's been a long time,' Gretje said.

In the tangle of sheet and shirt they met almost formally, checking bodies like goods on a market table. They were curious about details: dark flesh against white, hair against smooth, muscle marking softness, the blood that suffused skin with heat and threatened to bruise them.

A leg settled out of the pile of skins, and the cold was like nettles. Then they were all invested in push and take, eyes too close for seeing.

In the morning, Gretje said: 'You found anywhere to live?'

'Can I live here?'

She was not sure what she had meant when she said 'Yes.' No point in thinking that the Turk would stay around as doggedly as Hendrick, and no point in thinking she would be so virtuous again. He was present in the room—boots, shirts, breeches—but that wouldn't bother the other men who came in for an hour or so.

Anthony, having decided he should settle, was settled all at once. He signed off from the *Soutberg* and saw Governor Kieft about some Company land and some work splitting timbers and burning lime; it was very nearly slave work but it meant entitlement to food through the winter. He took a corner of Gretje's room and made it his own; he had the habit from being at sea. At night he liked Gretje to go to the bed first and he would ask to join her.

She'd be matter of fact, and suddenly he deferred to her. He drank furiously, then went about like a prizefighter in training for a few days. Sometimes they fought up and down the cold room so fiercely that the slightest pause left the sweat on them like ice.

That winter, too, the cold was a vice by December. Food was short; the Company sent ships up to New England to trade furs for potatoes and stockfish. Gretje found herself scrapping with the wife of Minister Bogardus over a can of milk. Anthony went out with some sailors to the north of Manhattan, a day's hard walking, with the notion that they would kill a deer and bring it back, but they met up with Indians and got almost nowhere, dependent in the end on the Indians' skills. The edge of the waters froze too hard to catch bass or find oysters.

'Next year,' Anthony said, 'we'll have our own food.'

'We can take from the Company store.'

'We'll have what we want.'

She was afraid he would think that settling was the same as being caught. He said he wanted to marry her, and she resisted very briefly. He said the marriage to Hendrick didn't count because Hendrick was dead. She said she didn't know that so she'd marry Anthony just because it might not count. He said it counted.

They got married before the Minister Bogardus, who was drunk. They were tied together now, and it made no difference to the wonder and the separation that both felt in their bed at night.

One night, Anthony said something about love. Gretje got out of bed and warmed some milk.

THE SKY SLIPS from the black of storm to the black of night. She pulls the shutters, lights candles. Nobody bothers with clocks in this cold. There's no money in the town to make things happen, no ships moving and no reason to separate day from night except by when you want to eat or drink. She guesses there are even people who stay in bed because their credit's stretched too tight to risk another raid on the Company store. The whole town will be sleeping soon.

No Tomas. No Pieter. She's not alarmed yet, not quite, but the boys are out there in the cold and dark, the boy who's mute and the boy who's soft. She cannot go out after them; she does not know where to begin to look, she can see no more than a torch will light up, and the snow is packed like dykes around the town, and nothing would keep her alive in the cold, not all the cloaks and furs she owns. This is a night when animals die, like the night that Anthony died.

She is grateful to hear commotion at the door.

She opens it, and old Beeche is standing there, eyes down like a nervous dog.

'Mistress Reyniers,' he says.

She doesn't want company.

'Mistress Reyniers, if I could ask you—'

'Come in.'

The huge, blown shadow from her candle pens him by the door.

'I'm so sorry to trouble you, and you in your mourning.'

She says nothing.

'In these first days of widowhood—'

'A gentleman wouldn't be calling. You're not a gentleman.'

Beeche frowns as though his lack of gentility has pained him terribly all his life. 'Mistress Reyniers, I'll come to the point.'

'Please.'

'My wife and I, we're honest people. You know that. But we don't see how we'll get through to the spring.'

'It's a bad winter.'

'If you could see your way to a loan, a small loan, at interest naturally, and if—'

'It's almost dark outside.'

Beeche looks puzzled.

'Would you have come here if it wasn't dark outside?'

'There's no shame in borrowing.'

Gretje says: 'I've gone to court before this to get money from you.'

'Sometimes things don't quite work as you expect.'

Gretje snorts. 'I'll look at the books,' she says.

She takes a candle and sets off down the corridor in a

circle of yellow light. She wonders if she ought to be alarmed. She is alone, he is desperate, she has money, he has force; he has righteousness lying upon him like the cold in his coat, and she is an impediment to the godliness of the town, and therefore nobody will dash in the dead cold night if she screams.

'Sit,' she says.

'Whatever is possible—'

She makes a show of opening the books. 'There's still money outstanding,' she says.

'Things are bad.'

'For me, too.'

'I would be most grateful,' Beeche says. 'Of your charity.'

'I can't.'

He shifts on the chair.

'At present, I can't. Maybe when the thaw comes.'

'But you haven't anything to spend your money on.'

'I'll need money in spring.'

Beeche stands. 'We'll be dead by then.'

'Ask the Company.'

'I'm asking you. You're the one who lends money. That's what you do.'

His presence makes the dark around the candle flame seem ominous. She stands up, defensively.

'I am glad to have seen you,' she says.

'Mevrouw, Mevrouw,' Beeche says. He never used that title before. 'Mevrouw Reyniers, I would be so grateful—'

'Give my regards to your wife.'

'I have always known what you do for other people, your kindnesses.'

'It's very dark out there. I hope you get home safely.'

'Everyone knows you've saved people—'

When they run out of these polite sentences, they are going to fight. They both know it. Beeche's arms are working inside his coat. Gretje is still, waiting for him to lunge into the light. She is trying to remember him in terms of weight and muscle and force.

'Tomas and Pieter will be here soon,' she says.

He pushes his face into hers.

'Where is the money?' he says.

'There's nothing for money to buy.'

She can sense all his righteousness suspended. He depends on her acting as Gretje Reyniers, the moneylender, is meant to act.

'Fine,' he says.

He goes clattering to the bed, pulls the curtains, digs in the sheets and furs, tugs the mattress. He bends down to see under the bed, but he also sees her coming, and he dodges backwards. The cockatoo's cage swings wildly, white feathers caught and caught again in the candlelight.

Gretje rushes at him. She wants him out of her house and her mind.

Beeche reaches up to a shelf, and Gretje meets his belly with all her force, and he sways and falls like timber. He knocks open the mouth of the stove. Gretje smells burning. Beeche screams for the pain on his side. Softly, the incandescent wood in the stove falls on to Beeche's cloak, falls in the gold and red of alchemy. Beeche comes up slowly from the ground. He is mottled with a slow, curling fire.

Gretje has picked up a broom. She has to smack out the flames, brush them out of the house before everything goes up. Beeche thinks he sees a gun. He would know she had no time to load a gun, but the smell of the flames is in his mind and he can't take chances on what she is holding. He knows he's burning.

He screams down the corridor, a great running bird shedding feathers of fire. Gretje runs after him, slapping at the flames. There is fire in the linens, she throws them down so they smother each other. There's fire where the money lies, but it hasn't caught. She's afraid the wood of the house will catch soon where the stove has dried it out, and then the roof will go and she'll be left with nothing.

He throws open the door, and the cold comes in like a blow. Gretje is at the door and she sees him running still where the snow is trodden down. He slips and rolls in the snow, and the fire dies.

But the fire in the house is not dead. She stamps where the meticulous wax is scorching on the boards; she throws down a blanket where the embers still lie around the stove; she throws herself down on the blanket on the floor as though she could hold the fire down with her weight, and her eyes close abruptly on a blank mind.

They'll have to come for her now. She knows it.

SHE WAKES UP smelling soot. She is cold. The candle on the table burns low. The walls no longer seem so solid, nor the house so certain a shelter. She hears soft knocking on the door.

She would open it to Anthony. She would give anything for that persistent rapping to be Anthony. If she can't have Anthony, then at least let Tomas and Pieter come back. She needs Pieter, who has begun to know about her story and may begin to know her through her story. She wants to be known. It is not a question of being understood, forgiven, predicted, let alone manipulated or prosecuted or plain carnally known, nor being gossip or in the records of a court, nor having a reputation that could go walking round the town on its own and be good-morninged and Mevrouw'd by everyone; she wants Gretje Reyniers to be known so she can know whom to be. She is terrified because she feels herself dissolving into sparks and embers and ash.

The wind pushes at the door to the stable. She stands up. The door catch clatters. There could be someone there, Beeche, Beeche's friends, men from the tavern, a posse that needs cash. She goes to the door. Beyond, the two horses fret in their stalls. She passes their hot breath and she goes into the yard.

The high moon makes flowers out of the snow.

She sees the coffin lid is not in place as it was before. She doesn't want to look down, in case the dogs have been here, but she makes herself; and she finds that the coffin is empty.

Someone, something has taken Anthony away. She has nothing left now, not even fear.

FIVE

GRETJE IS ALONE and cold. She remembers, so sharply, going out after Anthony in the cold, and coming down a sluice of snow to find the dog standing there. Its teeth were bared, but it was silent. She put out a hand, but the dog could not move: dead and cold. It had stayed out of loyalty, and its blood was ice.

Now she feels under siege from all the things that are missing in the house. Her physical memory of where a cup hangs, where linen lies, has been disrupted by Beeche's little ineffectual violence; so everything's strange. The polish on the table is smudged with smoke. She guesses that somewhere in a warm house down the street Beeche is telling a story, and his audience is full of spite and beer. And Tomas and Pieter are out in the snow, gone in a frozen dark that no sensible person could crack, and Anthony is gone in body as he is gone in soul, and Gretje is left, shadows of all these things mobbing her, but still alone and cold.

She went to touch the dog, calm him, and the dog toppled over.

She'd like to be one of a congregation, hanging her

troubles on God. She'd like to snuggle into the skin of some warm community, in a tavern, in an army, and be just another woman. She wants a city where she can walk and love the order and angles of the place, and rely on her knowledge of how it all works.

Of course, Pieter will come back. And Tomas. And Beeche. This oppressive peace can't last. She listens so hard the skin on her forehead is tight enough to hurt.

Maybe memory will help her.

In their first January together, Anthony and Gretje were at war in a bed.

No. She wants history, something less personal.

In that first January, Kieft summoned men who were not working on the rebuilding of ships for an expedition down the coast to the South River. He said the lack of news concerned him. Anthony volunteered, just as Gretje supposed he would; he went forward too eagerly. Their lives were about to be turned upside down, and all they could do was watch each other closely.

No. She's still too bothered by the present and the need to make some sense of it. She keeps thinking she sees Pieter in the shadows and guessing what he's doing. He is whittling a stick. He is out in the yard when someone tears out Anthony's eye. He is down in the fort, with a list of all her offences. He tugs the body back into the house and sleeps beside it, guarding a man he didn't know.

Her mind races. She thinks maybe Pieter cut out Anthony's eye because he was too late to kill him. She thinks Pieter has some reason for being at her side, that he means to kill her when he comes back. Tomas will be no witness at all. Then she's ashamed of thinking the soft, kind boy could intend such things.

She once thought the world was orderly.

SHE RECITES MEMORIES, just to keep down the clanging of those huge, round words: cold, alone.

Anthony went south and, when there was nobody to watch, Gretje felt a lack of occupation. All she did was scheme for food, turn tricks, visit the Governor.

'The shops on Warmoesstraat,' she counted off for him, 'beginning at St Nicholas's gate.'

A very few ships were clustered at the slips, bare-rigged like winter birds. She went visiting, dealing, carrying her purse and wondering if salt would be scarce in February and if maybe tobacco would be a good thing to stock. The deputy fiscal, the taxman's assistant, followed her for want of any other movement. He had spent the morning staring over the edge of the wharf, as though he was sure things were hidden in the water and might suddenly appear to the gifted eye: brandy and guns and barrels ready to be pulled back on board when the ship was about to sail. He counted ropes to see where the barrels might be tethered.

'Morning,' Gretje said.

'Mind yourself,' the fiscal said.

Gretje clambered on to the gangplank of the *Witte Paert*. 'You have no business there,' the fiscal shouted, when he meant the exact opposite. Gretje clambered down to the cabin.

The fiscal stomped on the wharf. He never allowed himself to imagine things, except for the public good; but he could smell conspiracy through the boards of a ship. And this was a company ship, unloaded days ago, not due to be loaded again for days; so the only business any person could have on board was conspiracy.

Down below, Gretje bumped up against her connection, the boatswain, a man from Scotland so pale that his features looked as though they had dissolved in water.

'Company up there?' he said.

'As usual.'

'There's nothing much for you.'

Gretje inspected the salt. It was lumpen and it would be a hard month before it sold. But February might be hard.

She heard the fiscal sniffing and whining above her.

'You'll have some brandy,' the boatswain said.

The fiscal stamped on the trapdoor.

'It's a raw day,' Gretje said.

The fiscal was full of authority and furious at being ignored. He shouted down: 'Explain yourselves.'

Gretje and the boatswain looked up.

'What's the woman doing on board?'

The boatswain clambered up the steps and pushed his head up into the fiscal's face. 'What's your problem?' he said.

'It is my duty—'

The boatswain made an elaborate bow and ushered the fiscal down the steps—face forward, arms akimbo, much too fast and trying to look as if he already knew it all. The room frosted up with propriety.

'It really is a raw day,' the boatswain said.

The fiscal perched at the end of the table like a crow.

The boatswain said to Gretje: 'We can talk later.' The fiscal nodded. Gretje climbed slowly up the ladder, the boatswain engrossed in the shifting and tightening of her haunches.

The fiscal said: 'I have reason to suppose there are furs on this ship that do not bear the Company's brand.'

Gretje waited at the hatch.

'Have a brandy,' the boatswain said.

The fiscal shook his head.

'We're none of us leaving port for a while,' the boatswain said. 'You got anything better to do than have a drink?'

Whatever the boatswain did, the fiscal took for a trick or a confession. He decided he was being stopped from a door to the right, and he went for it. The Scotsman let him pass. The fiscal decided he must be mistaken and went for the other door.

'By virtue of authority vested in me—'

He pushed the boatswain aside and looked past the second door.

Suddenly the fiscal had a sack over his head.

'This is most improper,' he coughed through the hemp. 'You can't do this.' He coughed again. 'The Company will know about this.'

The boatswain took a stick and tried to make the fiscal mind his manners, but he would keep talking.

'I have never—'

The fiscal stood up, and the boatswain side-swiped him with an iron bar.

'I really must say—'

The boatswain paused, and the fiscal sat down suddenly. He sounded as though he were speaking from underground. 'In all my days—'

The boatswain set him at the foot of the steps and signalled to Gretje to get thoroughly away.

'I shall be back with force,' the fiscal said. He struggled up the stairs, slipping on the wood.

Gretje swung herself down the gangplank and ran off the wharf to where she could see the *Witte Paert* but not be seen.

The fiscal balanced himself unsurely on the gangplank, a top that is about to stop spinning. He took one step and seemed pleased with it. A moment later, he thought to remove the sack from his head.

But then he remembered his authority and his dignity.

He had things to investigate. This rope ladder down the side of the ship must lead somewhere, he thought. It was his duty to know such things. He began to climb down.

The boatswain stood above him. The fiscal slid a little, and then found his footing. The boatswain took up something round and heavy and dropped it on the fiscal's head.

The fiscal looked up, discouraged. His hands slid down the ladder, and he sat, serious-faced, in the cold mud. Gretje stuffed a cloth in her mouth to stop herself laughing. The fiscal was trying, most earnestly, to grasp the reason he was there.

GRETJE SAW HIM later with the Governor. The fiscal recited the terrible things done to him on the *Witte Paert,* and Kieft looked stony solemn. The fiscal said in particular that when he had later sought to reprimand the boatswain, which was the very least he could do, the entire crew had threatened to mutiny. It was, he said, a Company ship and a most serious matter.

Kieft asked when the *Witte Paert* was due to sail, and was told it was past its due date. He said: 'Then there's nothing I can do.'

All across the fiscal's face, his feelings wrestled each other. He wanted the good of the Company. He wanted vengeance.

Kieft said: 'We don't hold up Company ships.'

SHE'S SO TIRED, she wants life to be safe again. She's even nostalgic for the Watch she used to hate, for having laws to break. Out there, in the snow, there are too many possibilities.

She won't hear footsteps in the snow, so she has to listen harder. She wonders if she could hear the crackling of the pitch on a lit torch, someone losing his balance, the effort of people trying to be quiet; or, much worse now, a blond boy coming home.

ANTHONY RETURNED FROM the South River with his face gaunt and nothing to say. Gretje learned more from the beer shops and the bakery and the Company store.

A settlement had been lost, they said. The settlers had put themselves in the way of some Indian war, and the houses had been burnt, and the walls broken to the ground. All around, the horses lay like wooden toys, legs in the air, frozen in place; they were the only certain sign of where the settlement had been. Because of the cold, the bodies of the three women and the twelve men had not lost their expressions of horror.

'This is Tomas,' Anthony said to Gretje, pushing forward a staring boy.

'Tomas,' Gretje said.

'He's going to stay here.'

Gretje said: 'I'll get beer.'

'I don't know if he wants beer. He's a boy.'

'He's a boy,' Gretje said. 'He wants beer.'

The boy moved awkwardly, even for his age; he stumbled at doorsteps. He looked at the beer. He screamed.

'He does that,' Anthony said. 'He was there when the Indians came. Sometimes I think he's still there.'

Tomas could talk in those days. It was soft talk, usually from memory, some story from a story-book; Gretje heard fragments of 'Jack and the Beanstalk', the farmer and the beans, the beanstalk spurting up, the giant. Each sentence was perfectly finished, and he hardly stopped for breath.

'How do you know all that?' she asked.

He went on. He had language in his head even though

177

he was not of a kind, nor of an age that you would suppose could even read. He had carved and intricate phrases, he had big, scented words, he had paragraphs grand as a merchant house and as full of expensive ideas: a book lying open in his mind.

Gretje said: 'You must have loved that story.'

When he finished, he began the tale again.

He was not concerned to be heard, or to impress; he simply repeated. And when she caught fragments, each one was familiar from the last telling and, in time, when he could not and did not stop, from the telling before that.

Anthony said: 'He could tell stories in the beerhouse.'

'Nobody would listen that long.'

'He could tell them quickly.'

But he never did tell his story quickly. He told it in exactly the way it had been told before. Gretje watched over him, alarmed by his thinness and his eyes, and she tried to keep other and more judgemental people away.

After a day or two, when the stories didn't stop, she wanted someone to explain Tomas to her, and for that she went down to see Minister Bogardus.

'You're a married woman,' Bogardus said. 'But you're still seen down at the wharf.'

'I didn't come about that.'

It was the first time she ever asked guidance from a minister, and he wasn't even grateful.

'And you still go to Governor Kieft. Diplomatic business, is it?'

'My life is my business.'

'You sin against the whole body of Christ in New Amsterdam, which is every man and woman. Your sin puts all of us in mortal danger.'

Gretje said: 'Now. I came to talk about—'

His virtue boiled within him. 'I have been in Africa,' Bogardus said, 'and I have been where it is so hot that man and animals mate together. Yes, animals—low, creeping, snarling things—and man. And I have seen their offspring. But I tell you, I have not seen monsters like the monsters of New Amsterdam. Their indifference—'

'It's about this boy from the South River—'

'They are monsters in the sight of God. They are ingrate. They are—'

Gretje said: 'I'm afraid of his memory.'

Bogardus's face was blown and red, but now he seemed to suck it back to the bone through his pursed mouth. 'You're afraid of what he remembers?'

'No,' Gretje said. 'I'm afraid of how he remembers it.'

Bogardus said: 'You're not making sense.'

She asked if Tomas could come to see the Minister, but the visit was not a success. Tomas told the story of 'Jack and the Beanstalk' under his breath, and Bogardus gave snippets of his sermons, strung together on an exasperated sigh. Bogardus asked if the boy had been baptized, and Gretje said they did not know. Bogardus pulled Tomas to the Bible. He opened the pages at random and told the boy to read.

' . . . in the valley of the shadow of death . . . '

Bogardus snapped the Bible shut. The boy went on.

' . . . I shall fear no evil . . . '

'Everybody learns the Twenty-third Psalm,' Bogardus said brightly.

When Tomas had finished the psalm, Bogardus said the boy had obviously been well taught at some point, and perhaps he had been catechized. But Tomas did not stop. He proceeded, in his high and snuffling voice, through the psalms in perfect order.

It was as though the words had passed from the book to

his eye to his heart and locked there. Bogardus stopped himself from saying that he remembered perfectly well when he was a boy and was made to memorize sections of the Bible, because he couldn't make that claim; it was Tomas who 'remembered perfectly'.

Gretje took Tomas home and slapped him because she was afraid of him. He looked up at her and after a moment, too late to be a reaction to the slap, he screamed, long and vividly.

She thought she understood at last. 'What do you see?' she asked.

Tomas stared round the room.

'You can tell me,' Gretje said. 'Tell me.'

'They put the knife into his head and they turned it against the bone,' he said. It was not, this time, from a book. The language was stumbling to keep up with things seen and felt and heard. 'His head fell. They took her and they cut down her belly. She was very white and she was very quiet. There were nine of them. Their names—'

He looked exhausted, like morning ashes. She stepped in front of him as though she could block what he saw, but she realized he did not see her at all.

'Get down,' he said.

He remembered everything—story-books, murders—as though they were happening still and in front of him in this smoky room as though his mother lay cut before him on the table with the pewter cups and the salt Gretje had brought from the *Witte Paert*.

'What was Minister Bogardus wearing?' she asked.

He said: 'A shirt, cream linen, a stain like a strawberry on the right sleeve, some blood on the collar. A waistcoat, plain black but lined in silk. A tear in the silk at the bottom, left-hand side. Moleskin breeches—'

She fought to keep him away from the South River in his mind. Games did not absorb him; she could never remember enough to ask enough. She borrowed a cosmographia, and immediately he could draw each map from memory. She handed him a sensational book the sailors brought with them and, while he did not seem to work on the words, he gave them back to her without mistake. He went to work for a while in the Company store, checking and numbering the pelts. At first he seemed almost to enjoy the job, the notion of concentrating, but one day he cut himself and though he bound the wound he continued to feel the cutting. At home he burnt himself, screamed, and, again, time and the coolness of the salve were not enough to wipe out the exact sensation of being burnt. He could not forget and could not, therefore, be cured.

Anthony said: 'He can work with me in the spring.'

GRETJE TIDIES THE linen. She is not quite awake, but her eyes are snagged open.

She has seen how close memory and madness can be and she's holding tight to the present.

She cleans the cockatoo's cage, stokes the stove again, looks around for a broom with which to shift the dust. She tries to think of new tasks. She remembers when her eyes were sharper and she crept across floors at the Van Welys' house looking for insects' eggs, the possibility of dirt to come. You needed strong light for that.

She is suddenly afraid of being in the dark with just memory. She goes to check the stores for candles. Above her, the wind is catching in the tiles.

Poor speechless Tomas out there in the cold, poor soft Pieter, the accidental children in her house. She ought to think of Tomas as a man now, but he can't speak for himself and, if he could, the whole town would know about the way his mind slips. She wants to think of Pieter as strong enough to cope with this cold, to know what to do, to bury them both deep in snow and keep out of the wind, but she has no such faith. Instead, in this warm, almost stifling room she feels as though the window glass was gone, the shutters torn and the cold wind cutting in from every side.

She listens for Beeche's friends, in case they come. She listens furiously. She wants to see everything beyond the wavering circle of yellow light in the room.

She can hear something above, carried on the air. It is the sound of wind in great bird wings, reedy and clear, as the geese beat south over the snow. To Gretje, it is the hounds of Gabriel passing.

IN THOSE EARLY years, she didn't know how to look for promise in this new land. It didn't run by the familiar rhythms of the North Sea countries. There was an April morning when the sky was blue like Heaven in a painting, but by afternoon, there was lightning prickling through snow, thunder rolling; the snow blinded the houses and drifted doors shut and made the horses pick up feet fastidiously and in fear. By the next morning, the sky was like Heaven again, and the snow was disorienting white, bounded by the black water of the rivers. She had never seen the island marked out so clearly.

She learned the stifling heat of the summers, the autumn trees like scarlet flames, the months the sea bass spawned along the river. Everything varied. She made notes in a book about what she would do to make money: how she would go into the salt business, how she would take a posse of slaves to the shore to cut up and render beached whales, how she would go to the end of Long Island where you could pick up the shells that Indians used as money; she liked the idea of cornering the money business. She wondered about a store for furs outside the bay of the harbour, so ships could pick them up without paying tax or the Company stamp.

Sometimes, too, she gloried in the place, walked with Anthony between the tall hemlocks, went half-heartedly fishing.

Gretje dipped for oysters, her skirts tied up and water-logged, while Tomas and Anthony worked lines from the shore. They laughed too much to catch things.

Then again, the perfect blue sky cracked once with lightning.

Anthony and Tomas tugged their lines, and brought back nothing. Gretje scrambled out of the water, feet cut on shells. At the top of the rise, where the lightning struck, a single tree had shaken clean of leaves.

Tomas stared. Anthony said the wind must have caught the tree, and Gretje said some animal must have brushed against it. Tomas did not even try to believe them; he could see that the tree was black like charcoal.

He screamed. He didn't point or gesture; the terror was all in his mind. The high, bright sound should have run up the air, but it held fast in the leaves and the shade.

'We are going a long way,' he said. 'We have five horses. There isn't a ship to take us so we go by land.'

Gretje said: 'It doesn't matter.'

'Trees. Pine trees. Fir trees. Broad trees. People moving in the trees.'

'Nobody's hiding here,' Anthony said.

'It's all empty. There are trees and grass and trees and rivers and it is all empty. We don't see a road or a house or a

183

line or a field. It is full of living things and it is empty.'

The river threw back so much light that it was hard to see. Gretje was used to scrambling for a lamp or a candle, being quiet when the dark came down and grateful for dawn, and here she was with the light itself blotting out her vision.

'Maybe we should head back,' Anthony said. 'There's a storm coming.'

They looked into a bare sky, and Gretje said: 'Coming from where?' But she was not keen to stay.

Tomas said: 'You don't understand. There is absolutely nothing there. Nothing that's to do with us.'

Anthony said to Gretje: 'He told us that when the Indian wars first started, they rode out of the settlement. They knew they had to get away. And they rode for five days until they didn't know where they were—whether it was safer or more dangerous than where they had started. So they went back to wait for a ship. And then they were attacked. Maybe he remembers the ride.'

Tomas threw himself face down in the mud. Gretje levered him up. 'You never told me anything like that,' she said to Anthony.

'What's the point of putting all that in your head as well? It's bad enough for Tomas.'

Tomas wanted the cool of the mud on his face. He rocked his face to catch on the shells. He wanted something to cut away memory. He forced his head down so he was half-stifled and had nothing else to do but fight for air. Gretje kept bringing him back, brushing off the mud, propping him so he could breathe easily. She knew already that it was a job to which she could devote the rest of her life.

'I'll carry him,' Anthony said.

He was thinking how Tomas changed everything.

Tomas screamed.

Gretje had no idea what pitched him out of the present and into memory. She assumed he did sometimes live in the present. She thought he might remember wilderness, being in places where nothing defined the place; because here, which must be close to New Amsterdam and was still on the island of Manhattan, had also become wilderness. The path was brambly and vague.

Anthony said: 'I need to rest a minute.' He had closed his eyes very deliberately.

'It's very hot,' Gretje said.

Tomas said: 'We go on and on because there is nothing to stop us. The men talk about it in the evening. They say there's no reason to stop here in particular, no reason to turn back here.'

'We'll be fine,' Gretje said. 'We can't be more than a few miles from home.'

Anthony opened his eyes suddenly, trying to trick the light. He said: 'That must be west.'

'You're the sailor,' Gretje said.

GRETJE HAS A paper before her, a bit of a quill that she can't quite control because she won't go into the dark to fetch a knife to sharpen it, and she is tallying herself.

The mother of two children, one in an orphanage in Amsterdam. That baby was taken away while she was still half-blind with the pain of giving birth. But there is also Maria, born in America when times were better and so much loved that she, too, is away in Amsterdam—sent to school to learn gentility, and living in the house of a man who sells furs. Maria she knows well enough to miss.

The wife of Hendrick and of Anthony the Turk.

The owner of four houses on Bridge Street and land on Long Island.

A trader on a small scale, but a widow of substance.

She melts candle wax to make plugs for her ears. The geese passing overhead, their low and grieving sound, have disturbed her. She knows they are only birds, but she also knows that Anthony said they were the souls of children who had not been baptized, abandoned in the endless circle of the air until the Day of Judgement.

She likes the quiet.

The room's full of hints of things in the shadows. She's tired enough for visions; there's life in the shadows already. She is suddenly in the presence of Anthony, afraid to turn round in case this feeling vanishes. She can almost taste the sweat on him, feel the hard heat of his muscles. He is touching her shoulder.

He is gone.

Just like that, she thinks, running out of his life like the tricks run away when they start to feel ashamed. She sees a black ship coming for him and the hounds of Gabriel singing him away. She sees a paper tied with a bit of pink ribbon, sealed up with wax, rising up in all its official glory and tearing against a corner of a wind; and on that paper is written the substance and tally of her life. The paper is burnt, drowned, torn; worse, it fades.

She pinches herself, hard. She will not dream. She will not sleep.

THE ODDEST, LEAST consequential memories can occupy her mind.

When there was a ship in the slips, she was down there working so there could be no doubt she was available; but, like the other women, she was careful not to seem as though she was actually looking for work. Instead, she carried a broom and looked useful.

Three sailors, green out of Frankfurt, bellies all fired up with brandy and their inclinations various, tried to saunter as best the drink would let them. Gretje said: 'Fine kind of boys we have visiting nowadays.'

The three men stopped. They liked what they saw: a cheeky, almost kind face, and a body full of roundness, the shape of fresh things that were missing on board, the shape of apples or peaches. They also saw a woman who knew the kind of thing they wanted to know, and would admit it.

'Fine women,' said one of them.

'Fine, fine,' the other two chorus.

'Nothing like the Dutch, of course,' Gretje said.

'We're stronger.'

'Bigger.'

'We got more pay than the others. We're just off the ship.'

'Money,' Gretje said, knowing they are interested in her and interested in each other's interest in her. 'What's money? It can't buy a woman a really good fuck.'

The youngest of the three said sweetly: 'Could it buy one for us?'

Gretje shrugged.

The three of them clustered around her, a wall of heat. She brushed against one, carefully; he smiled. She smiled. She knew each of them wanted the others to be excited, and she wanted to be in a warm beerhouse herself and away from this windy place.

'You might do,' she said.

The youngest one said: 'Will I do?' He put some coins in her hand.

She was hidden now in the middle of the three broad backs, and she slipped her fingers into his trousers. She tugged and edged his cock out into the cold air, red and proud. She did the same for the other two men, amazed, as usual, at how drink and lust could concentrate them in the cold.

She took up her broom and made a pantomime of checking cock against cock against cock: fat or skewed or mushroom-headed, long or unremarkable or stocky. The men were grinning like boys, eyes and mouths lolling wide. In the handling and the comparing and the shifting from foot to foot in the cold, two of them came.

It was a risky transaction, Gretje knew, being out of doors and in the last faint light before dusk. But she did the business wherever there was business to do and besides, nobody except the three men could be sure what she had done. But Mrs Bogardus noticed something and she denounced Gretje as precisely as if she had thought up the offence herself. Gretje paid a fine. She went back to Anthony and kept her account book in front of him, putting in the fine against everything they had, making sure he saw the connection.

She took Tomas to Kieft's house. Tomas recited from memory a list they had found in the cosmographia, the book of the world: streets of the city of Amsterdam, in order from the Rokin. Kieft listened as if to music; he loved the precision of the list, the fact that it could be repeated endlessly, unlike Gretje's scourings from a cloudy memory. At the end, he said Tomas was a good boy, and handed him a novel: the story of Gillias. He said he'd like to hear the story next time the boy came. And he said the Bogardus woman was talking again, talking always talking, like her husband.

'The Minister and Governor don't agree,' Gretje said to Anthony.

'It happens.'

'The Minister says everyone is a monster out of Africa; he said it to me once.'

'He was in Africa with the Company.'

'It makes you think,' Gretje said, not meaning it. 'If the Company does God's work, and it says it does, and the Minister does God's work, and he says he does, and they work against each other, then where's God in all this?'

'Wherever he was in the first place,' Anthony said.

That Sunday, all curious, Gretje went down to hear the sermon and found soldiers all around the church. The moment Bogardus began to speak, Kieft ordered the drumming of the muster. Bogardus drew in deep breaths and bellowed his prayers, rattling the shutters at the windows. Kieft tested the cannon, one by one. Bogardus clipped his words so they could cut more clearly through the noise. Kieft had cornets blown, and Bogardus sang above them. The soldiers crowded the church as the ostentatiously good came out from their service. The good pushed the soldiers, the soldiers pushed the good, and Bogardus stood at the church door like the dragon Kieft had called him: a scaly, fiery, furious and reptilian creature. Kieft strutted by, bombast pinched in a corset, offending everyone.

Anthony said: 'It'll be better in spring, when people can move again.'

'When there's enough food,' Gretje said.

'I got more pumpkin seeds. And I got maize.'

AT OTHER TIMES, they knew all too well that they were not alone.

Two men, two women came back from Staten Island because of the Indian attacks, they said; hogs went missing, a barn was set on fire. They said it was like two years back, when some other Indian nation was making trouble.

'They tried to take a ship, a yacht,' one of the men said furiously. 'The soldiers came across and they went after those damn Indians and they caught the chief's brother. Old Loockmans, he knew what to do. He took a plank and he smashed that Indian round the private parts so he won't be making any more Indians.'

'I don't like it,' his wife said, sure she had the beerhouse all enthralled and that someone else would be buying her next drink. 'You wake up at night and it's as if all these eyes are watching you, like animal eyes in the wood. Glinting, they are. They watch you and they're always there, and you know what they're like about the women. The white women, I mean.'

'They have all these grievances,' her man said, afraid that her last remark had died on the wind. His wife was a plain woman, and the Indian women were famously warm and lovely, so much so that Kieft made a law to keep the soldiers and sailors off them. 'They told me once Van Twiller sent a sloop up-river and he took corn from them, when they didn't have much, they said, and they only had two women to plant corn. And they kept saying our hogs and our cattle ruined all their crops. Well,' the man said, ostentatiously emptying his cup, 'you can't tell where an Indian plants. Nothing to tell you at all. They don't have fences, they don't have hedges. It's no wonder the animals go grubbing where they say they've planted corn; the animals think they're foraging in a wild place.'

'And another thing—'

On the way home, Gretje said to Anthony: 'I thought about what that woman said, about the eyes.'

Anthony said: 'You thought, did you?'

'I don't think she was right.'

'Were you ever out of Manhattan?'

'Not often,' Gretje said. 'I don't have business out of Manhattan.'

'Then how would you know?'

'It isn't the Indians who watch her. Nobody and nothing watch her.'

'That makes sense.'

'I mean nobody and nothing, they watch her.'

Anthony said: 'You've had too much beer.'

'What Tomas talked about,' Gretje said.

'Tomas,' said Anthony, 'is mad.'

'Don't say that.'

'He ought to go back to Amsterdam,' Anthony said.

'But he'd be on his own.'

Anthony said: 'He's mad. He's on his own now.'

They crept into the house.

Tomas was asleep in a corner, his face busy with dreams. Gretje looked at him and thought about abandoning him.

She said to Anthony: 'I don't know what you mean.'

She pushed away his shirt brusquely and it seemed she wanted also to push away his skin, to get to the heart of him. He lay very still; she thought she had alarmed him. But he understood what she was doing. She wanted to find him: she was bound to him, allied with him, and she wanted to know what he meant. The bed had become her settlement in a world of wildness and Indians, where the maps were all blank; this was the one place from which she could start out.

Anthony was in this bed. But how could she be sure about him? He could change, too, with nothing to hold him in place. He could be dangerous, even dangerously kind. She had to find his particular self inside the familiar turns of muscle because she was gambling on that self. She worked like a surgeon, with her fingers, with her tongue.

He turned her suddenly, using all his weight, and once he was inside her, he began slowly, muscle by muscle, to take back that weight and to translate it into motion. He watched her eyes. She expected something, some kind of answer in the rocking of their bodies.

Then they saw Tomas standing at the curtains of the bed, a gangly child in silhouette, but with staring eyes.

Gretje said with all the kindness she could find: 'Go to sleep now. Oh, for God's sake, go to sleep.'

OUT BEHIND THE house there was yelping and a scream like a man's scream. Someone shouted.

Gretje's so sleepy that she is not sure for a moment if this is memory. She undoes the wax in her ears.

It was the time she went out to find Anthony's dog, tangled up with the bloody flanks of a sway-backed pig. A black man was flailing at the dog, too afraid of hurting the hog to strike hard, and Anthony was shouting at all of them.

'You leave my dog—'

'My hog,' said the Portuguese, a square-built man, with all the passion of a man whose whole fortune is being ripped before his eyes. 'That hog is my hog. You call off your damn dog.'

The Turk shouted, but the dog was worrying at the pig's sides, drunk on blood and the fight, and would not be called off. The Portuguese threw a stone, a sharp bit of flint that caught his own animal and scared the dog. He ran forward as if to scoop up the great bristled weight of the pig and hold it and comfort it. He looked up to Anthony the Turk and said: 'I'll see you in court.'

Gretje said: 'The pig's still good for eating.'

The Portuguese had tears in his eyes, his wealth reduced to a dead weight. He said: 'I'll see you.'

After that, nothing went quite right. Bogardus owed some money, and Gretje said so, and Bogardus took her to court for slandering him; he lived famously on credit, and he could not afford to lose his reputation. The Portuguese took Anthony the Turk to court for the price of his pig, and, as the Turk said crossly, kept the pork.

Gretje took up with an Englishman visiting from Long Island called Huddlesdon, who wanted a kind of wife for his weeks in Manhattan. Gretje turfed Anthony out, since the deal was too good to turn down, and they had obligations, and Huddlesdon kept visiting. Two months later, Gretje found she was pregnant.

Then there were the rumours. The soldiers were said to be stealing chickens, tobacco pipes, even turnips to stay alive; they were bartering axes to the Indians for beaver pelts that they stored on their own account without bothering to tell the Company. The schoolmaster touched up some women on the street and took to bad-mouthing anyone who passed, said he cared for nobody in the country, said he'd had enough of everyone in New Netherland. Bogardus let it be known that he had to go back to Patria to answer charges, and Anthony said it must be murder—boring people to death. But the Governor, just to make trouble, wouldn't let the Minister leave because it was essential that the Church of God grow daily in strength. The Minister had been told at last that he was all-important, and he was furious.

Only Tomas seemed safe from all this, caught up in memory. He made himself useful on the small farm. He hardly needed to tend things; once planted, they seemed to grow unnaturally fast in the hot, wet summer. The pumpkins went from sprigs to strangling vines in weeks, the maize shot up to close to a man's height, the potatoes were a flurry of black-blue blossom and tiny berries. The ships plied in and out, and the Company made great scenes about stopping them, checking them, licensing and ordering them about, but it seemed to make no difference to the day they sailed, or where they sailed. The *Soutberg* brought in a prize, a Spanish ship full of sugar, and left it out by the mouth of the bay in case some other vessel came to steal it away.

The full weight of the summer lay on the town by July. If Gretje swept out the room, the dust seemed to hang in the street for days, glittering still in the sun. She lost subtlety in the heat. Tomas began to tell her things, and if she did not want to know, she said so. When she was curious about Anthony and his doings, she asked. One afternoon when the house was shut against the heat, she even looked through his sailor's chest, something she had never before thought of doing. She scrabbled at his possessions like a rat in a panic, finding only what she expected; because any answers to any of the questions that interested her would not be in shirts, stockings, breeches.

Tomas came back running from the town and said he'd seen one of the gunners shot at the gate of the fort. Gretje barred the door. She heard later that the man had quarrelled with some townsman over a woman, and the townsman came up with a pistol. Anthony polished his own pistol that evening and began to carry it tucked into his belt. The whole town was walking most carefully, everybody's manners neat and determined.

THE HEAT VANISHED overnight, but there was still no air, even by the water. Gretje grew huge and ungainly. But she had to eat, and Tomas had to eat, and she went down and around the ships, seeing if there was business to be done.

The *Soutberg* lay there, idling in the waters. She shouted up to the men she knew too well and asked when the Hell they were ever going to sail?

Now she was sitting down more, waiting to have her body back, she seemed to hear earlier all the stories that ran around the town. The gossips said Kieft had been hunting for pearls in the oysters of the bay, making the soldiers go fishing or else buying them; he'd put together a fine strand which he'd sold for himself, not the Company, in Amsterdam. The more the story circulated, the more self-righteous Kieft became. He took it into his head to prosecute one of the sergeants for theft and adultery, when the man's worst offence was to spend the whole night in the barracks with an Indian woman—unlike the other soldiers, who needed just a half-hour in a stables and an occasional change of partners.

Gretje sat at the table with a knife and a disc of cheese. 'I've got warm feet and a warm belly and cheese,' she said. 'What more could I ask?'

Tomas slipped through the room like a dog that expects a beating.

'I said,' Gretje shouted, 'what more could I ask?'

She had swelled up hugely. She swore the baby hiccuped inside her and dived suddenly from her heart to her groin, leaving her winded.

'You never stayed around before,' she said to Anthony. 'You never saw all this.'

'I've seen it.'

'You only saw me once when I was big with Anneke.'

'I've seen others.'

She said: 'Oh.' And then: 'You had other children?'

Anthony said: 'Yes.'

'You stayed with the mother, all the time?'

'It was hard.'

'And what happened to her?'

'You never talk about Hendrick.'

'There's nothing to say about Hendrick. We married, we lived together, I left. That's the whole story.'

Anthony said: 'I'm sorry for you.'

She was becoming her belly; she could hardly turn on her wooden chair for the weight of it. She said: 'You did so much better?'

He said nothing.

She said: 'She's alive? You're still married?'

He walked out. He wouldn't be caught with her haphazard notions, and the way she seemed to think she would breathe easily and walk lightly if only she could claw questions out of her way. He went down to the beerhouse and fumed in a corner.

She shouted for Tomas and, when he came, she told him to sit down. She wanted company, easy, effortless company like a daughter; the girl left behind in Amsterdam should be with her mother now. She wanted someone who cared only about the late, murmuring fly she was sure was in her hair or the glass of water she needed more than anything.

'You tell me a story,' she said to Tomas.

'I don't know which story you want.'

'Just talk,' she said.

SHE'S LOST TRACK of time, so she keeps hoping for a dawn that is not yet due. She's had more than a night of waiting, waking, talking to herself for the sake of company. Tomas has not come back and now he's missing after all she's done to keep him alive so long. Pieter has not come back; for that, she's almost grateful, except that he would bring Tomas home. Nothing's certain, nothing's obvious any more. She could almost welcome the friends of Thomas Beeche if they'd come to the door, all angry and drunk; at least she could stand out and defy them.

She starts praying, but doesn't get past 'Our Father.'

Then memory chokes her.

THE LAST TWO months she was pregnant with Maria were in autumn when there was all the work of making defences against winter. Gretje's solid passivity came to infuriate Anthony. He kept hinting at another wife, another child, another time, as though he could tease her into life. He went out drinking while she sat at home, left Tomas to listen to her complaints about the baby's kicks and dances inside her. In his day's work, he bumped up against foremen and shouted at them, and they made jokes about Gretje being big and unavailable, and he picked up his shovel like a weapon.

Gretje's pains started in the evening, before Anthony had made his way back to her. Gretje pulled Tomas to her, held on to his hands. He stared at her. She whimpered, feeling her whole body convulse around the movement of the baby. Tomas wanted to run for help, but she made him stay and see, his dark, wide eyes filling up with the sight of Gretje apparently straining to be rid of some bloody thing that had to be forced out of her with cramps and screams. He was afraid of what was inside her.

Anthony came in smelling of fire and beer and went out at once to find the midwife. Gretje was in the bed now, and Tomas brought her brandy. The midwife limped in, a thin woman whose arms hardly looked strong enough, but Gretje made up her mind to trust her. It was the only way. Anthony stood in the wind and smoked a pipe.

Gretje pulled Tomas to her. He was telling a story under his breath, a long one, and she could not make out the words.

The midwife said: 'Your second?'

Gretje nodded. She was straining still to hear what Tomas might be saying, for a little distraction from the pain that was filling her body and head.

'It'll be easier,' the midwife says. 'Always is. Besides, this time you know you're going to live.'

Her breath went in and out jaggedly for hours.

A head appeared between her legs, like a bloody egg, the eyes suddenly open, a little hair streaked back on a fragile skull and the mouth frowning at the shock of the air.

Tomas saw a bloody parcel and Gretje falling back. He saw the cord cut. He ran out of the room. Anthony tried to stop him as he went, to reassure him and take him back to see the baby, but he did not stop running until he could hide on the other side of the town fence.

'Is it like Anthony or is it like Mr Huddlesdon?' Gretje asked.

The midwife pursed her lips.

'I need to know,' Gretje said.

The midwife wiped the baby and held her so that Gretje could test her limbs and see her colour.

'You tell me,' the midwife said.

SHE WANTS A holiday from feeling. She wants sleep. She wants no more grief, no more anticipation, no more fear. She wants to face things, but it's the dead, vague hour before dawn and there's nothing stirring, nothing to face at all. She's never known emptiness like this.

As for her life, she's started the story and now she has to go on, get through the rest. It's not that she wants some varnished version, painted up and gilded; she lived it once, and remembering it can't be so bad. But she wants peace. There's a drum-skin stretched behind her eyes. She needs to be deliberate in order to move.

She tells herself she is not going mad. She will not go mad. And if she has to cling to the past, recite it in order, then that is what she will do. Out loud, if she has to, to infiltrate the quiet and frost all around.

'I REMEMBER,' SHE says to herself, 'that winter. There wasn't a real winter. The mud never froze into roads. There was no snow to make the sledges run. You put wood in the stove, and it only steamed. I used to stand there and thrash it, and all I got was ash. Rotten ash. And because the winter failed, there was nothing to expect when spring came.'

Anthony said the first wheat sprouts were up absurdly early, grew gangly and were cut back by the frosts that finally came in spring. Gretje said she couldn't do business with Maria, the new baby, to suckle; but she could manage the moneylending. That wasn't an answer. Since the price of food did not soar, as it usually did in winter, people needed less money than usual.

Tomas sensed that everything was wrong. He kept away, ate quickly and ran. At night when the baby cried, Gretje found him standing at the crib with a towel pulled tight between his fists.

But he was always talking, the soft progress of words like rats in the walls, one after the thousand others. She began to think blasphemously about him. After all, she'd made her own story out of all her possibilities, chosen her own place, and never relied on chance or God. But Tomas was pushed about by God. She'd like to give him back.

The thought made her ashamed, and she was kind to him at supper, heaping the fat bits of stockfish on his plate.

In return, he stared. Somehow kindness seemed like a punishment he did not understand. His world flickered between times, and it was hard to hold on to the present, but he was sure he was somehow to blame for the unsettled house. Maybe he had left undone some all-important thing. But to leave something undone would be to make a gap in memory, and memory besieged him; he couldn't escape it any more than Gretje or Anthony could escape the present moment.

Anthony took to playing dice in the Company store until all hours. He won, which was consoling, but his temper was thin. He was dyspeptic, frustrated, indecisive and alarmed. He took to carrying his pistol loaded.

And he was the one who brought back stories now. Some corporal had been hauled up as a whoremonger because he shared his bed with an Indian woman. And Kieft announced that anyone selling guns, powder or lead to the Indians would be put to death.

Kieft even summoned Gretje, despite the baby, with the notion that she could remind him once more of the street names of Amsterdam; but her thoughts about the place had gone stale. Besides, she was tired of being pulled about by a Governor's orders like some donkey, especially when the Governor himself was so manifestly scared. She said nothing and she did not go.

Kieft sent a soldier to bring Gretje to him.

Gretje thought: it takes ropes to pull a donkey. It takes only words to pull me down to where Kieft is. She was suddenly furious with the whole conspiracy of words, of power made up of papers and flags and sermons and anger.

She said she would not go, but the soldier would not take her refusal seriously. He walked her through the town, not quite under arrest, but so obviously escorted that people talked.

She walked briskly to get it over. She was furious at

being compelled, but she couldn't argue with a gun and an army. Before this, she'd seen the Governor for money, or to avoid his revenge; but she had never felt she had been led down to him. She had chosen to go with Mr Huddlesdon, too, although that was an easy choice because they needed the money, and who else was offering? Gretje chose what she did. But these grand people, these people with casual money and power, they were grating on her nerves because they thought they were the only ones who did the choosing.

She wanted to choose, to be free to be a bit of warmth in some back room for someone who wanted no more, and not a kind of animal to be driven about.

She broke away from her escort and went running into the open square of the fort where she bellowed, for everyone to hear: 'I've been the nobility's whore long enough.' That got the attention of the passers-by; they shone with interest. 'I want to be the people's whore!'

IN THE COMPANY store, men were hefting the stinking pelts. The foreman shouted once too often. Anthony, out of temper with the world, jumped down from the heap and flourished his pistol. He let his finger slip on the catch and shot through the roof.

A NEIGHBOUR WENT to tell Tomas that the pair of them, Gretje and Anthony, had been taken to see Kieft. Tomas only stared, and the neighbour, who was superstitious, left at once.

In the Governor's room, Kieft said: 'I've had enough.' It seemed that everyone remembered just enough, not kindness or honest dealing or salvaging someone from winter poverty with a little money at a reasonable rate, but trouble. Item: that Gretje was on the slips measuring the cocks of the Frankfurt sailors. Item: that she had asked the midwife whom her child resembled. Item: that she had sued and been sued, had claimed for slander and been accused of slander so often. She said she had only meant to defend herself, and Kieft glared. Item: that she showed her arse to the crew of the *Soutberg* and was called a 'whore'. She said she had been called that name before, and had sued for it. Item: that the wife of Minister Bogardus would not enter a house where she was.

'Fine,' Gretje said. 'I keep away flies and the Minister's wife. You should be grateful.'

Item: that she was notorious, and her husband, too.

Kieft turned to Anthony. Item: that his dog savaged a pig.

'It was a slave's pig,' Anthony said.

Item: that he pointed a gun at the foreman.

Kieft made a great pile out of all the grains of scandal, sat back and looked at it like Solomon. His stomach rumbled.

Kieft saw disorder in the pair of them, a steady insubordination. He also saw a rare possibility; when it came to this pair, he could be decisive and nobody would oppose him. He also resented what Gretje knew about him, sticky, intimate knowledge. He imagined New Amsterdam under a new and godly dispensation and he said: 'The sentence is banishment.'

The word echoed for a moment, and then Gretje laughed. 'There's nothing to banish us from,' she said.

Kieft said: 'You are banished from New Amsterdam.'

'From this hole? You don't even have a wall. How are you going to tell when we're here and when we're not?'

'Banished from Manhattan,' Kieft said, trying to make it sound as though he'd meant that all along.

'We'll appeal to the Company in Amsterdam,' Anthony said.

'I am the Company,' Kieft said.

Gretje and Anthony stared at him. This once, he seemed to have pulled the authority of a great merchant combine, and all its guns, around him. He was bright with power.

'Fine,' Gretje said. 'And where are we supposed to go?'

'You'll find somewhere.'

Anthony said: 'Fuck you!'

Kieft said: 'And the Lord be with you.'

TOMAS PRESSED HIMSELF against the flank of a horse in the stable, for support and for warmth. He tried to hold on to the exchange of heat, because it was something apart from the Devil's procession of his thoughts.

People were talking about 'banishment' in the streets. He thought of desolate, craggy places in books, where only Jesus could survive. He thought of heroes sent away from home and coming back with glittering fortunes. He thought of the white plain around the settlement, and his mother and father being pushed and dragged out through the door, out of the range of the stove's heat and into a world as blank as paper. He hated being moved.

He tried to concentrate, as Gretje always wanted, so that he could discover what thing he had done or failed to do which had led them to the word 'banishment'. But his mind would not respond. He panicked, as a cripple might panic on first realizing that his legs have failed, that his muscles will not cooperate. The horse shifted slightly, blowing into the wet straw.

He'd always had a memory like a book before him, to be read in order. At this moment, he had nothing to anchor him. He was tired of seeing and talking and remembering.

The angular wood of the stable, posts and beams, turned animate. He could feel warmth, but it might have come from fire or monsters; he had forgotten about the horse. Instead, he was in a room in the settlement, trying to make himself invisible because there were strangers in the room. He had a story in his mind and he was telling it out loud. His mother slapped him for speaking, but he could not stop. He was in some world of ogres and giants and magical beans, of princes and gold, and at the same time he was in the settlement room, and he was aware still of the warmth on his back; he felt dizzy at the times he was inhabiting, each opening into the other.

The Indian men came through the door. His father tried to block their way, and one attacker used a knife to slash down the arm that held the gun. Another cut his mother. There was the sound, so small, of a knife being driven through a man's temple and being turned. And Tomas was still speaking. He seemed to madden the Indians as much as he had annoyed his mother, but he could not stop. The Indian had a knife jabbing at his face, trying to cut.

Tomas fell. In the confusion around the room, the Indians collecting what they could, the faint pulse of life in the bodies, nobody could decide if he was dead. So he was left there. He knew he should keep quiet then. He knew, or thought he knew, that somehow his talk had brought the Indians. He knew he should have kept quiet this time, too, because he'd brought banishment on them all. No good could come of talking.

GRETJE SAID: 'WE'LL be fine.' And then she saw herself, the baby, Anthony and mad Tomas, working their way to some marginal bit of land, far from the protection of the city.

'We'll be fine,' she said. 'We've got money. We can trade. It's spring; we can plant.'

Anthony said: 'It'll be good to be shot of them.'

They opened up the house door. It might as well stand open now; they had to carry away everything that mattered and find a tenant.

'Load the sledge,' Anthony said. 'I'll get the horse.'

He scuffed through the straw of the stable, lining up reins and harness on his arm like bracelets of leather and dull metal. He held the horse's head. There was a curious sense of brilliance in the room, perhaps eyes. He untied the horse and coaxed it out of the stall; but the horse was restive and kicked back. He tugged the animal's head.

Gretje shouted from the house: 'Tomas!'

The horse shook away from Anthony. In the empty stall, he saw a dark mass pressed against the straw. At first he thought Tomas had crept into the stall and been kicked, because there was a fall of blood at the boy's mouth, his eyes were very wide with shock, and his face was the white of good soap.

Anthony said: 'Can you move?'

Tomas turned his head away.

Anthony shook him. 'Say something.'

Tomas opened his mouth; he might have been trying out a story. Anthony held him. Tomas opened his mouth on only blood and air and the stump of his newly severed tongue.

TOMAS IS SO much older now, more knowing. He checks Gretje's breath before he shakes her, not taking anything for granted.

She's down on the table, and the ink has spilled round her head, and she's cold. She shifts, the ink marks her like a badger, and she sighs very deeply.

Tomas shakes her again. She comes up blind from the table, and her eyes open slowly. Light is licking round the room, round the cleanness of it and the earthenware rims of pots and buckets, on the imperfect glass and on the immaculate bit of silver. Gretje yawns hugely.

Tomas wants to say something. Of course, he can't. His face is pressed into Gretje's face, and he tries to breathe sense into her. She sits bolt upright, masked with the ink.

'Well?' she says. 'Where the fuck have you been?'

There's enough light to get in among the shadows now, a false dawn that is amplified by the chill white outside. Tomas points to the door.

Gretje can't stop her smile, which is resigned and hopeful and adoring all at once, the instinctual smile on seeing a child. She wants to be stern again, but she also wants to hold Tomas, to see that he's not cold, to be sure that he's all right and Pieter is home and that they found somewhere warm to spend the night.

He won't let her touch him.

The door fidgets open.

She wants to sleep.

She tries to budge, but Tomas uses his weight to stop her.

She wonders if the stove is lit.

Through the door comes a body trailing shadows: a girl, skirt close, very young, with something brilliant and red draped all around her. The face is Pieter's.

Tomas bows to him and to her.

First, Gretje tries her scepticism, her reason. She asks: 'Who the fuck do you think you are?'

He and she sit in the same dress on the table, casual as play.

Gretje says: 'Where the fuck have you been?'

Pieter's eyes are stained black and his lips are vermilion and he says sweetly, insufferably, something that sounds as banal as: 'Mother.'

'Fair enough.' Gretje has picked up the metal poker by the stove.

Pieter takes her hand.

'You some molly?'

'I'm your daughter,' Pieter says. 'I've come back.'

This child is thirteen and portentous, grand in words but tangled in meaning, and he feels that he has to add: 'I mean I was Pieter, but I'm Anneke.'

'For God's sake,' Gretje says.

She stands up and he looks stern. She takes the poker and rattles cinders and ash out of the stove and leaves them where they fall on the shining floor. Pieter stares at the impropriety in such a polished parlour.

'I'm your Anneke,' he says. 'I've come back.'

She's determined not to indulge him by making a scene. She has come this far like the pilot of her own life, and this is not the time to lose control, not while her face is bloated with tiredness and she is tiptoeing over a great frozen field of grief.

Pieter or Anneke has climbed on to the table. Gretje has to admit it's a girl's clamber, not a boy's jump.

The skirt goes up like a curtain on a stage.

She thinks: he thinks I'm alive enough to shock, that there is still strength in me.

Pieter's hands are down between his legs.

'I'm Anneke,' he says.

She sees the lips of a girl and then pink like the shell of a conch, opened to prove the point.

'I'm your daughter,' he says. 'You want a son or a daughter?'

She says: 'If I wanted a child at all—'

'I wanted to know you. So I ran out of the orphanage and I went down to the Rokin and I found a man who was sorry for me. At least he said he was sorry for me. He had some boy's clothes, and I took them. And then—'

A bit of reason creeps back.

'How did you know where I was?' Gretje asks.

'I asked who paid the bills.'

'I don't pay the bills.'

'I didn't come to see you. I came to see Anthony.'

Gretje stares at the pile of ash on the tiled floor. She can't imagine how it came to be there.

'Say something,' the child says, settled ingratiatingly to one side and ready to smile. But you can't simply gather up a portent and kiss it better, like a child.

Tomas has returned from the stable and he grins like a fool in the doorway, like a man who's staged a grand senti-mental reunion, until something remembered breaks his smile as if it were a bit of glass. Then he scuttles on, hoping his household duties will somehow keep him clear of the great, visionary sea of the past.

The child says: 'I'll be Anneke now.'

'Wonderful,' Gretje says. 'At least that's decided.'

How can there be ash in a parlour that's swept appro-priately, dusted and cleaned and tended?

'You were a bit too good as a boy,' Gretje says.

'I could still be Pieter, if that's easier.'

She'd better go with the softness, Gretje thinks; it's easier to explain a girl who dressed as a boy to cross the ocean than to defend some wonder from a woodcut, a whale-man, a cockatrice, a species of devil that hangs in the chimney and sings like the plague as the draught goes through him. As a boy, Anneke's too odd: the whole war of man and woman in a single skin. Cocks, as Gretje knows better than most, are a fact that you can't deny; she'd made half her money on that assumption.

Anneke made a good boy. Gretje wanted a boy.

Once she knew about remedies for everything, how to open the mother vein to be rid of a baby, that parsley cures swelling, sweet milk cleans infected ears, a bit of oak in the mouth will guarantee your wind while you're running. She knew things. She knew fortune-tellers who could tell you how to get back stolen property, for a fee, especially when their brothers had stolen it in the first place. She knew women who could tell you the future, sitting over cards or a glass. She knew how to find a wise woman who knew what to do about sickness.

'You can't stay here,' Gretje says.

The child stares at her. The words are unexpected, so they can't be understood.

'You'll have to go,' she says.

It isn't selfishness, she tells herself, it is caution and sense and the need to keep herself together until loss and pain and absence are just words again, and not great painted figures in her mind.

Anneke comes very close to Gretje. She licks the ink on Gretje's face.

'I know you're my mother,' she says. 'Tomas told me.'

'Tomas can't speak.'

'He can write.'

'You can't prove it.'

Tomas is looking on. Gretje never saw such gravity in his face, as though he had stepped entirely into the present for once and understood what is happening.

'I belong here,' Anneke says.

'Mother,' she says.

Gretje pulls herself up out of her chair. She knows it's all true: that this is the child she never quite saw.

She sees ambiguity, vulnerability. That does not help. She's alone with two children. One is mad, the other must hate her.

'What do you want?' she asks.

She knows some things, suddenly. The girl wanted Anthony, wanted to be close and warm with him, wanted the father she'd missed. She hadn't expected to find a mother at all, because Gretje was missing somewhere in the world, and so she was puzzled. It would be fine to have a mother, but not necessarily this one, who deserted her in the first place.

But she's taken out the eye of a dead man, then moved his frozen body, then lost what remains of Anthony. She's been pickling a dozen years in her sense of abandonment and singularity, and she feels entitled.

Pieter couldn't take Gretje's life away. Anneke could just grow into it and steal it.

If he were a boy, she'd know what to do. She'd wink, lick her lips, offer him a breast. She'd get his whole attention so there was horror in his eyes and no possibility of this soft, consuming love.

'I don't know you,' Gretje says.

But Anneke isn't fooled. She knows she has crept inside the boundary of Gretje's self, as a lover does.

SIX

TOMAS BARS THE door, pulls a chair before it. Now he's determined about something, he seems much stronger than Gretje ever realized.

'What do you want?' Gretje asks.

She doesn't know how to distract the children. They don't want money, they don't want her to open her stays, they already have somewhere to live; they want something much more. Anneke wants her to be kind and firm and solid, a mother who'll give her shelter while she works out the conundrum of her life.

Gretje says: 'You have to say. I can't guess.'

The child is off balance, she can see, not solid on her feet. She doesn't have the words or the life to define what she wants, so she'll want everything, all the big words she's ever heard—love, mother, hope—played out in this place. But Gretje has only pain. And she cannot give the pain away.

She says: 'This is my house.'

She means: this is my own particular, private life, and I do not want you to come deeper into it.

'You never came to see me,' Anneke says. 'Anthony came. You never did.'

'I was here. I was a whole ocean away.'

'You were banished. It says so on the list of all the things you did in New Amsterdam. You could have come home.'

'This is my home. More or less.'

Anneke wants Gretje to show remorse, then she wants to forgive her, because she wants all these thirteen years resolved.

She says: 'I want to know what happened while I was in Amsterdam.'

AT LEAST SHE can laugh at this memory: Gretje Reyniers passing into exile, a merchant woman in a small rowing-boat, dressed in as many fine things as she can carry, sitting under the haunches of a horse; Anthony's black dog standing in the bows; the baby, Maria, strapped to Gretje's back.

She can still see the dinghy bobbing behind, full of axes and tables; chickens growing shrill in a cage; and Anthony pulling fervently into the currents of the bay with his eyes never leaving the desolate eyes of the horse. The water quarrelled with itself under the boat, flicking them back to Manhattan and on to the sea, turning them and tangling the ropes between the boats; the horse splayed its legs with a martyr's faded smile.

This wind, Gretje still hears, and sometimes the sound of a man, a baby, a horse, a dog gratefully breathing while they could.

They came ashore in a bay that was wooded and muddy, oyster shells crackling under their boots. The ground was the over-brilliant green of permanent damp.

The horse lay abruptly down.

Anthony, exhausted from rowing, stretched out in the boat.

The baby suckled on a cloth soaked in milk.

'Well, now,' Gretje said, counting the coins she had brought in bags.

NOBODY ELSE KNOWS this story. Anthony's dead, and Maria was too young, and Tomas had been left behind in Manhattan. Gretje said it was for his mouth to heal but she couldn't see how the boy would survive a life where everything had to be built or discovered or invented as they went along. So she paid a woman to take care of him, though she came to resent the idea because Tomas could still work, after all. And his new guardians would never have to hear his stories that ran on as formal as a litany.

Anneke says: 'I want to know what happened on the island.' She wants every taste and smell and hurt and breeze because she should have been there. She should never have been left in a town you can't even place, let alone see, from here.

But Gretje doesn't want to talk. There are memories out there on the island which are the very core of things. This girl, this girl who's all too good at being a boy, goes blundering into her memories like a goat in a cornfield, trampling and spoiling.

'You and the Turk,' Anneke says. The idea glows in the child's eyes; it's what she comes from.

'Three,' Gretje said. 'Your sister, too. And Tomas, later.'

'You made a house—'

'We dug a pit at first and put sod on it. You can see how far I'd come; the first place I lived on Manhattan was a pit.'

They face each other over the table. Gretje pulls her

clothes together, dresses up in her history. She's four-square with a past; Anneke is supple, with a future. Anneke can be brusque or she can be feathery, she can sing or shout, she can stamp or dance in the ashes on the floor.

Anneke says: 'What did you eat?'

Gretje doesn't think to stop herself; the question seems so innocent.

'Oysters,' she says. 'You throw oysters in a pail, put the pail on the fire and you've got dinner.'

She realizes her mistake; now Anneke looks expectant.

'Ferns, too, when they first come up in spring.' She's making an encyclopedia out of a simple answer. 'We had money so we could buy from the English settlements. Fish, of course. Berries when the season came. There were wild grapes—only good for vinegar, though. Walnuts and mulberries. We could have had a farm full of silkworms and a business in fine silk.'

'You two—'

'Venison,' Gretje said quickly. 'You see how rich we were? We could have had silk and venison. Turkey, too. There were chestnuts and sturgeons and huge mullet, the biggest I ever saw. And clams. When we built the house we had cedar for the cupboards and oak and hickory on the fire. You've no idea how grand a life . . . '

'You had each other,' Anneke says.

She sees: that Anneke is painting a moral miniature of a love, the kind from which she wants to have been born, and filling it with all the kinds of yearning and devotion she's learned in songs and gossip. But in doing so, she's making Gretje confine the fussy business of a life in words, catching her sentence by sentence.

'You're tired,' Anneke says.

Gretje won't give in, won't sleep.

'We still have the land,' she says. 'Land with this damn red weed you could never get rid of. And you don't just walk out on the land like on some polder. You have to cut the trees. You have to burn the trees. You have to cut the bush. You have to burn the bush. You keep cutting and burning just to make a space in all that wildness.'

Anneke says: 'You miss him.'

She knows at once she has said too much. 'Were there wolves?' she asks quickly.

'Everybody knows about the wolves.'

'I don't,' Anneke says.

'Everybody knows.'

'You know more.'

She thinks that's true. But she can't open her eyes any more.

'I think you were very brave,' Anneke says.

Suddenly, it seems much better to be asleep. Gretje loses concentration, loses light. She is in some marshy corner where a stream runs through. She has baited a basket with bits of chicken, and slipped it into the water. She tugs at the rope, and it feels heavy. She reaches for the basket, and something smooth and cold cuts through her fingers. She can see dark things turning over in the basket. She shouts to Anthony and brings up the basket, and the eels break out like silver in a fountain. Gretje snatches at them, the eels snap at Anthony's arm, Gretje holds on to one twisting fish and chases it down the stream. Anthony and Gretje, together, kill what they can land.

ANNEKE SHAKES HER awake. She won't let Gretje escape so easily.

'I waited for you,' Gretje said. 'All last night.'

'We had things to do.'

'What kind of things can boys—' She stops; of course, only one of them is a boy.

Anneke lays out on the table three knives.

'It isn't safe,' Gretje says. 'The Indians come down to the store sometimes. You never know. It's so cold you can lose a foot or a hand.'

Anneke says: 'You don't want me here, do you?'

'We had to leave you in Amsterdam.'

'But you just went away.'

'You were warm, you were safe.' She hears the pleading in her voice. 'They never let me see you,' she says.

Tomas is snorting at the door.

'I lost my mother when I was twelve,' Gretje says. 'I was on my own.'

'But why did you just leave me there?'

She can't say: because they took you, and so I learned not to think about you. She can't look easily away from the three knives on the table. They are small and set out with precision. One has either rust or blood.

'I'd have to tell you about my whole life,' she says.

'Then tell me. Tell me.'

Anneke has picked up one of the knives. Gretje half expects her to lunge at her, but instead she holds the knife over the palm of her own hand and looks directly into Gretje's eyes.

Memory takes her back where she never wanted to go again—lying in the new pit out on the island, but between the last of the crisp linen from the Manhattan house. Above and below the sheets is the must of pelts.

She describes how the night moved.

Anneke still holds the knife. It's as though by threatening to cut herself, she can make Gretje into a mother, someone who cares if a child is cut or hurt. Then there's the question of what she means to do with the two other knives.

Anneke is waiting.

'I didn't understand the sounds on the island.'

She was used to the settling of a house, the lap of still, contained water, the sound of rats or mice in the walls, all sounds she could account for. Here, she understood nothing and heard everything. She wondered if human beings went past in the night, silent except for their breathing. They could be hunting food or taking war to a new territory or going out to meet a devil in the woods. She liked to remember other human beings who tumbled down lit streets, full of hope and gin, shouting, brawling, singing. The sheets were all tangled around her, and Anthony got up to crouch by the bed in his nightshirt, and the baby cried. She woke suddenly, and she went to quiet the baby at once, in case the night found them out.

'Why did you leave me in Amsterdam?' Anneke asks, again.

Gretje doesn't know the answers to her life; she just lives it.

She gets up from the table, legs shaky, skirts heavy as lead. Anneke rises, too. Tomas, at the door, hiccups, and Gretje wonders what time and what place his mind is in. Then he includes her in his stare, and she knows he's here, now. The three move with elaborate care, as Gretje makes for the door.

Tomas blocks her. He's a big boy now, she thinks. Anneke pulls out the chair and, play-acting courtesy, encourages her to sit down.

Gretje panics. The warmth of the house is a trap, the cold wild outside is a trap; she has only a choice of traps. The children get what they want, and they don't even have to speak. She doesn't know how much patience they have left.

Finally, she says: 'I'll tell you about the island.'

THE MORNING AFTER they first landed, Anthony said: 'I can build a wall, or I can build a house. Which do you want?'

She said at once: 'I want a wall.'

He ran at the trees with an axe, brought them down like players in a game. He planted and tied the timbers in a palisade. This wall around the pit was much more than a defence against eyes and claws and arrows; it was the physical sign that he and Gretje had cleared, dug, burnt, cut and built a place for themselves. He came back from his labour hungry, feeling both tired and strong across the shoulders, and tumbled into Gretje's arms. They fell on the grass and fucked for the sake of the wall.

Now she's thinking about Anthony again, as a limb that's been cut away. The limb's gone, but the brain still feels it in place. You try to live, but you can't walk on a severed leg, sew with a severed hand, love in a severed life.

She's casting around for a children's story, something to keep them distracted until dawn, but all she can think of is the pit.

The wall guarded them, but it also needed guarding, which meant Gretje was trapped there. She strapped the baby to her back and went to help Anthony strip land to plant maize, but she was always within sight of the wall.

On the eighth night, Anthony opened a bottle of kill-devil rum and sat by the fire. The spit and sparkle of the flames made his face look reckless. Gretje settled the baby and climbed gratefully out of the dirty air of the pit. She teased Anthony, said she'd go outside the wall and walk for a while. He stared into the fire. She said the fire made demons play all over the wall and she'd feel safer outside. He drank more rum. She touched him gently, but he did not respond, not even pulling away.

She said: 'I might as well be alone.'

She stood outside the wall, reading the stars for want of books.

TOMAS CLEARS AWAY the ashes and lights the stove again.

'You're cold,' Anneke says.

Gretje finds the child's stillness more disconcerting than her suppleness; as though she was both Pieter and Anneke, defined in a single skin and able to be easy with the fact.

She notices that Tomas hasn't unblocked the door.

Anneke has put himself in the bowl of light from the candle. She pricks the end of her finger. The blood wells up, more black than red.

Gretje can't see the limits any more, the limits that define who Anneke is, nor the limits to the child's taste for making a theatre out of this room.

She says: 'I have another story.'

The quiet makes her other senses work. There is the faint smell of wood cooking in the stove, and the light, gassy wind that catches the back of the throat when the flames break up. She remembers how she used to think that the smell of burnt wood on her hands, in her hair, could hide her just as well as smoke.

'Very well,' Anneke says.

She's pompous like a boy, like a judge, but like a boy, she's made a mark on the table with her blood and now she's sucking her finger carefully.

THEY TUGGED THE dinghy down to the dunes, Anthony taking the rope, Gretje guiding from behind, the baby taken for granted on her back.

She thinks she remembers that she didn't want to be there, that she looked out blankly across the endless, grey-green scales of the ocean. Somewhere in that distance was Patria, and everything settled; in between was this world-wide void of angry water. She knew that this void, to Anthony, was currents, shoals, ice-banks and islands, a distance between places, something to be read and understood; but she didn't have that power to make charts out of the reality in which she stumbled about. For safety's sake, she stood rooted in tussocks of sand and briar and mallow.

She never looked for detail in the sea, but today, past the first lines of surf, something rose from the water, grey and diffused like the smoke from chimneys. She saw the same jet rise in a different direction—and again, and each time the sea around the smoke was churned white like hoar-frost.

Anthony's eyes were burning. He manhandled the boat, and she pushed behind him into the surf.

She said: 'We didn't bring the gun. We don't have anything.'

Anthony drew the oars through the roll of the water with all the power in his body. She could see the strain in his shoulders and arms, and she caught the sting of the wind in her face and her hair. The fear had gone; there was only salt, the way the water caught on the bows of the rowing-boat, the hunt.

She could count the great jets of water: nine of them, from creatures that were gone in the glass of the water one moment, then reappeared the next, black and flat through the glass, tiny, sardonic eyes cased in weighty hide, as crusty with barnacles as ships, and from whose heads spouted water. The whales could come up under a boat and beach it on their backs, or go suddenly down and flourish their tails on a boat; they were indifferent. From a small boat, they were like continents gone wild.

She heard sea sounds and also a cacophony of metal like bells and drums, like charivari when the neighbours come out to teach moral lessons in the streets. Canoes came on fast, with half a dozen brown men rowing and shouting and banging on pots and bells, chasing after the crashing authority of the great animals.

A canoe came close, and one of the Indians stood up as though he were firing a gun. Anthony looked down on the floor of the boat, mimed a search and shook his head elaborately, exasperated. They had only lines, and lines could not hold a monster.

The canoes made a wide circle around one whale, cutting it from the others. A hunter picked up a twelve-foot pole with a blade at the end that shone a full foot and a half. His canoe edged closer to the mass of the animal; its play in the water now seemed watchful. As the hunter drew nearer, he held the lance ready to pitch. The whale lay at the surface, still, its small eye fixed on the approaching man. There was a long moment in which man and animal stared, each calculating how to stay alive.

Then the lance flew, sudden and straight, and caught deep into the fat flank of the animal. The whale threw up its tail and dived down and down. The rope from the lance could hardly keep up with the force of the dive; it seemed the canoe would be dragged down through the whirlpool to the cold sea floor. Gretje held her breath. The rope pitched off the canoe, and she could see there was a bladder of some kind at the end, a floating marker to where the whale lay.

The men in the canoes were whooping and shouting, ringing the bells and banging the pans.

The whale surfaced. It bulked too large even in the mass of the ocean to need the mark of a lance and a bladder; it was almost unimaginable that men in canoes could find a way to kill it. Two men threw lances, and in the cuts and blood Gretje tried to read words, warnings, prophecies. The great creature threw up a column of broken water and went down leaving curls of blood on the sea. Gretje knew she was meant to see oil, meat and cash, but instead she saw a sign—a catastrophe coming, an enemy about to invade, an emblem of God's attitude now sculling strongly down below the water and dragging a little nest of bladders with it. When such beasts came ashore in Patria, they were examined, measured, prayed over and feared, painted and engraved for posterity, their exact significance debated in sermons: great fish, sea monsters come out of their element for some purpose. Here, there was a ring of them, running and bleeding, and men, not even Dutchmen, to harass and cut and bully them.

The whale came up under the surface. Its black mass made the water into a perfect gleaming mirror; Gretje looked down in awe. For the first time that day she felt fear for her baby, who until now had seemed only part of Gretje. She worried that the beast would move suddenly, that the muscle of its ear or the great boat of its tail would capsize them, and the confusion of its dive would take them down.

The creature lay insolently still.

The men beat their drums and kept their knives and lances ready, for the moment when the creature surfaced again and lay in a circle of screams and blades. The more cuts opened on its sides, the more it seemed to change from omen to carcass. But Gretje still believed it could somersault these little wooden boats and break free to where the rain was creeping forward like mist.

The whale broke surface under a canoe, turned suddenly and split the boat in half. The men hit the water on their bellies. Anthony rowed forward into the thrash of the whale's panic. Three of the men pulled themselves aboard and made the small rowing-boat wallow. They were salted like meat. One of them asked in gestures if Anthony had a gun, and again he was disappointed.

Suddenly, the whale came under the circle of boats and began a dash out to sea, the bladders running like a school of fat fish in the water. The canoes followed quickly, hoping to catch up when the beast again came to the surface, and the boat went after them, one of the Indians rowing alongside Anthony. By the time they caught up, there was breath and blood and water rising from the sea, and the whale lay in a tight net of hunters. They cut, stabbed, hurled their blades, and the creature twisted away from them.

The whale's eyes, hooded and judging, looked back at them, and its great mouth opened on ice-white teeth. It was as though they could not kill it; they could only persuade it to die.

Then the sea filled with blood.

Gretje imagined tides going down so far that fish would feed in them and taste and smell of blood. The blood was a fact huge enough to dwarf the cut monster at its centre. It came up in their faces when the men rowed, stained their skin and clothes. It made the wind stink.

And the whale was gone. The rain out at sea, a smoky curtain coming in to land, gave it a kind of sanctuary, and its exact movements were masked by its own blood.

Between the canoes raged a debate that Gretje thought could only be about turning back. The Indians took the oars of the rowing-boat and Anthony sat, weary and blank, next to Gretje and the baby. In these bloody waters, they looked like some family in a moral picture.

Back on shore, the men nodded to Anthony, and he nodded back. It might matter that they had been defeated together, but they had nothing to celebrate for the moment. On the other hand, they would try to find a language if they happened to meet again.

Gretje tried to stand on the wet sand but she shook and stumbled, using her arm to hold herself off the ground. Anthony sat her on the rower's seat in the boat. The grey-white sea was shrinking with each minute as the rain came into shore.

NOW GRETJE'S WORRIED. She told that story for Pieter, but Anneke was the one who listened, and it was not what the child wanted.

Now she doesn't know how to calculate which stories to tell.

She wonders why the child is here at all. Something brought her across the Atlantic and made her choose a place that's just a gap on the maps. It can't be ambition; a girl at thirteen doesn't know how to think about her fortune.

That leaves one possibility: hate.

Anneke makes a triangle out of the knives.

'What do you want me to tell you?' she says. She can't hide the fact that she really wants her to say.

The room is growing light.

'Tell me,' she says. She tries smiling.

Anneke's face is all shadow against the light, just the glimmer of the candle in her eyes: she's a monster, an omen, an invention, a horror, and if she's known hate, Gretje thinks, then this is a hate twisted out of the ordinary emotion.

'We couldn't have brought you to the island,' she says. 'We could hardly look after ourselves.'

She catches Tomas's eye, but he doesn't think she would talk to him; he's away drowning in some deep past, and catching his eye means nothing. Gretje turns to her daughter. If Anneke wants the truth, how's she going to know what's even likely to be true? She knows about truckle-beds in an orphanage, courtyards of stone, breasts of a dozen inter-changeable wet-nurses, tables so long a child feels lost there; but she doesn't know enough to trust Gretje.

'I always asked for news of you,' Gretje says. 'If there was someone to ask.'

She sees herself in Anneke's eyes: a whore who couldn't tell the face and name of her own child. Fair enough, she thinks. She's a wall without feeling, without heart. She is, to Anneke, everything she ever feared she might become.

So let her think that; it's better than having to go back to the island in her mind and, besides, it's almost day. When it's light, she'll be free again; it's only night and shadows that give the children their power. But the light at the window is the wrong light, a swamp of light diffused by the snow, not beams that can catch directly at the ice and make it ring with colours. The snow's still down, the trap's still set. She wants to cry. She wants to sleep.

She'll have to go back. It's her last shot.

BEGIN WITH MARIA, the baby, swaddled and cosseted, screaming for breath, her face brick-red and wet with tears. She warms to the thought.

'I have to stay here,' Gretje said.

Anthony said: 'Fine.'

She watched him tug the horse away.

She sat down on the chair they had brought from Manhattan and stared at the wall. She wanted so much to get to the towns, Dutch towns and English towns, do a little business, offer money on terms. She needed to see what was possible, find out what the Indians wanted to sell and buy. She took up the baby, who tugged at her nipple like a lover's hard fingers and grew quiet; but when the baby fell back, Gretje imagined again.

All she knew was the lack: of roads, of houses, of smoke, canals, maps or signs. She had seen wilderness painted, of course; there had been golden wilderness, with mountains sliced abruptly like bread and high islands of forest, on the walls of Artesia's grand house. Each branch and leaf was sharp against the sky. She had seen green, tangled wilderness, too, and a ship landing at precipitate rocks; the Van Welys had a picture of people landing, with guns, in a place that looked cold. She tried to put those pictures on the wall like windows and see through them.

'They never did what I did,' she thought.

She was tethered, but the edge of the woods was very close. It had a frayed look, cut up with axes, trunks splintered in sand browns and the underbrush stopping abruptly at the line of the cut. It was as though the edge hid the woods. The baby was quiet, and she stood at the gap in the wall, looking out. She remembered all those women she had seen standing longingly at doors, waiting for trade or lovers.

She walked into the breeze; there was never enough breeze inside the wall. She passed the new edge that Anthony had cut for the woods. Inside, tall hemlocks graced the light; she thought of high windows in empty churches, and white light running in channels across the air. Birds cut up in panic out of bushes and beat for cover. She could smell the sweet process of the woods, mast and seeds and leaves turned to soil, the spin of an animal in a bush, birds shouting alarms, the faintest movement of a deer that was trying to stand stock-still.

She kicked her way forward through old leaves, to make sure they all knew she was there.

She felt heavy after the baby, hips swelled and breasts big, but sheer curiosity made her light. She scrambled up minor rises because she needed to be at the top. Sometimes, she ran because the pull in her muscles and the air on her face felt good.

When she stopped, it was perhaps half an hour later.

Gretje had left the baby alone in the pit, and she would be hungry. She looked around the trees full of sun, and each way looked exactly the same as any other because she made no mark between the springy bushes. She ran at the sun where it swelled like hot metal between the trees, and then back at her own shadow, dodging until she had to acknowledge that she could not possibly know her next move.

She had found nowhere; she was fixed there.

Panic set up in her belly like a cramp. She stood and turned slowly in a circle, hoping to recognize something specific in all this vague loveliness. The light was so diffuse in the woods that she had not noticed whether she was walking towards or away from the sun. She chose a direction and ran, and the flicker between the trunks and branches made her fearful. She longed for an axe to make a mark, to begin to define this place and use it. But as it was, she could define her position only in time and memory.

A bird, red as fire, clattered beside her. She smelt cedar.

And then she knew, abruptly, just how much streets and churches and markets and walls and civil order were an anchor in the present time and a defence against memory. You looked at a monument and saw your present duty of respect or reverence, not the man or the battle the monument commemorated. You walked down a street and you had to deal with trading, jostling, standing, things so intense that they hid the history of why things were as they were.

But here, memory stung her like the flat, shiny leaves that poisoned her bare skin or the briars that picked at her skirts. She was without defence. She was not the Gretje who worked the streets—whore, businesswoman, mother—but a catalogue of all the Gretjes who had lived in her skin. She was the Gretje who left her mother under the hedge, not the Gretje who remembered the action and justified it as merciful. She had walked out of the fair and on to the *Soutberg,* still in the full and certain passion of that moment. She was every act and every moment shared with Anthony the Turk, and not just the position of his wife, nothing so easy it could be promised before a Minister and written down in a register. She was, she thought, like Tomas.

And Tomas was mad.

It always came back to madness, to the terror of one day not finding the boundary between memory and now. But these leaves, sharp against the sky, were much like the leaves she had seen an hour ago, or the leaves in some fantastic painted wilderness; the bush, the birds were the same. She was no longer sure of boundaries.

She was afraid that the baby would be hungry. She could hold on to that.

She was tangled in light. She could easily imagine curious shapes in between the rooted things: shapes that could lift as well as turn, that were immense and then narrow as sticks, always on the edge of her eyes and still more real than the mass of the trees. She thought she heard the baby wailing, and she blundered in that direction. Tiredness made her skin itch against her clothes; her nipples had begun to put out a little milk. She felt all the wrongs she ever did laid on her back to weigh her down. She knew no particular prayers to rid herself of the burden of thoughts, no book to explain the way out of a cold place; all she could do was think, and for herself, by herself.

She heard movement in the trees behind her, even whistling—a deliberate, off-key tune.

'I WAS ALONE,' she's saying. 'I was alone.'

Anneke says: 'But there was someone whistling.'

'I was alone. I was separate from everyone. Even Anthony.'

'You felt alone. That's different.'

'It was like dying. You have to understand that.'

The child can't grasp it, can't comprehend it in her unused, unhurt mind. She's good for grievances and not for emotions. She doesn't grasp what frightened Gretje—or why, in that moment, her mother came as close as she ever will to redemption, or else to falling off the edge of the world.

She says: 'You want me to go on?'

'You can go on.'

She wonders if Anneke is giving permission, or being compliant, or simply keeping control as a child tries to do.

ANTHONY GOT DOWN from his horse, still whistling.

'I'm hungry,' Gretje said.

He broke off some bread and passed it to her. She ate, and for her it had the warm, reliable taste of the city.

She said: 'Take me home.'

He didn't say she should not be wandering in the woods and he didn't ask where the baby was. She wondered if he was so used to Tomas being there, a third person who could take responsibility, that the issue never crossed his mind.

They came to the wall around their pit. Gretje unlaced her bodice before she scrambled down the ladder.

Anthony stood by the door. He spat into the bush, and a bright lizard scuttled out.

Gretje reached into the pelts where she'd left the baby lying and found nothing. She looked around. The beds were as ordered as they ever had been. She looked at the floor around the crib, but saw no sign that anything—anyone—had been moved. She tore the linen sheet out from between the pelts, so she was sure nothing could hide there. She looked about to see if the baby could have crawled anywhere in the pit, because she knew perfectly well no child could manage the ladder up to the air. She imagined the child waking to the presence of nothing and nobody, and then perhaps to some stranger, or to an animal.

Anthony said: 'Where's the baby?'

Her horror was immaculate, with no possibility of excuses. Her face was burning.

'Gone,' she said.

He doubted her at first, then came down to search, then ran up babbling about cats or wolves or Indians. After a while, he came back and said: 'Too many tracks. There might as well be no tracks.'

She'd never had time for loss before.

They went back and forth in the woods until the sun went down in orange fire that made their wall look alive and dangerous. She could remember the baby pressed under her heart and against her belly, the exact weight and taste of the child.

'I went to Breukelen,' Anthony said. 'I could see our old house across the river.'

She couldn't listen. 'I looked and looked,' she said.

'We need torches,' Anthony said. 'If we go out with torches, we'll find her. She'll see them. And if an animal took her, the fire will scare it.'

They crashed about the woods, torches flaring in their hands and sometimes catching at a dried branch and making it flame. They tussled with brush that had seemed open in the daylight. They could find nothing as orderly as a maze in the woods, no starting-point for the path they needed.

They came back to the fire and passed the bottle back and forth.

'A couple of people bought me drinks. There's been a mutiny,' Anthony said. 'I thought you'd want to know. The soldiers stopped taking Kieft's orders. They said they weren't slaves even if they lived with the slaves, and they weren't working, even for extra pay.'

'It won't be safe there,' Gretje said.

'Maybe,' Anthony said. 'Kieft had the ringleader shot.'

'We're safer here.' She stared into the ashes of the fire, wondering what safety could mean now Maria was gone.

'And there are new orders from Amsterdam. They ring a bell in the morning and everyone starts work, and they go on working without a break until the bell rings again. The same orders for everyone.'

'Do you think she's safe?'

'You know Kieft. He thinks the rules are for everyone.'

'Nobody's going to pay any attention.'

'And,' Anthony said, 'Kieft wants all the English living around Manhattan to swear some oath of loyalty. Most of them signed, but it won't mean a thing if there's war.'

'Maybe someone took her.'

Anthony drew up to the fire. 'Who?'

She said: 'In a war, they take children, don't they? The English or the Indians.' Then she couldn't bear thinking about the one thing that mattered, so she said: 'You bought seed?'

'And turnips and onions to be going on with.'

That night they slept in the open, Gretje settled into his belly to keep warm, because it seemed wrong to go below and risk hearing the woods less exactly. They woke with raw heads and an overwhelming sense of sadness. Gretje wanted to talk about exactly where they would search for Maria, and Anthony wanted just to be away, beating down the bushes and hallooing for the baby.

'And the Indians,' he said. 'If they came down for whales, they must be around here somewhere.'

'Maybe they came along the coast.'

Gretje was less and less confident that any ordinary agency had taken the baby: an animal, a human being hungry for company or a tribe that found a child alone. She thought Maria had gone to the same nowhere that Gretje stumbled through yesterday. Maria still depended on her mother's body and milk, still could not grasp that she was separate from Gretje; she had no words to shape who she was. She was the kind of nobody who could so easily slip away to a place that was not mapped or known, a cloud of blood and gas and tears that was not quite yet a child.

'You don't give up like that,' Anthony said.

He was angry at how separate Gretje seemed, full of thoughts she would not speak out; he had seen her so often as lover, as merchant, as practical as stacked wood, and now she was playing at being the moon, flooding and ebbing with feeling. He put his hand on her breast, but she pushed it away. He came close to her, and she let him make love to her, but she was neat as a professional all the way through. At the end, he felt he should pay and get away.

But they still had to find Maria.

She stayed behind, in case someone came. He went into the wood. He ran into a few of the Indians, who were dragging back a pair of racoons they had caught—biting, snatching animals with neat nails. He tried to mime a baby, a baby lost, and they shook their heads.

'I THOUGHT ABOUT praying,' she says. 'I thought I'd find the saint of lost children, and everything would be fine.'

Anneke is stroking the white cockatoo.

The door is unbarred, but the room still feels like a cell.

She says: 'I thought there was nothing to be done.'

She can't tell Anneke these things. She looks at her, a child who's only recently learned all the old certainties, who will cling to them and not think again until she is grown—a fresh conservative, who won't care to put herself in the wild along with Gretje.

Herself or himself; Gretje can't even be sure of that. Even dressed prettily, that's Pieter stroking the bird.

She'd like to explain that in the woods she knew she didn't have the faith even to choose a direction; she felt dependent on chance. She believed in Anthony, but only on each given day. Now she had to do something to bring back her baby Maria, and she did not know how to scheme or invest or pray. It was shocking that, this time, she was not the one who went away.

Anthony quartered the woods, put up markers to show where he had been, followed tracks of small animals and what he thought were human tracks; but his skills lay in reading water, not land. He went at the hunt with brute energy; he fell asleep after eating. There was cold, thick matter settling in his chest, and he had to fight off falling sick. He was at the very limit of his strengths.

They slept a fourth night on the ground, waking if an owl cried. In her dreams, Gretje was back on the *Southberg*, alone on a ship held tight by a sea of worms and grass. Anthony was on a carousel at a fairground, and Gretje on a horse across the way from him; he could never reach her. Gretje dreamed of a great cat that carried the baby very gently in its mouth, but she could never see where it was going.

Anthony woke up angry, staring at a face made of stars in the sky.

When the dawn came, he woke Gretje. He waited patiently for her to lose the sleep in her eyes and stretch. He hit her across the face.

'You lost her,' he said. 'You fucking lost her. Like you lost Anneke.'

She fell out of bed and then stopped by the ladder, very cold. 'They were taken,' she said. 'Someone took them. Anneke was gone before I'd got my breath back.' She picked up a bucket, and found she had nothing to do with it. 'It must have been animals that took Maria. Maybe it was Indians. I don't bloody know, do I? I don't bloody know!'

The bucket clattered out of her hands to the floor.

SHE HAS ANNEKE'S attention all right. The price she pays is remembering all this, which is much too close to how she feels now: tears just stopped by a membrane, desolate and angry and stinging.

GRETJE WASHED AND went outside. The day needed strategy, and she made one up: since they had looked everywhere by land, they might as well go down by the dunes and the sea. There had never been human tracks down by the sand, and she didn't know an animal that would snag prey and drag it to the water, but at least she had somewhere to go and something to do.

She crossed the scrub and reeds, the last wave of soft dunes, and walked on the road of flat, wet sand by the sea. Ahead of her, the line of the shore stretched straight with nothing to break it. She turned around. There was one indentation in the line of sand where a stream came into the sea. Something could hide there.

As she walked, she thought. The ordinary procession of ordinary events had been force enough to move her forward, until now. What she needed now was hope.

Where the stream came in it had cut a channel in the sand, neat as a knife would make. The water retreated in among reeds, twisting back to a salt pond, but there was a smell far stronger than the sea and the weed. She climbed over the next dune, sand tugging at her feet, and she looked down.

The next beach began with a huge blur of blue-grey. It was a cathedral of a beast that had been torn and slashed, broad ribbons of hide taken from its sides, leaving black blood and fat. As for the smell, it was a secret smell, that was supposed to live only where a body was consigned to the sea or the earth, but which had spilled out with the guts of the creature on to the beach. It was the smell of pain, Gretje thought.

She slid down to the whale's back, closed her eyes and ran her hands over the rough hide; it was cold as the sea, as intricate as a map. She put her hand into the cuts and sniffed them. She edged around to the huge, articulate tail, and to the belly of the creature. Its penis lay out like a bent staff; it was bloodless and vulnerable on the sand. She edged up to the creature's mouth, believing still that its jaws might fall on her and its teeth cut.

Maria lay there, swaddled in bright, unfamiliar cloth, fed well enough to be sleeping.

Gretje fell on the child and rolled her on to the belly she came out of, where she could be warm. The mouth of the whale was open above them.

When Maria began to stir in her bindings, Gretje smiled at her, called her name, cooed and whistled, determined that she should acknowledge her mother. The baby's eyes opened, and she cried monstrously, echoing in the cavities of the whale. Gretje took out her breast and pressed it to the child's mouth, and slowly Maria began to steal her mother away by the act of suckling.

She bound Maria carefully into her own clothing, carrying her at the front where she could always see her, and she ran up the first dune. Anthony saw her running and saw the weight at her front. They caught up to each other and hugged with the baby dazed and smiling between them. Gretje undressed Maria and ran her fingers over her plump flesh, afraid to find breaks or bruises; but there was none.

Anthony worked it out to his own satisfaction. 'Whoever took her,' he said, 'didn't mean her any harm. They found her in a pit, after all. They must have wanted us to find her again, so they left her on the shore because that's where they knew we went, and in the whale because we were bound to look for the carcass. You see? You see?'

But Gretje was too busy swiping and cleaning her child, and dressing her like a talisman in a piece of lace she had been keeping for her christening. She wondered at all the perfect ways this child could grow.

GRETJE LOOKED DOWN on the whale, axe in her hand, sled tugged behind her, and she looked at Anthony and together, whooping, they fell on the great creature.

They prised out the teeth for ivory, each on its stump of blood. They tore off strips of the blubber and cut down to the baleen, the flesh splitting neatly as wood. The cuts took them close to the shiny, purplish membranes that held all the bile and shit in the animal, but nothing could stop them in their harvest. They had oil and wealth piled up on the sled. They were justified before God, at last.

'BUT ANTHONY DIED,' Gretje says.

One minute she's singing with all that godly wealth, defying any authority to get between her and glory; her luck is so good that nobody could keep her banished. The next she's sitting in this stuffy room like a prisoner, giving up the lot.

Anneke's studying her.

'You want to know how he died?' Gretje asked.

She'll get to Anneke, she will. She's angry at the child's detachment.

'You want to see him die?' she says.

Anneke's edgy. To reassure herself, she's taken up two of the knives, one in each hand, as if she were waiting for dinner. Tomas has put himself at the end of the table, which Gretje thinks is a defensive position.

'He could have died here,' Gretje says, 'in this room.'

For she can bring Anthony here to die. She wants the fact of his death to shock this child out of her stillness, to make her be one thing: fluid or fixed, winsome or brave, a person who reacts instead of allowing Pieter and Anneke, male and female, to cancel each other into nullity.

Anneke has her left hand gripped on the knife, and her right hand brings the other blade to her own wrist.

Gretje knows all rooms see death in a sturdy house; it just takes time. But this particular death, in this particular room, is a fact she has not yet acknowledged out loud.

The child sits there, old enough to change sex when it suits her, old enough for anything except pity. She holds the blade against the pale blue veins under her milky skin. She lets it run across her skin. And again. And again. Gretje is surprised that the blade is so good; the cut is too fine to bleed yet.

Anneke is staring.

'You're supposed to be angry with me,' Gretje says, 'with me and with the Turk.'

She's checked where the poker lies in case the children suddenly rush her and beat her for being what Anneke missed, what Tomas wanted. And now the blood begins; it makes a perfect letter 'A'.

'Be angry with me,' Gretje says.

It's pleading. It's affection. She wants Tomas to stop Anneke hurting herself; she can't simply lunge forward because they're at war, the child and its mother, each afraid of sudden advances. She's gone in a moment from horror at the woodcut monster she's borne, her shape-changing nature, and wanting only that she lives all through this hot, spilling anger. She wants Tomas to take the knives away.

'I remember,' Gretje says.

She wants Anneke to look where she looks, hear what she hears. Telling a story might do that.

'There's a skinny man on a sad horse and a woman clinging to his back; they're here on Broad Street. They go riding down the street, and their mouths are wide open as though they are screaming. They come up under a rope across the street, and they bite at the air, and the horse just goes rushing on. It's a game,' she says. 'The next couple circle their horse and they go riding down the street, and their mouths are open, too.'

Anneke sits like alabaster. The blood sweeps away from the cut as though it were being blown. The letter spoils.

'It's a game,' Gretje says. 'They have to bite this eel that's hanging from the rope. It's struggling and twisting, and they have to bite it.'

Anneke spreads the fingers of her hand on the table and takes the second, heavier knife and drops it from a height. It catches in wood, not flesh. Tomas is laughing.

'You want to know what it was like on the island, then?' Gretje says. The child's playing with anger now, she thinks. Gretje wishes she knew her better, knew her at all.

'We farmed,' she says. 'Traded. We came back into Manhattan from time to time, even though we were banished. They didn't know how to banish people. They didn't have a place to banish you from. They didn't even have banishing posts. I bought this house two years after we were banished,' she says, 'and it was three years more before they said it was legal for us to be where we were and doing what we were doing.'

It isn't enough of a story to hold Anneke. Gretje puts out her hand, and Anneke pulls back from the edge of the table. 'You have to know how he died,' Gretje says quietly.

Anneke's eyes are huge. Gretje sees her clearly now: someone who came across an ocean to be sorted out and settled and found a dead father and a mother who was too far gone in grief even to know and hold her. She sees the blood spread like a straight-sided banner from the cut on Anneke's arm.

She begins: 'Tomas came out to us on the island after a while and then he went back to Manhattan. Then people began to stare at him, and he came back to us.'

Then she says: 'Anthony had a bad tooth. The tooth-puller came round, pulled it, but maybe he just broke it in the jaw because the pain went on. His face swelled. His breath was deadly. He had a fever at night but he wouldn't stop working. He said if he stopped using his body, his body would stop. Like that.'

Anneke is listening now. Even Tomas seems to be

involved in Gretje's story.

'The winter came down on us, and I tried to keep him warm,' Gretje says. 'At night, in bed, he'd sweat so much I had to change the sheets. And then in the day, he'd take all the force he had left to cut wood or go out hunting.

'The winter locked us here. We were afraid the rivers would freeze and there'd be no food coming from the English, and then the whole harbour turned solid. We were walking on the water. One night there was snow, and the next day was hardly a day at all, and the next day, and then the houses were just points on this huge, blank paper that went from here to as far as we can see. We were afraid of being hungry. That's it. We were afraid of starving.'

But she knows they were afraid, also, of being in that place she had reached in the woods: that nowhere, where no direction is better than any other and nothing leads anywhere, so you might as well sit down and die.

'The ground was solid. You'd break a pick on it. There were black shoots on the trees because the frost never lifted. It was—' She looks directly at Anneke. 'You've seen how it is.'

After a moment, Anneke nods.

'The fever came and went, the swelling went down for a while. But the cold hurt him, I know; hurt his face. Then he wanted to go out after deer. He took the gun and went to the farms.'

'And didn't come back,' Anneke says.

'It was like that last night when you didn't come back. I used to think it didn't matter. People had other business. I'm good at disappearing, too. But that day, Anthony didn't come back, and I didn't like to leave the house in case he came back sick, so I waited and waited. And it was unreasonable. The sun wasn't down. It was full moon, anyway, so he'd have light all night. Maybe he wanted a drink at the tavern.'

She tells Tomas to pass her the rosa solis.

'I didn't mean any harm,' Anneke says very quietly. She's looking at her wrist.

'What did you say?'

'I didn't know you, but I wanted to be with you,' she says.

Gretje knows she can get up now when she wants. Tomas is spluttering. She gets up and brings a clean towel and ties it around Anneke's wrist. The girl feels blood stop in her fingers and she's afraid, shaking her hand. Gretje slackens the bandage.

'You want my story?' Anneke says.

Gretje concentrates.

'I walked out of the orphanage,' Anneke says. 'I just walked. I went down the street and I kept going. There wasn't anyone to stop me. I remember thinking I was magic, that they couldn't do anything to me while I was dressed as a boy—I was too much a boy for the Spinhuis and too much a girl for the army. So I felt safe.'

Gretje says: 'I couldn't stay in the house that night, not with Anthony out in the cold.'

Anneke says: 'The last few days on the boat, the cold was like knives. We came into the harbour, and there were these great islands of ice, and I hung over the side so I could hit them and push them away. They all thought I was younger than I am.'

Each knows the other is listening.

'The moon was like pewter,' Gretje says. 'I remember that. I went out by the road to the Bowery, but there wasn't a road so much as the traces of the last people who had tried to go that way. The snow was shining, like salt does when you spread it out. The ice and the moon and the wind, I remember those.'

'I asked for Anthony,' Anneke says.

Gretje nods. 'We couldn't send you away.'

Tomas stands by the window, looking out, and Gretje wonders what and when he sees.

'I tried to follow the tracks,' she says. 'He'd taken a sled, I knew that; he'd have to have. He said he was going with some other men. So I was looking for sled tracks and footprints that went together, and the prints had to be a fair distance apart—men walking fast. I hobbled in the prints. They were frozen, like glass, and worn away around the edges with the wind.'

Anneke says: 'I was glad you were here.'

'I walked for most of that night. You get scared when it's cold enough to change the shape of the town. I was walking easily enough, but that was out on the ice in the river, on the rapids; you can tell by the folds in the ice. I kept thinking I would die or find him.'

Gretje wants Anneke to know that this story is a gift to her because she will hide it from everyone else.

Anneke says: 'I couldn't just say, I'm Anneke, could I?'

'I think there was colour in the sky, a bit of green and blue and red, but very faint. I was back to the outbuildings at the farms by the Bowery, and there were the tracks of a sled down to a shed. It looked as though the sled had run down of its own accord. I don't know why I thought that.'

'I wanted to be with Anthony, and with you, and with both of you. But Dad—'

Gretje can't stop herself; she grins. 'You want to hear my story or not?'

'You want to hear mine?'

ANNEKE SAYS: 'I wanted him to be warm, which meant dragging him inside. Tomas helped. I wanted to care for him. And you. So you'd tell me about who made me.'

Gretje says: 'I always remembered my father, even after he went. The smell of tobacco and beer in his moustache. The warmth of a chair when he got up.'

'I was angry that I'd got here late, angry he'd died, and I thought it was my fault. You had everything settled, and I came, and then everything was over. And you looked so numb, as though you couldn't care for me even if you knew who I was. And it's hard to explain,' Anneke says.

'It certainly is,' Gretje says.

'One night,' Anneke says, 'I was in the yard and I opened the box and I looked at his face. I couldn't believe he was dead. I thought maybe his eyes had gone white in life; you see people with white eyes sometimes. I thought he was pretending to be dead because I was here, and he'd come back to life the moment I went, but I couldn't go—because of the ice and the ships not moving. I stood there and I tried to make him talk to me. But he wouldn't budge. If he wouldn't see me, I didn't want him to see at all. I took a stick and I hit at his eye.'

Gretje doesn't breathe for a minute.

'Then I went away because I wanted you to notice me.'

Gretje says: 'And now, do you want to hear how he died?

'I SAW THE dog first. It was still. I went to touch it, and it fell over.

'I could see the sled by the grain sheds. There was a deer on it, stiff. People can keep warm in the bowels of a dead animal. I felt the velvet on the deer's antlers—no reason in particular, nothing to be learned from the velvet. I just didn't want to go on.

243

'It was colder than I've ever known—there was cold all through me. If I'd cut myself, the blood would have stayed put. I went round the corner of the shed, and he was there, looking as though he was trying to open the door against the snow, but he'd fallen forwards. He was a terrible weight. I pulled him up a little, and he went back down into the snow. It was the end of the night and the end of my strength, and I didn't know if I could ever move him. I didn't want—' She pauses a moment. 'I did not want to know,' she says.

'But I turned the body over. He looked as though someone had kicked him in the belly and the chest, and he'd folded over the blow and collapsed, dead from shock. His heart gave out. He'd been feverish and he'd struggled through that damn snow all day and he'd found a deer that had come down to the sheds in the hope of finding grain, and he'd managed to load it up on the sled, and then—then he stopped. I looked down at him and I couldn't believe the pain on his face was over.'

Anneke, this time, puts out her hand.

'I couldn't believe,' Gretje says. 'It's taken me all this time to believe.'

Tomas is restive, shifting from buttock to buttock.

'We couldn't bury him because of the frost and we couldn't have a service for him because Bogardus won't stand for that kind of papistry. God's greedy for the dead, apparently, and doesn't see why the living should mind.'

Tomas slips out of the room.

Gretje smiles at Anneke. 'You and me,' she says, 'we've lost something.'

'Tomas and I—'

The rosa solis is burning the charity out of her, and Gretje's back, brusque and big in her chair. 'You can do too much confessing,' she says.

THE DOOR TAKES a beating, the air quivers like a string in the hallway.

Tomas is out about some business in the stable, Anneke is lying asleep on Gretje's bed, so Gretje goes. She isn't in a mood to trust anything sudden, so she listens by the door for a moment. There are people waiting, several of them, trying to be quiet.

She opens the door.

She sees: a deputation, a line of people who don't much like Gretje Reyniers, never did, never trusted her, never took to her way of living, but who came to borrow money or rent a house or do a little business that couldn't be arranged in their own shops or beds.

That's fine. She knows how to handle them. They need her, so they hate her, but their need is strong.

It is daylight now, but they are all carrying lit torches. Some of them have pots, pans and drums. They begin to beat the pots as though they are beating the sin out of Gretje. There are horns and a sheet of metal that shivers and sounds like thunder. The noise begins like music and then it builds up to jeers and discords and cacophony.

In the middle of the line is a figure she knows: Anthony the Turk.

He is propped with a plank against his backbone so that he seems to stand, but uncertainly, as though he'd made it home at last after a good wild night. They've stolen him, enrolled him in their number, put his face among their own slipshod faces, and they look out smugly at Gretje.

One woman makes a show out of keening and grieving, hair switching at the snow. She's doing the mourning for Anthony that Gretje didn't do, that Gretje couldn't do, being only the town whore. She's teaching Gretje a lesson, mocking her.

For a moment she thinks they've cut up Anthony like a steer, because they're hungry. She sees she's wrong, but the rage comes up inside her like bile. They're counting on her love to make a mockery of it. They're expecting the fury she feels and they're enjoying it.

When they beat the metal, it's like a storm, like God's voice shouting down the drums and hooting. They want her pale and faint and running.

They'll kill her, she's sure. Nobody will ask for an explanation. She's a woman grieving and therefore mad, and the authorities down in the fort will tidy away the papers on Gretje Reyniers with a grateful sigh.

But they want more than that. They want a confession: all her pain, spelt out for them so they can relish their own virtue and save the town from her sins. The beer and the gin fuel them, keep them shouting, drumming, jeering. They want a sight of Gretje Reyniers, broken.

She stands there. The cold stuns her, her heart's gone, the light's so generalized by the snow that she can't find a horizon or an escape route. She smells the pitch on the torches.

One man, a sailor maybe, supports the plank that supports Anthony. The flicker of the torches makes Anthony appear to think, even to smile.

She wants him alive. She wants that more than anything.

They play the torches round his clothes. Sometimes there's a smouldering, a break of fire, and then nothing. They're going to take him away with fire. And there are dozens of them, their noise now beating on to her mind directly, without the intervention of drums or horns.

She smiles at Anthony. She opens her arms. She acknowledges him, dead, and that she loves him.

The deputation leers, hot with virtue, but their shouting stalls for a moment. Gretje doesn't seem to see the fires they brought out into the dawn, or the heavy sticks they use to beat the drums, or the gun that Beeche has slung on his shoulder.

She walks towards Anthony. She ought to be afraid of him. The circle's still swaying, grimacing, drumming at her with too much momentum to stop, but each of them is aware the body is not perfect any more. Each of them can see the blind eye, the way the organs hang inside slack muscles, the new scars where cold has broken the man's skin. Anthony isn't some moral example like a shocking story; he's human and ruined, propped up on a board.

So Gretje receives him, like a lover.

The drums can't stop. The men don't want to look.

She sees they have beaten the body. Angry they couldn't get to her, she thinks. Angry at the cold and the ice and the stillness all around that maddens all of them—a town come together in a community of fury and drink and frustration.

She kisses Anthony on his dead lips.

The drumming stops.

The judgement stops with it; for the women and the men all stand, blankly, as though they didn't want to imagine the old, wormy taste of that mouth.

TOMAS AND ANNEKE come out of the stable. The deputation lets them through, whispering. Together, the children lift Anthony on his splint as if it were a coffin, and they carry him reverently. They half-expect stones, blows, even Beeche's long hunting-gun that looks as though it ought to make music.

Gretje says to the deputation, quietly: 'Fuck off.'

The men look offended, as though they have never

heard words like that before, but they can't quite look at her. There's charcoal under her eyes, and the cold has startled her skin, yet she's alight with love. They can sense the way the muscles yield when she holds him and the corruption that's to come.

A man drowns his torch in the snow. Another man murmurs: 'No shame. No fucking shame.'

The men are fading back into the snow, they kick down the lane, remembering to forget all this. When they sober up, they'll face the substantial, respectable Gretje Reyniers again, guarded by each last foot of her property and stuiver in her purse.

ANNEKE AND GRETJE and Tomas wash the body with melted ice and rose-water, carefully so as not to break the fragile skin. Gretje imagines she can feel some warmth in the wind.

They lay the body on the sled, which Tomas pulls, and between them they make a procession. They're following Gretje, so she does not need to explain her idea, which is that if the ground will not take Anthony, then perhaps the ice will break at last and the water will.

Bogardus and his wife stop in the street as the three come grandly past, slow and steady, their solemn faces as potent as guns in keeping the onlookers serious. Bogardus wants to complain, but his wife tugs his sleeve. The soldiers, as they pass, take off whatever they've kept on their heads against the cold, but Gretje doesn't see the tribute. Each step has a message as clear as a sermon: that a life has ended, that the end is absolute, that she is entitled to the horror of sorrow and that she will survive.

Tomas and Pieter stop at the edge of the water, but Gretje goes on. She takes the reins of the sled.

There's no water, of course, only a lock of ice, with pack

ice tucked in blocks by the shore and then quicksilver like the backs of cheap mirrors. Gretje goes forward, the ropes over her shoulders, Anthony lying like a martyr's statue on the sled. The ice out here rucks up where currents run and then goes on, flat and ridged and flat again. It could be a cold tarpaulin stretched tight across the water. It could be pewter, waiting to be turned on the lathe and polished. Gretje thinks in these terms again: goods for sale, quicksilver, mirrors, tarpaulin, pewter.

She throws herself forward into the blank light. She has only ever heard what she wanted to hear, but this quiet makes her listen to the terrible weight of air.

They have turned away from her on the shore, frightened by the sight of passion. She goes alone, at surprising speed.

The ice catches her. She falls and waits a minute to consider the fact that she has fallen and then she rocks herself back to her knees and stands again. She's offended by this winter: it holds up ships and it keeps the sailors in town long after their money is gone. But she's also grateful for the way light and ice and sky became a grey skin for her eyes and spare her the trouble of seeing things any more. She wants to find the nowhere where Anthony can be at peace.

To the soldiers on the fort, she's a comma in their view, bent by the fumes from the brazier. They go back to their talk. She might as well have passed into cold, white mist.

Only she sees the shadow coming over the ice, like a black ship, its sails stiff with ice. It is a sixty-tonner, no more, a fragile thing in the vice of the cold. Its masts are charcoal, its decks frost, and it does not resist the glass in the bay.

Gretje Reyniers pants a bit, and when she stops, the sled butts into her calves. She looks back at the little pencilled trails of smoke coming up from the village on

Manhattan, at the ropes on the wharf that have frozen into hemp rods. Nothing seems to move. All that moves is out here with the dead.

There is a sound like Bridge Street, like birds in a coop with nothing to complain about. Above the dark ship, like its attendants, the geese straggle south, shocked by the cold wind that sings in their wings.

She can hear ice being splintered by the boat, but the ice stays whole. She isn't alarmed; she's glad. She tugs Anthony off the sled and lays him out, his arms cracked to a semblance of prayer over his chest. The first of the thaw will take him down.

The sled she takes with her.

THE SOLDIERS SEE her skeetering back to shore. The twilight is closing in on the town already, but there's no moon yet; on the plain, bare paper of the bay, there's nothing else for them to see.

Gretje squats down, throws her thick skirts up and around her and pisses a yellow sun in the ice.

'Right,' she says out loud.

END NOTE

THERE WAS A Gretje Reyniers, who did sail to New Amsterdam in the colony's early days, and became notorious. This book is a version, but only a version, of her life.

She left no trace in Amsterdam, as far as I can tell: not in the notarial records, the confession books or any of the court records. So she is available to be invented. But she did travel to New Amsterdam, and bits of her life appear in the colony's records: a prodigious list of debts demanded, debts welshed on, slanders uttered and complained of.

So it is a fact, as good as any other fact told in a court, that she said certain things to the crew of the *Soutberg*, was married to the Turk; measured the members of three sailors on a broomstick; asked the midwife whether the baby looked like her husband or Mr Huddlesdon; charged into the fort and demanded to be the people's whore because she'd been the nobility's whore too long. It is fact, too, that she was banished from Manhattan and within five years was back in a house on Bridge Street, from which she saw her daughters married well. But there is no more fact about Gretje Reyniers.

Sometimes she has to be conjured out of other people's generalities. In particular, I have drawn on A. Th. Van Deursen's wonderful and modest *Plain Lives in a Golden Age: Popular culture, religion and society in seventeenth century Holland* (Cambridge, 1991) and on Simon Schama's *The Embarrassment of Riches: An interpretation of Dutch Culture in the Golden Age* (London, 1987). But the most important source has been pictures and prints, mostly in the collections of the Amsterdam Rijksmuseum and the Amsterdam Historical Museum; some of these appear in Van Deursen or in Schama, some in *Masters of 17th Century Dutch Landscape Painting*, edited by Peter C. Sutton (Boston, 1987). The circumstances of New Amsterdam are synthesized in Oliver Rink's *Holland on the Hudson* (Ithaca, 1986), and in my *Maximum City: the Biography of New York* (London, 1991), which is where I first encountered Gretje.

I have invented her in this book, which is dangerous. If she isn't satisfied with the flesh I've found for her, I know I'll hear.

M.K.P.
New York City, November 1994